Toxic Soup

by

RR Rowley

Toxic Soup

Cover Art by *The Wild Rose Press, Inc.*

The Wild Rose Press, Inc.
PO Box 708
Adams Basin, NY 14410-0708
Visit us at www.thewildrosepress.com

Publishing History
First Edition, 2022
Trade Paperback ISBN 978-1-5092-4116-3
Digital ISBN 978-1-5092-4117-0

Published in the United States of America

Avoiding a sandbar, they swung into a backwater eddy. Spooked ducks sprang into flight in front of them. Gliding, they studied the depth of the water, avoiding the chance of running aground. Some sickly grasses stuck out from the bank. Was this it? She brought her kayak closer, excitement rising. Pointing to a spot upon the bank, she called to Rex, "See that? See that? Is that water trickling out of the ground over there?"

He removed his sunglasses and squinted. "You're right. I see a wet spot."

Straggly, yellowed grasses drooped away from the seep edge. They moved their boats to get a better viewing angle. A foam rose from the trickle of liquid and spread to a nasty orange and pink gunk smeared over exposed rocks. "I see it!" Rex cried out, a jolt of fear zapping through him. "Radioactivity!" He quickly backstroked. "You've got your evidence. Let's get out of here. I don't want to be anywhere near that stuff."

"Okay, okay. Take it easy," Casey said while joining Rex in retreat. She had her proof. Toxicity still flowed into the river. How many other places existed? Perhaps beneath the water, much worse. Nobody doing anything about it other than talk. Untouchable Hanford getting away with whatever they wanted. But what could she do about it? Launching an attack from the shoreline seemed hopeless. Attack what? Attack whom? Her taking on security a ridiculous notion. Frustration wrenched her nerves. Something needed doing, but what? Not only for Charley but for the birds, the fish, and all the little creatures suffering at the hand of man's dereliction of duty. Suddenly, she knew what she must do.

Dedication

To the whistleblowers who reveal the truth.

Chapter 1

Sun-baked dirt crunched beneath Charley Long's boots. Every step tested his will to carry on as he plodded uphill towards the high desert knoll's summit. When he reached the top, he bent over and braced his hands upon his thighs, lungs billowing. Sweat pearled down his face. A rancid smell of sour washcloth wafted up into his nose from inside his airtight, protective suit.

He stood and surveyed the daunting valley before him, where steel and concrete storage tanks puffed in a row out of the desert sand like muffins in a pan. His jaw hung in anticipation. He knew that within the tanks, slushy atomic fusion excrement gnawed against its confinement. Nuclear waste remaining from the Cold War ballistic weapons era. Spawn of split plutonium atoms. Stored up God-awful stuff, no one knew how to get rid of but kept on producing anyway. A cringe crawled under his skin. He sensed the innate desire of what festered before him, to devour all life force.

The city of tanks beckoned beneath the hot sun. He would be among them soon enough. Nausea gurgled in the pit of Charley's stomach and seeped into his throat, wanting to expel. He winced from desperation, and tearing at his mask, pushed it up onto his forehead. Freed from the covering's restrictive filtering, he sucked the fresh air in heaves.

Nausea quelled, claustrophobia released, and with a sense of duty commanding, he willed his body to soldier down across the desert sands towards the tanks. His mouth soured again as he gained ground. The chafing of his protective suit rubbing between his legs scratched his nerves. Everything about this mission rubbed him raw. He clenched his teeth and ordered himself forward despite it all. Earn his damn paycheck. That's for sure.

He knew he'd be in proximity to radiation when he signed on to work at the Hanford Nuclear Reservation. What surprised him was getting sent to the front lines for leaking tank inspection and repair. But the money was good. The federal paycheck and the benefits were way better than anything else available in the high plateau desert on the eastern side of Washington State. The job, a shot at saving the money he needed to buy that plot of homesteading land shining in his dreams.

He twisted his head and checked behind him. His team advanced but remained a good ways back, so he decided to wait for them. Enter together—strength in numbers.

Without warning, a deep, moaning growl cracked the silence of the desert. The frightening bellow reverberated from deep within the tanks' bowels, sounding like the prelude to some angry underwater symphony. The sludge awakened. Charley jerked to attention and froze. A shudder rippled through him, and his eyes stretched wide as his ears tensed for any other sound.

The ground rumbled and shook in its depths. The sludge stirred. Charley crouched to steady himself, spreading his arms as if ready to jump. While he poised, a turgid, hollow bubbling sound burst into an erupting burp, giving forth like a giant-stomped pumpkin. The sludge spoke. Its breath came unseen, mistily reaching through the ether for Charley. His hands sprang to clutch his face, sizzling in excruciating pain, and he smelled the stench of unholy dread. Inhaling the toxic spew, he crumpled to the ground, writhing in agony, darkness engulfing him into a sea of fire.

Chapter 2

Casey Long climbed up from the rushing White Salmon River with her kayak snugged against her hip. Halfway to the top of the trail, she paused to catch her breath. The air rising from the snowmelt water smelled sweet. A smile graced her face. When she engaged with the river, nothing else mattered. The troubling world fell away, and there was only oneness with nature.

She turned from the river and ascended the switch-backing trail. Reaching the top, she went to her trusty Honda parked alongside the country road and slung her kayak up onto the rack, breathing a sigh of relief to have finished the trek up from the river with the boat in tow. Arching her back and bunching her hair behind her head, a light breeze feathered her sweaty neck.

Her phone rang from within the car's glove box. She opened the box and took out the singing device. "Hello."

"Hello. Is this Casey Long?"

"Yes. Who is this?"

"This is Clair Wright calling from the Hanford Nuclear Reservation. Casey, I'm afraid I have some terrible news for you. An accident has killed your brother, Charley."

Casey's heart clenched. Her hand flew to the side of her face in shock. "No! Dead? What the hell happened?"

"I'm afraid he got caught in the wrong place at the

wrong time. A tragic accident that no one could have expected. Casey, we are so sorry for your loss. Our thoughts and prayers are with you."

Casey stood stunned. Charley's death, unfathomable. Images of him, from child to man, whisked through her mind. She squeezed her hands and quaked, calling to the sky in wide-eyed exasperation. "Why, Charley? Why him?"

Her attention fell back into the phone, Clair's voice speaking into her ear. "He got exposed to radiation and toxic chemicals, and we are holding his body in a special ward."

Casey answered with a tremor in her voice. "What does that mean, and when can I see him?"

"I'm not authorized to share all of the details, but I can arrange for someone from the Department of Energy to meet with you. Can you be here tomorrow morning?"

Casey exhaled, "I'll be there."

"Good, Casey. Something else you should know. We must handle Charley's radiated body properly, and it requires burying in a special way." The word, buried, made Casey's head spin. What would Charley want? Burned or rotted in the ground? She remembered them encountering a decaying deer carcass in the woods as children. The squirming maggots had freaked him out. Burned—that's what he would want.

"Don't worry. We can talk more about that tomorrow. Follow the signs to area 200 West and then HPMC. About eleven o'clock? Is that good for you?"

"It should be okay."

Casey lowered the phone. Reality slapped her. She stomped her foot in the dirt and spun a circle, crying out, "Oh, Charley!" Her eyes squeezed and her tears flowed as the hurt overcame her.

Casey's housemate, Frank, came up the hill from the river. His wet suit, peeled down to his waist, revealed his buff, inked arm that clutched his kayak as he made for the Honda. A slash of dirty blond hair hung over one eye, and a grin showed the pleasure gained from his run down the White Salmon. He saw Casey slumped against the car; her arms locked across her chest, her eyes blankly staring, her puffy red face laden with pain. He set down his boat and hurried to her side. "Casey, what's wrong?"

"My brother is dead," she croaked, and surrendered to his open arms. They held each other by the roadside, rocking in the moment. "He got nuked somehow at Hanford," she furthered. Her words sickened her. She had never faced death before. Where did he go?

Frank gently held her. "What happened? How could he get nuked?"

She pulled away and wiped her eyes with her arm, her face tightening. "I don't fucking know. But I sure am going to find out."

"What happens now?"

"I'm driving out to Hanford in the morning. I have to talk to some special Department of Energy person to get answers," she said with a doubting curl hanging at the end of her lip that she often held as if scrutinizing the world, not expecting much.

They changed and drove upriver to drop Frank at his truck. Frank broke the quiet between them. "Typical Feds," Frank said, snugging down his straight-billed, snapback cap with 'Wicked' in red letters on the front. He shifted his head side to side as if they might be watching. "They try to make like everything is cool out there. You know, talking about how great their safety programs are, while in reality it's a leaking cesspool of the most deadly shit on earth. What got into Charley to want to work out there anyway?"

"Lured by big money, I guess. Thought if he toughed it out for a while, he'd get ahead. Not everyone is sitting fat like you." Frank rolled his eyes and shrugged off her red-neck roots getting the better of her. "I'll find out the truth about what happened. You'll see. Somebody is going to pay. They're not going to get away with murdering my brother."

"Whoa, girl. I get you being upset, but like what? You're going to take on the Federal government?"

"Whatever it takes, Frank. I'm saying I'm not afraid of them, and I'm not going to buy into any bullshit. I'll find out what happened to Charley and who's to blame."

****

At the bottom of the hill, where the White Salmon met the spring melt swollen Columbia River, Casey swung east towards the town of Bingen. On mental auto-pilot, she headed upriver back to her shared 'little run-down but cute' home, an estate agent might say. Out of her car window, she saw the big river dotted with kite-boarders launched from the tawny sand bar fingering from the Hood River into the grey-green Columbia. The kite-boarders ripped across the channel, capturing the winds that blew steadily from the west off of the Pacific Ocean. The multi-colored sails, set against a clear blue sky, flew across the water like a kaleidoscope of butterflies luffing into the wind.

Dashing the picture of wind filled colorful sails, an

eye-blinding headlight barreled around a bend in the river. It appeared to be coming straight at her. Like breaking the sound barrier, a one hundred car coal train roared into Casey's brain. It thrust through her, and it's roar and clamor of vibrating clatter of wheels obliterated all other sounds. It's inertia gutted her. The force of it leaving her hollow, blowing past her like the life of her brother. Here, then gone, then emptiness and silence. She tightened her grip on the wheel. She just wanted to get home.

The trains through the Gorge ran relentlessly. Following the river banks, they tunneled through basalt cliffs and found their passage from the eastern plains through the Cascade Mountains and down to the sea. The coal and fracked oil trains transported the drilled and dug remains of eras past that greased the present's wheels and tarred the future. A chunk of loose coal blew out of a train car and bounced off her car's hood.

"Fuckers!" she screamed, pounding on the steering wheel.

Past the six-block, downtown strip of the lumber mill town named Bingen, Casey turned and drove three blocks before hitting the side street that led to the wood-shingled bungalow. She came to a halt in the large carport, perfect for hanging wet suits and gear. Scattered in front of her in the yard were Frank's toys: kayaks, windsurfing and kitesurfing boards, sails, a couple of dirt bikes, snowboards, and a snowmobile. Between two glacier peaked volcanos with countless miles of National Forests veined with rivers, the outdoor playing never ended. But today, the sunny fun clouded behind the darkness of death.

Frank parked his pickup beside Casey's car and

joined her in stowing their gear. They walked to the house in silence. The screen door flapped and Jett, a housemate, came out to greet them. He emerged with his dark hair tousled, wearing protective eyewear and a mask dangling on his chest. A peculiar odor clung to him. "How'd it go, guys?" he said with a welcoming smile.

Casey walked past him.

Jett's head jerked back.

Frank raised a finger to his lips and led Jett into the living room, where he sat Jett down and told the sad tale of Charley's accident.

"Well, that explains everything," Jett said, dropping his voice to a near whisper. "Damn awful, isn't it? Killed by radiation and toxic chemicals. Gruesome, man." He hung his head. "Poor Casey. She told me how Charley took care of her growing up in Spokane."

"Yeah, it's going to be hard for her for a while. You know—sad, angry, and maybe even spiteful. We need to help her get through this tough time."

****

Casey flung herself onto her bed, clutching a pillow to her head. Questions bombarded in a repetitive circle. What had happened? People aren't supposed to die when they go to work. Charley—gone? Death, a stranger.

She wished it a bad dream she could wake from, but it remained valid. Tomorrow, she would learn more. Determined to hold herself together, she got up, showered, and changed for work. She hoped carrying on with her regular schedule would distract from the turmoil of her mind. How she'd make it through the night, she wasn't sure? Break out the melatonin, she guessed. Tomorrow, she'll see him—or what's left of him. She grimaced at the thought. What did radiation do to a person anyway?

She needed to talk to her girlfriend, Lolly. To hear her voice and to share the overwhelming grief with someone intimate. She called. Lolly answered. "Hey, Casey. I was thinking about you, too. Funny how that works. I should be leaving Portland and coming out your way later next week."

"Something horrible has happened," Casey said and managed to tell of Charley's death with agonizing difficulty.

"Oh, Casey. Poor Charley. What a terrible shock. You sound devastated. Are you all right? Look, I'll get off work and come straight out."

"No, don't do that. I'll be okay. Just hearing your voice is what I need. Sweet of you to offer, but things are happening quickly. I go to see Charley first thing tomorrow, and decisions need to be made about what to do. You don't need to get involved in all of that. Bad enough that I will have to see his dead body. No reason for you. "

"Sure you don't want company?"

"I'll get one of the guys to go with me. Bring some big hugs when you come out next week. Okay?"

"You seem upset. I should come."

"Let me get past tomorrow. You know, seeing him and all that. I'll keep in touch."

"If you say so. Call me if anything changes. You know I'm here for you."

Lolly's words were magic to Casey's ears. All her life, she had needed someone to feel that way. "I love you," she said.

"I love you too. Call me."

Jett moved cautiously towards Casey when she entered the living room dressed in her work outfit for bartending across the river in the larger town of Hood River, Oregon. He reached out to her. She came to him. Eyes watering, he hugged her tenderly. She melted into the comfort of his arms. "Casey, I'm so sorry to hear about Charley. Can I keep you company on the ride out to see him tomorrow?"

Jett said what she needed to hear. He had a way of knowing her insides. Casey gripped him at arm's length and found his eyes. "I'd like that." She turned and walked towards the front door. The thought of leaving to see dead Charley in the morning slammed her. She stopped before the door. Her shoulders dropped. Her face darkened, and she threw back her head. Shaking her hair defiantly, she cried out, "Fucking Hanford! Why did he have to go there?"

Chapter 3

They left at seven in the morning. It would take three and a half hours to follow the river upstream to the Tri-Cities in Eastern Washington. Casey white-knuckled the steering wheel, eyes glued on the road ahead while her mind tossed and emotions flipped. Sorrow, then a rising head full of rage. How could they have allowed Charley to die, and why didn't they protect their workers? What were they doing out there, anyway? Sadness tumbled back in. How had I allowed myself to lose contact with him? Why hadn't I kept better in touch? She had thought he'd always be there.

Casey's eyes squinted and her cheeks drew back in pain. "What will Charley look like, Jett? What did the stuff do to him?"

Jett shifted uneasily in his seat. He turned his head towards the side window and raised his voice. "Probably not pretty, Casey. Radiation burns. Prepare yourself."

She lifted her chin and blew air. That sight would come soon enough. One that she will have to bear for a lifetime. She determined that she must hold herself together. Be strong for her brother in the end like he was for her at the beginning of her life.

An image from the past swirled into her mind, and she allowed herself to reminisce on a time when it was only the two of them, Charley and she, adrift in the world, depending on one another like orphaned children. Together, they found the comfort and strength required to face life on their own. She wanted to hold him and take care of him as he had her. Heal him. But, too late for that. Cracked road pavement jerked her back into the present, hands upon the wheel, traveling at sixty miles per hour down the highway. "So, Jett, what's going on at Hanford? All I know is out there is where they keep nuclear waste. Charley said he'd be safe. What do you know about the place?"

"It's a monster of nuclear toxicity out there. The Hanford reactors made the plutonium for the World War Two atomic bombs and SIXTY THOUSAND of this country's nuclear warheads. The radioactive waste unforgivably was first thrown into thirty miles of ditches and buried into the ground on-site. The rod cleaning water dumped directly into the Columbia River. Now the stuff is being stored in leaking tanks built on site. FIFTY-THREE MILLION gallons of it! An environmental disaster! A hidden disaster. Everyone thinks of how beautiful the Columbia River is. Hurts to talk about the damage done to her."

Jett's words shocked Casey. She had no idea about the history of Hanford even though she grew up in the Pacific Northwest. "How do you know all that?"

"I hung out on the fringes of the Earth Liberation Front when at college in Seattle. They used to talk about Hanford and schemed to do something but never got anywhere."

"Why not? Horrible, what's going on."

"You'll soon see. Easier said than done. The place is a military fortress. Top security for nuclear business, you know, and the waste is untouchable."

They fell silent; minds lost in their thoughts as they

drove alongside the Columbia on Washington State route #14. The river wound through the hills of the Gorge like a long, relaxed ribbon, appearing cobalt blue that day in the rising sun. Passing by towering, basalt cliffs, they traveled on until the landscape sprawled into ragged stony moonscapes randomly graced with fairy tale rock castles made by some God's hand, dribbling stone into towers and turrets like child's play with wet sand at the beach. Lines of grape arbors and fruit trees tucked into pockets of riverside vales. And, all the while, white snowy peaked Mt. Hood shone in the rearview window.

Casey barely noticed, her mind stewing on Hanford. In disbelief, she said, "So they threw the nuclear waste in ditches by the river?"

"Yeah, making two hundred square miles of contaminated groundwater and radiating the river."

"What's that have to do with Charley?"

"He probably was killed working near the storage tanks. There're one hundred seventy-seven steel and concrete tanks full of the hot sludge they could manage to pump out of the ditches after people found out and pressured them to do something. They're leaking now, the stuff inside so caustic it's eating through the walls of the tanks, joining up with the stuff seeping along in the ground with twenty thousand years or whatever of half-life left."

Casey tried to envision one hundred seventy-seven tanks full of brewing toxicity, a scene out of a sci-fi horror movie. Unbelievable. How had Charley gotten himself so involved?

Farther along the road, they passed by towering, immaculate white wind turbines perched on hillsides like sunflowers reaching towards the sun, only to catch the wind. Spinning like Mercedes Benz emblemed pinwheels, they harnessed the natural power. Jett pointed out of the window towards the hillside. "Now, there's some clean energy production we can be proud of."

Casey said. "I didn't know about Hanford."

"Many people don't. That's the way they like to keep it."

****

George Marshall, head of the regional Department of Energy, leaned forward in his leather chair and placed his elbows on his desk. Holding a newspaper in his hand, he read from an article, "Man killed by toxic emissions at the Hanford Nuclear Reservation. Six men are in the hospital. Spiked radiation levels from the release of hazardous materials into the air monitored as far away as Chicago." Letting the paper flop to the desk, he wove his fingers into a bunch in front of him and squeezed them while his eyes bulged over his reading glasses. "It certainly doesn't help our tattered image a bit when someone dies on the job." His accusing eyes darted back and forth between Richard Shorter, his Director of Operations, and Bill Glibson, his Public Relations man. He launched at Richard. "What the Sam Hill happened, Richard? I want to understand it fully."

Richard ran his fingers through his thinning hair, laying like chicken feathers against the side of his head. He cleared his throat. "Same thing that's been going on, only worse this time. Built-up hydrogen in the tank contents burst through the confining crust on top, causing a mini-explosion, in this case blowing out the filter, something that hasn't happened before. A dose of radiation and toxic chemicals escaped into the atmosphere. That's why the watchdogs have monitored the 'burp.' There is no controlling the chemical reactions happening in the tanks. It's a bloody toxic soup with a mind of its own. We can barely get near to them without suiting up like we're going to the moon. That guy, Charles Long, was downwind and near the tank when it spat. He got a direct hit while the others luckily only got exposure."

"If you could call that luck. Was Charles wearing a mask?" George asked.

Richard adjusted his glasses. "Damn if I know. We're investigating. The WRPS subcontractors have been using non-union men, allowing them to remove the masks when they want. They say the masks slow down work. You would think he'd have it in place that near to the tanks. Whether he removed the mask or it got blown off, the bottom line is he inhaled the spew."

"Bill, keep that under wraps, and Richard, send a memo to WRPS that everyone must wear masks for the short term. The press will undoubtedly want to view the site." Rubbing his smooth head, George continued. "Miserable situation. I don't know what more we can do about the ongoing 'burps.' Comments?"

Bill threw his hands in the air. Frustration etched his forehead. "It's a witches brew going on in those tanks—changing, morphing, growing with a life of its own. The dead man is a one-off. A case of being at the wrong place at the wrong time. How do we control fate? We're doing the best we can with a complicated containment situation. Until D.C. comes up with a solution, we're merely storage monitors." Exasperated,

Bill searched his comrades for support. No one chimed in. "Of course, we're concerned with safety, and our record and programs speak to this fact, but there is always the wild card factor—accidents can and do happen. Everyone knows this is a dangerous business."

"But not how dangerous, Glibson. Our duty to the program is to retain public trust, assuring that we control the situation. The genie is in the bottle, so to speak," George added with a raised eyebrow, pleased with his metaphor.

Bill answered. "Until there is some other solution, like a deposit site or the blasted vitrification plant, we have to work with our situation. Hanging on and containing the material is the best we can do. In the meantime, we must assure Americans that they don't have to worry. The situation is in good hands," he said with a dismissive wave.

"Very good. I'm glad to hear that," George said wryly. "When you meet with that man's sister later this morning, Bill and Richard, please give to her my condolences. Work out with HPMC how to dispose of the body. Keep her calm. We don't want this blown up any worse, and no names of his family get given out. Keep those damn reporters at bay."

****

Casey's gut twisted as roadside signs for Richland appeared. Not long to go before they reached the Reservation, she hunched over the steering wheel, urging her four-cylinder car up one of the pitched, seemingly unending grades rising from the low-lying river onto the high desert plateau. She rocked back and forth in the seat, eager to have the long ride over and to see Charley. Squeezing her legs, she had to pee.

With less than thirty miles to go and nowhere to pullover, green patches of vegetation sprouted out of the sagebrush and sand hills. Cookie cutter, American dream houses appeared in clusters as if transported from some idyllic suburban community somewhere gentler and more hospitable. Homes for the executive elite. Hanford's economy, the lifeblood of the region. Government money poured in, but real hope for solutions existed years in the future. Subject to variable government oversights, which changed with each passing administration, new technologies were obsolete by the time they became mandated.

They pulled into a mini-mart in Richland for a bathroom, gas, and snack stop. Eerily quiet in the hazy light of the vintage ranch housed town, something appeared not quite right about the cash register guy. Stringy-haired, grey-skinned, and staring blankly through dark socketed, absent eyes, he robotically made their transaction. Jett felt he had landed in the dystopian future. Clenching his jaw, he whispered into Casey's ear, "Zombie town. Stuff must be in the water."

She furrowed her eyebrows and frowned, knowing that Charley had lived there. How repugnant a thought and worse was that she, so caught up in her own life, couldn't be bothered to visit. She could have convinced him to do something else. Come hang out with her or work in Portland or something. Anything but here.

Getting past the military checkpoint with an ID show, they followed the signs to area 200 and HPMC medical services. The hidden and blatantly posted surveillance cameras followed their route. Lifeless, grey concrete edifices haunted from the roadside, joined by confining cyclone fences and tortured crucifixes of electrical poles and wires, the ground below them seeping with the killer of all things living. Casey bit her lip. Fear clutched her heart as she got closer to her brother's corpse. Would she be able to keep it together? Should she? Impulsively and out of character, Casey crossed herself while traveling across the unholy ground and prayed for Charley's soul.

Industrial sized Petri dish-shaped tanks loomed ahead. They and a complex of offices came into focus out of a hazy mirage shimmering off of the asphalt road before them. Inside the flat-roofed, linear medical facility, refracted light through long narrow windows glinted off shiny, sterile surfaces. Waiting for them inside, a tall, noodle thin, Peter Pan haired woman stood wearing a crisp, white lab coat and owlish glasses.

"You must be Casey?" she said pleasantly. "I'm Clair Wright. We spoke on the phone. I'm overseeing Charley's case."

"Yes, and this is my partner, Jett. Where's Charley, and when can I get him out of here?"

"Please sit down, Miss Long, and I'll tell you."

Casey flicked her ponytail like a wild horse. "I don't want to sit down. I just drove over three hours to get here, and I want to see him!"

"He's in a special room. You can't go in."

Casey's mouth dropped open.

"His body is contaminated. He received a high exposure to radiation and chemical gases. I have arranged a viewing for you. He is in a specially sealed covering." Clair dropped her head and spoke with upturned eyes. "I must warn you. The viewing will not be pleasant. His face is disfigured." Clair leaned back

19

and let the image sink in. "Are you sure you want to see him? You don't have to, you know."

The words startled Casey. The vague but frightening description locked her where she stood. Her mind wobbled through horrible, disfigurement imaginings. Jett sensed her shock by the vacancy in her eyes and gripped Casey's hand. She abruptly brought the reel to a halt. One last time, she must see him and witness what the accident did, what Hanford and the stuff had done to her brother. "I want to see him."

The click of Clair's flat heels echoed in the hallway silence as they left the office and walked down a long, tunneling corridor, seeming to go on forever. Clair's warning stuck in Casey's mind.

They turned a corner and approached a glass-windowed viewing room like in a maternity ward. Casey trembled and let out a choked back whimper at the sight of the body bag lying on a table. A white-uniformed man with space suit headgear turned to face them through his clear, face shield. Clair's voice echoed through a monitor. "We are ready for viewing."

The man acknowledged and unzipped the bag down to the body's chest and spread the opening. Casey's fingers dug into Jett's arm. What she saw, not the Charley she knew. His face, a rusty—red, hideously melted blob. She turned away from him, holding her mouth like she might be sick. Inside she screamed NO! Jett reached out to comfort her, but she broke free and went to Charley, slapping her palms against the glass surround; her face twisted in agony, her tears uncontrollably falling.

The man in the suit zipped the bag closed. Jett gently hugged Casey, and this time she let him. He silently stroked her back. Slowly, she caught her breath, then patted Jett twice on the front of his shoulders. Turning to Clair, Casey growled through her tears, "I want to get him out of here. Away from this stinking place!"

Clair reached a hand of sympathy towards Casey, but she flinched and pulled away. She pressed her face and hands back against the glass. She went to him, lying dead and silent before her. "Oh, Charley."

Out of the corner of her eye, Casey caught the movement of a man entering the viewing area. He slowed, straightened his tie, cleared his throat, and put on a consoling face. He spoke to the air between them. "Such a terrible misfortune for your brother. I'm sorry, Casey." He put out his hand. Scowling, she refused it. "I'm Mr. Glibson with the Department of Energy. We're truly sorry that something like this could happen. Our hearts are with you," he said, placing his hand over his heart like getting ready to sing the national anthem. "Safety is number one for us."

"Then why did this happen? How did it happen?" Jett said.

Glibson explained the accident as concisely as he was allowed. "This is a dangerous business out here, and people are well aware of that when they sign on. He spread his hands and peaked his brows, lines creasing across his forehead like a wise preacher. "Sometimes, accidents just happen. The tanks are extremely volatile. They are reacting on their own accord. Almost as if they were alive," he said, surprising himself with his insight. "Charley never saw it coming. It happened quickly. He didn't suffer."

Casey rifled doubt at Glibson. She found the man's

words hard to believe after witnessing Charley's melted face. Glibson held his position. "I guess we never know when we are called." For a moment, he cast his eyes downward as if engaging in her suffering but then puffed himself and gave her a sympathetic smile saying, "Find strength in knowing that he's gone to a better place."

Casey's breath gushed in disbelief. She stepped hotly into Glibson's face. "What the hell are you smiling about?" She pointed to the glass. "Did you see his face?"

"What kind of bullshit line is that?" Jett screeched. "You guys created this mess and can't figure out how to fix it. While we're waiting for you to come up with something, the nasty A-Bomb shit continues to disable and infect human and animal lives. Gone to a better place? Is that all you can say? You religious nut bag."

Glibson cautiously stepped back, caught off guard by the fomenting hostility. Jett held firm, fouled by Glibson's repugnance, which stank like a freshly laid turd. Casey shouted, "I want to get my brother out of here. Away from this horrible place. You hear me?"

An approaching figure answered with a voice of authority. "I'm afraid that will not be possible, young lady."

"Who the hell are you?" Casey blasted back.

Richard straightened himself to his full five foot four and adjusted his glasses. Proudly, and with a stern tone, he addressed her. "Richard Shorter, Director of Operations."

Casey stepped in close and stood over him, ready for a fight. "Oh, the big man himself. I suppose the one responsible for the killing of my brother."

Richard raised his head to meet her eyes. "Your brother's death was an accident. His remains are highly contaminated, and his body needs special handling."

"He's my brother. I want him burned. He never wanted to be buried."

Richard, accustomed to showing authority, lifted his voice to take command. "Burning would release radiation into the air and contaminate a facility. His body is in our charge, and we will deal with it properly. We will place it in a sealed container in a concrete-lined grave. These are the ordained facts and procedures, and fortunately, for everyone's benefit, we have logistics planned for this kind of situation. There is a private location that will enable the entombment. His body is unacceptable to any other cemeteries. Don't waste your time thinking about it. I am sorry for your loss, but these are the rules. There is no need to criticize us. We are only doing our job as mandated."

"Why is Charley's death so meaningless? I feel no sense of remorse or guilt coming from you. Just another accident, you say? You seem more concerned with covering your miserable asses than about Charley."

" Casey, we're sorry but we're only doing what we have to do."

Richard let her words pass through him. He held power and knew that the accident was not his fault. She had no idea what they were up against on the site. No way would he waste his time schooling this belligerent piece of trailer trash. He had reviewed Charley's file and knew their story. "A date for the burial will be soon. We can't hold him in this protected space indefinitely. These are the facts. You need to contact anyone in the family that needs to know. The burial will be nearby in the Richland area. Clair can give you details."

"What? I get no say in how or where he can be buried? I got rights. Charley has rights."

"Not here. This Reservation is Federal and Atomic Energy Commission territory. You can have a choice of flowers."

"How nice … Real generous of you … You self-righteous weasel."

An incredulous look sprang from Clair's eyes while Richard's face glowed red, eyes bulging. Turning away, momentarily defeated, Casey returned to her silent brother behind the glass. She touched her heart. "Charley, why did you have to come here?"

Jett grasped hold of her hand. "Let's go, Casey."

"Call your folks. The funeral is in four days. Don't be concerned about the costs. We will cover everything," Bill said.

"Small favor for killing him," she said over her shoulder while making for the exit.

Ms. Wright caught up to them in the long hall. "You'll need my pass card to exit. I'll call you, Casey," Clair said while buzzing open the door.

They sat shattered and shaking, gathering themselves in the sanctuary of the Honda. She put the car in gear, and they gladly left the tanks, the hospital, the whole sordid Reservation, and that nasty little man behind. Charley remained. The big river valley opened before them as they coasted down the long grade. Disillusionment dispersed into the spacious skies. Dirty cobwebs of disgust, hurt and anger clung to them.

"Can you believe that shit?" Casey cried out. " I want to scratch that guy's eyes out!"

"I can't blame you. Those jerks are in total control. Seem to want just to get it all over and done. On with the show. Business as usual. On to a better place, huh?"

"Well, I hope so."

"He looked horrible, didn't he?"

"Yeah, fried. Poor Charley never had a chance. To them, his life was meaningless. It's not for me. Down in my gut, what happened to him makes me want justice. I want to get back at them. Get back at that whole damn place. Change something. Make them care about what they're doing to the people working there and to the environment."

"Good ideas, but how?"

She lifted her eyelids and shook her head. "I don't know, Jett. I don't know."

Chapter 4

A sign for their return route appeared by the roadside. The Cascade Mountains beckoned from the west, but Casey resisted taking the easy way home. Thirsting for more answers about what happened to Charley and what Hanford consisted of, she questioned Jett. " Is there somewhere out here where I can get an overview of the Hanford Site?"

"Hmm. Let me think about it," Jett said while scrolling through the encyclopedia of his retentive mind. "I recall that you can get up on a bluff out in the Reach. From there, you can overlook the river and down into Hanford. It's on the Oregon side and east of where we are. Hell, we're out here with plenty of daylight left. I'm good for a look-see." He held his belly. "My stomach is talking. Let's get something to eat first."

She sailed past her turn. "Mexican ought to be good around here."

Casey extracted the Washington State Atlas she kept under the car seat. It showed the Oregon boundary side as well. After scanning the back roads route to the Hanford Reach, she found the turn-off and set out across the dirt road framed by rocky buttes and sage pocked hillsides. Billowing clouds of dust lifted behind them. The washboard road kept the pace slow and challenged their digestion. They bumped along for about fifteen miles until they reached an overlook and pulled over. She wished she had binoculars.

Across the Columbia River, the nuclear Reservation stretched into the steamy distance. In contrast, the snaking river flowed through clusters of small islands that provided shelter and food for wildlife. The river view, beautifully alive and picturesque in how it wove a green, watery swath of life through the arid countryside, transported her beyond lingering indignation remaining from the flash encounter with that vile little man at the hospital. Focusing on the watery sight below, she merged with the river's flow and accepted that Charley's burial was out of her control. Theirs to do what and how they pleased. After all, he was dead, she reckoned.

The far side of the river spread brown and stark in contrast to the living corridor. Ghostly tombs of concrete ruins stood grey as cigarette ash with nothing alive anywhere. She wondered if even the ants survived. Sure weren't any birds happily chirping. High voltage towers jolted skywards out of the burnt toast landscape and more trailed off into the barren distance. Something deadly, against the forces of life, had occurred there. Antimatter remained embedded in the ground, seeping along, following gravity, in underground plumes that led into the Columbia River. To the west, steam rose in fluffy clouds above concrete box, windowless buildings. Casey pointed, "What's that, Jett?"

"I'm guessing that it's the Columbia Generating Station, the last of the nuke power plants still running. I'd forgotten all about it. They sure keep everything hush-hush. No one ever mentions it anymore."

"So, they're still making the shit." Scowling, she

swiped her hand across the site in dismay. "The place is huge, isn't it?"

"Yeah, from down below, you'd never know anything was going on. It was a good idea to come up here. You can get perspective on how all locked up tight it is down there. A squad of Green Berets couldn't get in. You know surveillance has got to be state of the art." Jett turned to the Cascade range and introduced it with his hand. "Meanwhile, over here, there's a whole line of volcanos waiting to erupt, and there is no protection from earthquakes. The 177 tanks could rumble and burst, or they could just randomly explode in a bigger burp than what got Charley."

"Gee, wouldn't that be sweet. No wonder they propagandize that it's all cool, under control, no worry. Don't want people to freak out now, do they?"

From her vantage, she tried to imagine that seismic event. Too terrible to comprehend, she switched her thoughts back to the river where life and death met side by side. She chose the picture of life and stroked towards the river, her hand like a paintbrush. "Look how gracefully it carves through the land. A green stripe, a wildlife sanctuary in this bare-scape. The Mother doesn't give up easily, does she?"

"No, she doesn't. I believe RiverKeepers float through this stretch, and Native Americans fish it," Jett said, moving to her side.

Casey brightened. "Floating the river. That's a good idea. See the complex from the river. The back door might have an opening."

"Worth a try, but don't get your hopes up. No one has ever been able to do anything to nuclear waste other than storing it in a big can. You should look into

RiverKeepers. They monitor river issues. You know, Rex. He's a member. Check him out. So, ready to get a move on?"

"Almost."

Casey remembered that she should call her mother. Stepping back from the car, she leaned against it in preparation for her reaction to what usually came when she spoke with mother. It pained to have to talk with Sally. Why she held any sense of loyalty to her un-mothering mother, she couldn't figure other than an obligation to Charley. He would want Sally to come to his funeral. He had held a certain attachment to her despite her selfish neglect all through their childhood. Sons and mothers, Casey guessed. A strange male voice answered, half laughing, half talking. "Long Tall, Sally's."

Laughter and "Stop it, Jimmy. Gimmie the damn phone," garbled in the background. "Hello."

"What's going on, Mom?"

"Casey, is that you?" she chirped. "Having a little par-ty with Jimmy boy." She cupped the phone while giggling. "Stop it. I'm on the phone with my daughter—How are you, dear?"

"Have you heard about Charley?"

"Oh, poor Charley. Yes, they called me. Such terrible news. Very sad. Have you seen him?"

Casey would have slammed down the receiver if she was talking on an old-style landline. Sally could be so self-centered and heartless. "Yeah, I've seen him. He's dead. Cooked and horrible looking. It wasn't Charley lying there. You didn't miss anything."

"How dreadful."

"Here is the situation. The Feds have total control.

He has to be buried in a certain way at a certain place because he's contaminated."

"Oh, my God. When?"

"Like in four days. You should get a flight or drive up to Richland soon. You are coming to his funeral, aren't you?"

"What did they say about the costs? All that special handling sounds expensive."

"They said they'd cover all the costs."

"What about my costs? Do they say anything about that? Anything about the damages?"

"No, nothing was said. Forget about it. You owe Charley to come up and say good-bye."

"Of course I do, honey. I'll work something out. Get Jimmy to cover the tickets. How are you holding up?"

"I guess I'm still in shock. Dry-eyed for now, anyway. Don't know when the tears will come next. It doesn't take much: what a scary place out there and a horrible way to die. Charley was nuts to go to work there. I'll miss him."

"Yes, I know. He was a good boy."

"Look, I'll call you with the details as soon as I get time and place, but get up here and leave your phone on. They said four days."

Casey lifted her head to the fluffy clouds sailing past. The afternoon sun bore down, and the phone shone in her hand. Still digesting the call with her mother, she rang Lolly, hoping to clear the distaste of dealing with Sally. The voice mail prompt came on. Casey assured Lolly that she was doing okay, missed her, and looked forward to being with her when she made her upriver swing. The truth of the matter was that Casey didn't want Lolly anywhere near her mother. Least of all, at an emotional funeral accompanied by some Jimmy guy. The extra drama of whatever her mother could cook up, she preferred not to risk. Besides, she felt ashamed—no need for Lolly to see so deeply into her roots.

Chapter 5

Casey dragged herself down the hallway to her room. It had been a long day. When she closed the door, she turned and caught her reflection flashing back from the mirror attached to the vintage dresser against the wall. Her body's image startled her. It seemed such a strange vessel that held her essence. She thought of how the person held inside Charley had left his ruined body. No longer there, where did he go? Where do we all go? From where do we come?

Mangled Charley crept into her mind. Her stomach churned. Yanking her door back open, she urgently went to the bathroom and splashed water on her face in vain. No splash of water would wash away the horror of seeing him lying like that. She wondered how she would find peace. Perhaps, she wouldn't.

She had no use for religion. She felt forgotten by the white-bearded father God and his Son found in churches. But anyway, perhaps that DOE guy was right; all she could do was pray. She could pray to the Goddess. She clasped her hands together and prayed for Charley. Prayed that he would be at peace. Her mind spun like a gun barrel, chambering on vengeance.

****

Jett took a PBR beer can from the cooler and flopped his lanky body into the lazy boy chair adjacent to Frank. He half drained the beer in one slug.

"So, how'd it go today up at Hanford?" Frank

asked out of the side of his mouth.

Jett blew air like an emptying balloon. He gripped his thigh and leaned into Frank. "Man, Charley was messed up bad."

"How bad?"

"Melted with a scabby, red blob head, like someone threw acid on his face and stomped him. And that's just what we could see through the glass window. What the stuff did to his insides, you can only imagine. He took a seriously high-level dose of radiation and toxic chemicals. Scary place, man. There's some bad energy hanging around out there. All the years of unnatural things going on. Know what I mean? Some slick-talking DOE guy tried to smooth us with religion. They said it was a freak accident, making like they don't know it's all ready to blow at any time. I couldn't wait to get out of there. They're burying him in concrete in a few days."

"Damn."

"Casey's hurting. You know how close she and Charley were. You should talk to her. Let her know you care."

"I don't know about that. I'm always saying the wrong things."

"Just come from the heart, bro."

****

Casey rummaged through her chest of drawers, searching for her old photo album. Inside the album, she found a selfie. One of her and Charley huddled by the big pine in the forest behind their trailer. The big tree was their special place. By the tree, they nestled in the sanctuary of nature and found refuge as children. Later on, it was there, when she was sprouting, and his stubbly beard stood dark upon his face that they held one another and shared their struggles with an unkind world. She grasped the picture close to her chest and felt the sadness of memory. She kissed his face and placed the image on top of the dresser, propping it against a unique shell. Had Charley ever made it to the beach? She took hold of a candle that stood to one side on the dresser, placed it behind the photograph, and lit it. The flame rose and glowed a soft yellow in the mirrored backdrop—a grotto formed for the memory of him. She laid on the bed and held the picture and the wavering candle in her mind's eye. She went to him, searching for a way for him to remain close to her. Letting go, she allowed the Universe to carry her to the realm where his spirit lingered, seeking one last embrace.

A knock sounded on her door. "It's me, Frank. Can I come in?"

A weak "all right," replied.

He cracked open the door and peeked in tentatively. Casey didn't object, so he slid into the room and sat beside her on the bed and waited. She rolled over his way, hair rumpled, dark rings showing under her eyes. She seemed lost. He reached for her and held her like a child. His touch comforted. Vulnerable, she felt open to him in a way she knew he liked but rarely ever allowed herself to show. "I'm sorry, Casey, about what happened. I know, seeing Charley like that has to hurt. But you're my rad girl. You gotta carry on—stay strong—know what I mean?"

"Yeah, right. Always about you, isn't it, Frank? Wanting me to be the way you can handle it. Your go for it, Casey girl," she said, with a harsh, mocking voice which sadly contradicted the softness she had been feeling.

"That's what I mean. Hold on to that Casey attitude. Stay on top. You know, go with the positive flow. Right?"

Her mouth arched down. "Frank, I don't want to hear that flow shit right now. You're not helping."

Frank recognized he was floundering, and before he lost the goodwill of his intention, he got up from the closeness of the bed and moved towards the door. Turning back with his hand on the knob, he threw his last pitch. "We're hitting Swell City tomorrow. I heard that the wind will be kicking. You should join us. Catch a good blow. Go to Church—Know what I mean?"

Rising from her grief, she consented, understanding that Frank was trying in the awkward way he could to lift her spirits. "I guess so."

****

At Swell City, the wind picked up mid-morning. It funneled through the Gorge from just the right angle. The wind pushing against the downriver current peaked the water into rolling waves, which added an extra lift to the windsurfer's perfect ride. The waves, easing off shoreward, lapped gently against smooth rock slabs of basalt tonguing from the river bank. Casey could almost smell the sea in the air as the breeze whistled by, even though Swell City sat more than one hundred miles away from the ocean. Already, windsurfers streaked across the river. They dashed through waves, dancing around a tug and barge that pushed to ports near to Portland and closer to the Pacific Ocean.

"All right! Looking good," Frank said, as they pulled on wetsuits and lowered their boards and sails off of the truck rack.

"Lot of tourists," Jett said, noticing the out-of-state plates. "The words out on the spot."

Frank shrugged. "Don't matter. There's plenty of room on the river, and the vibe is bitchin."

Casey walked with Jett down the rocky path towards the flat stone slabs that jutted into the river. Their smooth surfaces next to the water made for easy launching. Jett's damaged knee kept him off of the water. A snowboarding incident had put an end to his windsurfing days. The icy cold water and lateral strain were too much. He kayaked once in a while, but he mostly hung out by the big river, conducted a little product business, and enjoyed being at the scene. "Feeling better today, Casey?" he asked.

"I'm trying to," she said, managing a sliver of a smile. "Yesterday was hard, but today I'm holding Charley in my heart, sending him my love."

"I'm glad. I'm thinking of you both." Jett locked eyes with Casey. "The wind will help your heart. Go to Church!"

Across the wide river, rolling waves white-capped from the stiff breeze. The whites breaking off the tops of the waves splotched the dark river like seagull droppings on a rocky shoreline. Casey gathered herself. Her blood pumped, and she launched. The wind popped open her sail, and off she flew. She leaned back and cut through the waves on her board, her mind and heart opening to the wind's rush propelling her forward.

Reaching the far side of the river, she tacked, filled her sail, and reversed course. The stiff breeze in her face felt marvelous. Water sprayed in rainbows and rolled up and over her head as she pearled through a wave. She laughed at the good fun until fear gnawed at her perception. What was in this water? How safe could it be? The Hanford leaked into it! She grimaced, imagining the poison and radiation in the water, while revulsion and paranoia began to rack her nerves. She raced to the far side, avoiding spray in a near panic.

Stripping off her wetsuit beside Frank's truck, she frantically searched for a towel to wipe herself off. She shuddered, thinking the stuff had got onto her skin, under her nails, and God forbid, into her mouth.

Rex, a friend of hers, prepared his windsurfing equipment next to his truck, close to where Casey scrambled in desperation. "Casey, what's up? Step on an ants nest or something?"

"It's the river. It's poisoned. It's got radiation in it. I know. I can feel it. It's all making sense now."

"Hey, take it easy. What's making sense? The radiation levels are negligent. There's nothing to worry about."

"Who says it's negligent? Who's fooling us? What about 'river nose' and these skin rashes we get, and who knows what's going on inside us. We windsurfers get more exposure than anybody except maybe for the Native Americans who eat so much fish. Some of us are getting wet almost every day."

"I always shower off afterward. Look, the State has done tests, and they say plain old pollution is causing river nose. There's plenty of agricultural and industrial runoff going into the river too, you know."

"They would say that. I thought you RiverKeeper people were smart. You've been up in the Reach. What have you seen?"

Rex's face scrunched. She could see his wheels

turning. "Well, I guess we have seen evidence that contaminated groundwater is traveling through plumes, a kind of underground spring, making its way into the Columbia. The poison is still in the ground, leaching. No doubt spawning fish and aquatic creatures are being affected, but I still think we're safe."

"Oh yeah? So what's being done about it?" Are you people keeping it secret too?"

"Hey, you know how powerful those guys are."

"Yeah, I was up there yesterday. Right in the middle of that hell hole."

"Frank told me. I'm sorry about your brother. I can't blame you for being upset. You should come to one of our meetings. We want people involved who are concerned and are willing to speak out."

"Thanks for caring, Rex," she said, managing a smile. "Maybe I should check out your meeting. You know, connect with some activists. I need to do something about what's happening with the river. She's too beautiful to be ruined by contamination." For now, she held her vengeful thoughts tight to her chest.

"That's for sure," Rex said, lifting his board. "Check us out online and come join us at the next meeting." He turned towards the river. "Gonna catch a ride."

"You're in denial," she shouted at his back.

****

Bill Glibson sat out back of his two-story, big-box home in his padded lounge chair. Hot out in the Eastern Washington high plateau, his covered porch provided some comforting shade. He watched his two children frolicking in the backyard pool and reflected on his blessings: an eight-year-old boy and a six-year-old girl, a loving, tending wife, church on Sunday, and a well-paid job with all the benefits being part of the royal family of government provided. Life is good, or so it should be, he thought. But he was bored stiff with the same-old-same-old and troubled by the uncontrollable aspects of his toxic charge.

His wife Janet brought him another icy gin and tonic. He gladly took a sip. "The pork roast is in the oven, and I've made a salad," she said. He gazed into the distance. "Problems at work?" she asked.

Bill lifted his head and showed her a frown. "They never seem to end. The latest burp incident that killed a man has the unions on our back. His body is lying in a contamination ward, and I have to go to the funeral." He found the compassion he desired on his wife's face and continued his unloading. " His sister and her punk ass boyfriend were in today, and when I tried to give them some spiritual comfort, they got confrontational. Environmentalist types—plenty to bitch about but no answers. No telling what kind of trouble she and her buddy will cause."

"Well, you can hardly blame her for being angry, can you?"

Bill took a big slurp of his gin. "Of course not, but she should show some respect for us. There's no easy fix for the situation we've inherited. The funding keeps coming up short, and the science swings like a pendulum. I know it must have been horrible seeing her brother like that and believe me; I didn't like it either. But, I'm sick to death of everyone pointing the finger at us, as if we made the stuff. All those tattooed and pierced haters of our kind of world weirdos need to get a grip. They don't have a clue as to what we're up against."

"Should I get a tattoo?" Janet asked coquettishly. She turned sideways, sucked in her stomach, and held her chin up questing for approval.

"I love you just the way you are," he said and took hold of her hand, his eyes angling upwards to inconveniently dwell upon her double chin plumped by her appreciative grin. His reflective sunglasses hid his inherent apathy.

"Oh Bill, you say the nicest things." She gave him a peck on the forehead. "I'd better check the roast."

That went well. I haven't lost the touch. Maybe I'll get some tonight, Bill mused. A stir tingled below, and he fed his arousal by drifting into the dreamy, sensual world where his often-attended erotic fantasy awaited. Eyes closed, that fine piece of ass dancer he fancied from the strip club materialized from the pulp of brain where she resided. Saucy and willing to tantalize, her arched back and spread legs offered him her dark-rimmed, fleshy-lipped orchid. That ruby stoned hood piercing guiding his eyes to her bulging clitoris. He stiffened.

"Okay, kids. Out of the pool and get changed. Dinner is almost ready," Mom yelled from the poolside.

Chapter 6

Dressed in black in the warm June sun, Casey stood next to her mother at Charley's gravesite. A fat rope cordoned off the concrete-lined pit like at a museum exhibition. Jett and Frank flanked Casey on one side while red-eyed Jimmy held Sally's arm on the other. Jimmy profiled a walking cliche of a washed-up casino casualty in his bursting at the buttons rumpled suit, western hat, and turquoise bolo tie. Mom could sure pick them. However, Casey had to give Sally credit. Clothed smartly in a black dress and wearing a prim hat with a veil over her face, she portrayed the picture book grieving mother. Indeed, she had much to suffer. Glancing sideways, Casey saw real tears on Sally's face as the solemn preacher began to give Charley his last rights.

A pile of freshly dug dirt stained the air. A floral arrangement of white lilies in a stand-up vase stood at the head of the grave. Charley, a lump in a sack, lay in the bottom of the concrete vault. Casey hungered to feel him, but he was not there. She brought her eyes to study Bill Glibson's face. She watched him reverently listening to the words of the preacher. His entitled aura symbolized a class of people to her, ones who had always set themselves above her, like the entitled kids who ostracized and made fun of her underfed, red-headed looks, her untrendy cloths, and bad address. A channel opened. Anger and hate flooded in. Now, they had killed her brother.

Casey gripped her fingers into her hands. Past and present merged into one. Though the pit lay before her, closure would not come. She watched as Sally tossed a handful of dirt onto the corpse. Casey took the cue and followed. Time stood still as she clasped a handful of cold, freshly dug soil. She raised her clenched fist of dirt to her pursed lips and gathered her thoughts into an unspoken vow. Slowly, she hour-glassed her intention into the awaiting grave. Her eyes burned into Glibson as the dirt fell. He felt their heat and warily acknowledged her, glad that her brother lay in rest.

With no wish to linger, they moved away from the burial site. The waiting backhoe fired up and placed the concrete lid onto the tomb, and began to backfill. The remote gravesite conveniently was situated in a far corner of an old pioneer cemetery in Richland, Washington.

Away from the commotion, en route to their vehicles, Bill approached and introduced himself to Sally and her friend Jimmy. "I'm sorry about your son's death, Mrs. Long. He was a hard-working, respectable young man that found himself at the wrong place at the wrong time. It was an accident no one could have predicted."

"So, what happens now? When do we get compensated for his death?" Sally said sharply.

"Have you been dependent on Charley for income?"

Sally quickly thought of an answer to tide her over until she could come up with something better. "Oh, he was a good son and, of course, sent me money. He knew I needed help. Why do you ask? For sure, the government has to pay for his wrongful death?"

"It was an accident, Mrs. Long. Charley signed a release form when he came on board. He knew the job was dangerous. I'm afraid that, according to the law, only his dependents, such as wife and children, would be covered." He leaned towards her. "But if you have proof that he regularly sent you money and that you were dependent on that money to cover your bills, you may be considered a dependent."

Her lips slid to the side. "Sounds like I need a lawyer."

"You can do that if you wish. But I'll warn you. The law is precise."

"Well, damn. What kind of outfit are you? Kill my boy and leave all of us with nothing. I just may have to lawyer up. In the meantime, you could at least offer to pay for my air-fare up here. I had to borrow money from Jimmy here to make the trip. And while you're at it, he should get a ticket too—part of your funeral expenses. Get away with murder and don't suffer a penny. What kind of people are you?"

He reached into his inner coat pocket, drew out a card, and handed it to Sally. "Send me a copy of your receipts, and I'll submit your request for consideration. I'm sorry for your loss." Turning from Sally, he gave a sympathetic nod to Casey and walked away, disgusted by the whole scene. Thoughts and prayers were all he could offer them.

Casey gave thanks that no reporters were present. What good would they be anyway-showcasing a dysfunctional grieving family, at best? Digging into who they were, where they came from, and what they wanted. Her mother making her needs clear. Sure, another complaint about the Reservation would splash the news, but people have been damaged there for decades. Countless stories had already been written, voices raised in protest, and the stuff remains the same, joined by a steady influx of fresh barrels.

The group circled. Jett and Frank kept quiet, allowing the family drama to unfold. Frank's truck stood ready to clear out Charley's things from his apartment. "I need a drink," Sally belted out. For Casey, getting drunk with her mother was the last thing she wanted to do. "Come on over to the motel room and join us in a toast to Charley?"

"We've planned on going to Charley's apartment to clear it out. Want to come with us instead?" Casey said.

"Nah. It don't matter anymore. Can you believe it? Not even a dime for us survivors. I'm having me a good drink, toast Charley, and fly back to Reno tomorrow. Who'd a ever thought my fine boy would end like this? Give me a hug, Casey. Nice to see you, girl. You're lookin' good. Nice meeting your boyfriends, too. Come on, Jimmy. Let's blow this place."

****

They found Charley's apartment upstairs in a two-story motel looking complex. A grey stubbled, buzz-cut apartment manager guided them to Charley's unit and unlocked the door. "Sad about Charley. He seemed a good kid. He always paid on time, and he didn't make no trouble. Some of these contract workers drink up a storm and make a lot of noise. A real pain in the you know what."

Jake pushed open the door. To her surprise, Casey crossed the threshold into a perfectly clean space;

everything in its place, nothing personal about it. A comfortable chair, a sofa, a TV on a stand, and some bar stools butted up to a kitchen island decorated the room. Washed dishes stood starkly in the rack. Counters were clean, and carpets seemed recently vacuumed. Who lived here, she wondered. It struck her that the time she spent discovering herself since leaving Spokane caused her to lose contact with who Charley had become and what filled his life. It dawned on her that the place represented the antithesis of their trailer growing up. From that point of view, it all made sense, him wanting to make his life better.

"Well, I'll be, look at this place. Wish they all kept their apartments like this. You wouldn't believe how trashed some of these places get. People do the darndest things. Take out all of their frustrations on the apartment, like it did something to them. No problem getting the cleaning deposit back on this unit." Sally missed an opportunity.

Wandering about the apartment, Casey searched for signs of the brother who once was so close to her. She opened cupboards, checked the fridge, and walked down the hall. She poked her head into the bathroom and then swung to the closed door of his bedroom while Frank and Jett investigated the refrigerator's contents. Quietly, she opened the bedroom door. A wisp of breeze from the adjacent window floated by her. The bed lay rumpled and unmade revealing a sign of life. Entering the room, she turned and brushed back the louvered door of the closet. She remembered childhood games and wanted to cry out, "I found you."

His smell, from off of a rack of hanging clothes, surrounded her. Captured in its familiarity, she surrendered to memory. She closed her eyes and laid her head on the sleeve of a soft sweater. A vision whooshed through, transporting her to where she found herself face to face with Charley standing in the desert sands. He flashed his panic to her as an unseen force gripped him and knocked him to the ground. Gasping, she backed away. She listened for sounds coming from her friends. They remained in the kitchen. Re-entering the closet, she stroked through his clothes, searching for the connective thread. She needed to be with him again—feel him close. Shutting her eyes, she immersed herself in his clothes and whispered his name.

He answered her call. This time his soul reaching out to her with a pained and questioning expression upon his face. His arms hung at his sides. His turned palms implored an explanation. His eyes drilled her, blackening with anger, then fading to disbelief. She willed her form to move closer, to be together again, but he retreated. She shook her head side to side, disgust on her face, mouth downturned. Her thoughts turned bitter. "I won't let them get away with this, Charley." Their eyes locked in the psychic plane, and he nodded.

"There you are," Frank said, bursting into the bedroom. "Man, Charley was a clean freak."

She abruptly stepped away from the closet, shaking inside. She answered Frank with a mumbled explanation. "Probably a reaction to the cluttered, slob hole we lived in as kids." She gestured to the closet. "Take a look at his clothes and see if there's anything you want."

"This poncho is kinda cool," Frank said, scanning the rack. "Jett's gone to the truck for some boxes and black plastic bags. We might as well keep the provisions. Don't you think?"

"Sure," she said, distracted by opening the top drawer of his dresser. Her hand went immediately to a silver chain necklace with a blue-green earth stone pendant on it. She thumbed the smooth surface of the stone then held it to her chest with eyes shut. Charley whisked through her again, this time as a memory of Christmas past. The necklace, a present given to him the year he went off on his own. She put it around her neck.

"Here are some bags to put stuff in." Jett tossed them on the bed.

"Check out this poncho, man. See if there's anything you like before we bag it," Frank said, shuffling hangers.

Jett stepped into the closet and ran his hand through the clothing. He checked the sizing. "I'm too tall for this stuff. Besides, it's too weird for me. Hey, after we finish up here, let's do the kitchen. Pack up the loose stuff we'll keep and toss the rest in the dumpster." He put a hand on Casey's shoulder. "How are you doing?"

She murmured, "I'm okay... .You're right. It is weird, but I'm connecting," she said, reaching for a framed picture of a young woman sitting on the dresser. She wondered who the woman could be.

In the kitchen, Jake said, "Y'all got a place for the furniture items?"

They looked at each other. "Not really. I figure we'll take them to Goodwill. Maybe keep the TV," Casey said.

"Tell you what. I can do you one better. I'll give

you two hundred dollars for everything and rent the place furnished. What do you say?"

"Beats having to haul it down the stairs," Frank said.

"It's a deal, Jake. Thanks," Casey said.

Chapter 7

Lolly slipped into Casey's room. The window curtains fluffed in the evening breeze. Casey lay curled on her bed, the sheet scrunched in her hands, worn out from the emotions of burying Charley and clearing his apartment. Setting down bowls of warm soup on the bedside end table, Lolly eased herself onto the bed's edge and gently stroked Casey's cheek. Her eyes opened, glazed from her inner world. "Lolly, you're here!" Casey cried out, lurching upwards to embrace her. Lolly moved onto the bed and propped herself against the headboard. Casey nestled into her, resting her head on Lolly's mothering chest. With a heaving breath, she surrendered.

"How are you? It must have been a very long day?"

"Yes. A sad, long day. At least he's buried and loose ends wrapped up."

"I can only imagine what you must be feeling. Even though I didn't know Charley, I know from you how much he meant to you. It's hard to lose a loved one, but the memories will always be there. Keep the good ones and let the rest go. They won't serve you anymore." Casey snuggled tighter. Holding Lolly provided the physical touch that she needed. It gave her a release from the mental strain that lay heavily upon her. A peaceful feeling rained over.

"I brought the wonton soup from Chinatown that

you like." Without waiting for an answer, Lolly got up and delivered the bowls. "Sit up, Casey." She sat, and Lolly passed the bowl. The smell of the broth promised comfort. Pressing, shoulder to shoulder, they spooned nourishment.

Glamorous, more sophisticated, and outgoing than Casey, Lolly posed as the big sister Casey never had. Though only a year apart in age, Casey followed Lolly's lead right from the beginning days in Portland, Oregon, where they met by chance through a mutual friend. Someone who Casey vaguely knew from Spokane and who Lolly had befriended in the Portland bar scene. Having no interest in mainstream paths and escaping from a stifling, small town, wrong side of the tracks upbringing, they shared an affinity along with their family scars.

Released from the miserable situations that held them down, they reveled in the awakened freedom found in the hipster city of Portland. A fast friendship flourished. They took waitress jobs and a small apartment. They cruised the bars—spreading their wings, exploring their sexuality, and along the way, unexpectedly uncovering an unknown calling that brought them into each other's arms.

Waitressing lasted but so long. Growing restless, they needed more. Lolly dreamed of a life as a showgirl in Las Vegas and figured a job dancing in a strip club could get her on track. She could save money while she enhanced her theatrical talents, at least the seductive dancing side. Lolly had the goods, and besides, the thought of dancing naked in front of men, teasing them with what they couldn't get, excited her. Frequenting the steamy strip clubs, she studied the dancer's moves and soon took it to the stage.

Stripping was not Casey's scene. More of a tomboy rebel, she preferred outdoor adventure. She couldn't imagine herself getting naked on stage, which the Portland clubs had the dancers do. On a weekend trip up the Columbia River to Hood River, Oregon, she found an outdoor adventure lifestyle that beckoned. So they developed separate lives but remained emotionally close. Lolly became more urban, and Casey wild country. Lolly's stripper circuit up and down the river made for keeping them close and their fire lit.

In silence, they rested. The warm soup and companionship comforted. But, it was not enough to quell what roiled within Casey. "Those bastards are going to pay," she growled into the quiet.

"Who? What are you talking about?"

"Those miserable Hanford bastards that killed Charley. Somehow, I'm going to get payback. They think they are untouchable, but they'll see."

Lolly stroked her head. "Easy girl. Now is not the time for those thoughts."

Casey allowed herself to draw back into Lolly's chest. Her softness pillowed the inner edge that burned inside. Her warm and promising flesh transformed the turbulence within Casey into lusty desire. She thought it strange, perhaps even sinful at first. But she needed to feel loved in the physical world.

She slow circled her hand downwards to touch Lolly's special parts. Lolly responded by spreading her fingers on Casey's back and pulling her closer. The touch sparked arousal. It juiced and ran in their spines. The emotional stirrings from the intensity of tragic loss triggered an awareness of the precious now of being alive. The life within their bodies flooded to the touching of skin. Compassion morphed to passion. They kissed deeply—tender and fulfilling—the loving, easy between them, no male-female ego games getting in the way. They loved and gave woman to woman, satisfying each other from a knowledge of their like body's' desires.

Laying entwined, they savored their lovemaking, thankful for the gift of each other, grateful for the gift of life, mindful of the loss of Charley.

****

Frank and Jett stood coffee cups in hand in the morning—yellow kitchen. Curiosity running high, they observed Lolly and Casey entering hand in hand. "There's coffee in the pot," Frank said and zipped his loose lips before he found himself in trouble. Only yesterday, Charley buried. He wasn't sure about Casey's mood. Her aura shone brightly at the moment, but how will she pick up the pieces and go on?

"If anybody is hungry, I can whip up my buckwheat-buttermilk pancakes with boysenberry syrup," Jett offered with an elegant roll of his hand.

"Yeah!" They cheered. Casey and Lolly helped themselves to coffee and joined Frank at the table while Jett did his kitchen magic. His cooking expertise equaled his flare with cannabis chemistry.

"So, how have you been, Lolly?" Frank said with the table his focus. It took an effort not to fixate on what poked out of the front of her thin tee-shirt. He couldn't help himself from being attracted, and it took real willpower to not stare like a hungry dog. She, so beautiful that guys paid money to look at her. Devoid of make-up and with unbrushed bedroom hair, his imagination tweaked further. He raised his eyes to find hers.

"Keeping the boys well entertained as usual," she said, probing him with her violet eyes. He squirmed uncomfortably in his seat. She enjoyed the power she held over men—so predictably easy to stir. "You know, everyday life in Stumptown. Pretty God-damned awful what happened to Charley. Thanks for being there for Casey yesterday. "

"I'm always there for Casey, we're buds. But yeah, sucks about Charley. Everything about that stinking Hanford sucks. But they sure have their asses covered. Safely hiding under the shield of government self—righteousness and getting away with it."

"Not if I can help it," Casey spouted.

"Right, Casey, what a great thing to wake up the world, but how the fuck are you gonna do that?"

"Burn it down," Lolly said.

"Bullshit, then the whole place would explode with radiation flying everywhere!" Frank practically yelled.

"Get the media involved." Casey wasn't so sure about that, not wanting to be the center of attention.

Frank went off. "Just another nasty incident reported in the press. Another gone bad day at Hanford. People are numb to what has been going on and can't figure out what to do. Everyone stuck in the sludge." He gathered his thoughts. " It's not an easy one to figure out, you know. Damaging the place in any way, even if you could, would only hurt countless numbers of innocent people. It's like the place becomes protected by its potential for destructive evil. The government can't even control what's going on out there. They don't know what to do with what they've got, yet they keep generating more waste. Besides, the area is under surveillance. No sane person would want to do anything that released any extra radiation onto the planet or into the ozone. That defeats the point."

"Well, damn it! Who's to blame?" Casey yelled.

Jett placed a stack of pancakes on the table and returned with butter and syrup. Before anyone could go off again, he answered Casey in a calm but firm voice. "The damn nuclear waste. Completely guilty but innocent in that it's only doing what antimatter has to do; kill living things. Otherwise, I suppose the Department Of Energy. They're calling all the shots. Have been from the beginning. There's the do-nothing Congress, and then there's the WA River Protection Solutions. They're the contractors running the show, allowing workers to be injured."

"Some of those guys come to watch me dance out in Umatilla," Lolly interjected while forking some pancakes onto her plate.

"Well, next time that pretty ass of yours is pumping in the air, fart in their faces for me. Will ya?" Casey said to their astonishment.

Lolly about choked on her mouthful of pancake. "Those sick bastards just might like that."

Chapter 8

Casey decided to attend a RiverKeeper meeting held in downtown Hood River. As hard as it might be for her, she would try to keep an open mind. She knew that she had to do something in order to find a clue towards getting retribution for Charley. Nothing had come to mind so far, which left her in a quandary. Checking out RiverKeepers seemed as good a possibility as any. Jett wanted to go, too.

While driving to the meeting, she called Lolly. "Hey, babe. Thinking about you. How are you doing?"

"Casey, hey! Still wiggling my ass for the cowboys. Sorry, haven't farted on them yet." Roars of laughter broke out on both ends of the phone. "But, I'll see what brews. It could be a special effect for my act. Keep me lingering in the boys' minds," she said with a Mae West tone of voice. She waited for Casey's laughter to die down. The laughing felt good. " Listen, Love. I'm afraid my timeline is running tight. I'll have to drive by on the way back to Portland. Are you okay?"

"As good as I can be, I guess. Anyway, I'm on my way to a RiverKeeper meeting. I am going to give them a try. Thought I'd let you know and say a quick hi. I miss you."

" That's sweet. Glad you're going to the meeting. Maybe you'll find something you can get your teeth into."

"Yeah, something to bite into."

"Watch you don't bite off more than you can chew, girl. Keep it together—will you? Hey, I'm sorry, but I'm getting ready for work, so I have to go. Miss you too. Bye-ee."

****

A crowd of people gathered outside of the RiverKeeper office. Casey slapped palms with some familiar faces from the windsurfing and kayaking scene. Her community—a place and a set of people where she had found a home.

She followed the herd into the building. Jett went in his own direction. Spotting Rex, she took a seat next to him. Joan took the mike, welcoming and introducing Johnathon Law, who proved to be a charismatic speaker. The primary subject of the evening, salmon. The rising temperatures of the water in the Columbia River, caused by dams not releasing water when they should, caused migrating salmon deaths. He threw out a disturbing number. Only three percent of the fish from Lewis and Clark's time now made it up the River. His words struck a chord. The dam's actions represented another strike against nature by man's disconnected self-righteousness. But water temperature problems for fish didn't further her quest.

Johnathon brought his pitch to a crescendo. A disgruntled murmur tumbled through the crowd. Someone yelled out, "Blow the dams!" Casey liked the sound of that. The threat sat her up straight in her seat, wanting to hear more. Johnathon reined them in with his raised hands and replied, "the dam operators are ignoring the law, impeding the flow of the river to keep the turbines spinning. Energy profits prioritized over our salmon legacy." Loud boos and hisses rang out. "We can't let these dam operators break the law. We're filing a citizens suit, which will demand that the operators must obey the law. Save the Salmon!" He cried with a raised fist. "Save the Salmon!" The crowd echoed. "Save the River!" He yelled. "Save the River!" They cheered back. "Write your congressmen. Keep the issue in their face. Let them know that 'the people' are behind the suit."

A lot of good that would do. She enjoyed the emotional chanting, but lawsuits and political activism could not satisfy the anger she held in her heart. All manner of protests for decades had already been done against Hanford with next to nothing to show. After more than sixty years of horrible incidents, deaths, and contaminations, it remained a bleeding cancer upon the environment. Now that it had killed her innocent brother, it became personal.

Johnathon ended his speech by praising all the achievements that activism had brought towards halting the oil terminals and liquefied natural gas platforms that would have added more potential problems for the Columbia River beyond the damage currently being done by the coal trains. He also heaped praise on the backbone of the organization, the river monitors.

Casey looked around at the nearly all-white crowd of politically correct people and struggled with where she fit in. Always an outsider when it came to groups, she cast a glance back at Jett, who offered up a shrug. Next to her, Rex remained intently involved, lapping up the group's solidarity. She mentally ran through the list of possibilities she could join. Door to door knocking? Definitely no. Testing water for E-Coli? It seemed covered. Carrying signs and chanting slogans? Nah. It appeared that fish held the power platform. Probably because of all the different groups it pulled together. The idea of working with Native Americans felt good, but how? It didn't seem like anyone at the meeting would be willing to do something radical. Protest at best, and that was not what she had in mind.

The crowd thinned, and Jett left with some friends. She approached the sign-up and information table. A friendly, grey-haired woman with tortoiseshell glasses wearing a RiverKeeper T-shirt asked if she was looking for something in particular. " I heard about a kayak trip in the Hanford Reach?"

"There's our annual float coming up in a couple of weeks. Are you an experienced kayaker?"

"Does a fish swim?"

The woman's body stiffened, and her face puckered at Casey's smart-aleck response. None the less she muddled around among the sign-up sheets. Finding the one for Hanford, she handed it to Casey to sign and give her details. Casey filled in the paperwork, handed it over, and smiled at the woman. The smile worked. The woman took a second look at Casey. Perhaps that spunk could make for an ardent protestor. "I'm Andrea. Good to meet you, Casey. First time here?"

"Yep."

"Know about Hanford?"

"Sure do. I want to know more."

"It's the stuff out there you can't see that's scary, all those depressing old relics, too. I've floated the Reach once and have no desire to do it again. It's too weird for me out there."

"I noticed that Johnathon didn't mention it tonight."

"Plenty of more winnable battles to be fought. Hanford is an unmovable object. We just bounce off the walls of that one," Andrea said, putting her head down while gathering all of the paperwork, eager to call it a night. "We have your number. Someone will contact you."

Casey left with a feeling of accomplishment. At least the next step had come out of the meeting—a trip onto the river running alongside Hanford. Despite being in the company of people who cared about the river, she remained alone in her radical thoughts.

Outside, a few stragglers gathered in a circle, voices raised in a discussion about fracked oil trains that now passed through the Gorge. Only recently, a train had derailed, spilling oil and starting a fire that burned for three days. A frightening fire because no one out there in the country had equipment designed to handle an oil fire. At least this time, the spill didn't go into the water, soaking into the land side of the track instead. Rex turned away from the group when Casey appeared. "I noticed you went to the sign-up table."

"Yeah, I signed up for the Hanford kayak trip."

"Hey, I'm on that float, too. There is lots of wildlife out there. It's been a reserve for sixty years on the side opposite the old nuke buildings. Someone will give you a call or a text." He gave her a Cheshire cat smile. "Maybe me."

She returned the smile and started to turn away. "Stop by the club sometime. I'll give you one on the house," she said over her shoulder. With her hands tucked into the pockets of her light-weight hoodie, she continued down the sidewalk, stepping over the cracks, winding her way towards work at the saloon, one small notch closer to finding some way to get justice for Charley.

Chapter 9

The Hanford Reach kayak group met at the Park and Ride adjacent to the Interstate. It was a blue sky day in the glorious early Pacific Northwest summer. They loaded their boats and gear into a dual-wheeled cargo truck and then climbed into a four-bench express van for the ride out to the Reach. Only nine of them, they spread out and got comfortable. Casey sat beside Rex, the only person that she knew. "You'll like the river out there," he said. " It's the last free-flowing section of the Columbia before all of the dams."

"What about the old nuke stuff?"

"I think you'll find it more interesting looking for wildlife on the Oregon side, but the old sites are still visible."

"Always the optimist, aren't you?"

"Why not? There's enough negativity in the world. The plutonium reactors are long gone."

"Maybe, but not the waste and you know it. Just don't tell me to chill like Frank does, or I'll have to pop you one."

Rex jokingly covered his face with his arms, and they settled in for the long, highway journey. Julie, the trip guide, barked out from the front passenger seat against the road noise. She talked about safety stuff and shared information about possible wildlife they might see, including some pelican colonies. A hardy, sun-spotted woman with short-cropped, salt and pepper hair, wire-rimmed glasses, and a floppy sun hat, Julie reminded Casey of what a camp counselor might be. She muttered under her breath to Rex. "Please, no campfire songs."

They unloaded and stretched their bodies at the Vernita Bridge landing site to prepare for the nineteen-mile drift in the confining kayaks. Julie explained that only one beaching would happen over on the Oregon side of the River, where it was legal. With a steady current, the trip estimated out to be around six hours duration. With anticipation building, excited by the blue sky above and the shining river of water before them, they brought their kayaks to the shoreline and put on their wetsuits. Julie instructed. "Try and be respectful of the wildlife living here by keeping voices down. People on boats are the only ones coming through here, so it's a sensitive area. The water looks pretty calm now but keep in mind that anything can happen. Be aware. That is important. I know you're all pretty experienced river people so, I won't harp anymore. Let's stay somewhat together and share along the way. Any questions?"

They moved towards the water, but before anyone could launch, Casey spouted out, "I've heard that there are some seeps of radiation coming into the river in this section. Is the water in this stretch more contaminated than elsewhere?" People stopped in their tracks. Unspoken concern passed among them. Some turned and frowned disgustedly at her like she was bumming their trip.

Julie answered with a yes and a yes. "We're only floating through not handling anything. We'll wash off our exposed skin with fresh water when we land. There's no need for concern. I know it might seem scary entering this section of the river. Nobody here is ignorant of the fact that the Hanford Reservation is on the Washington side, so we'll try and stay to the center of the river and beach in Oregon. We'll see some of the old buildings. Think of yourselves as observers. Take note of what you see, and we'll talk about it later."

They launched their boats, and the Columbia River quickly engaged. Smooth and waveless on the surface, it ran dark and deep underneath, the only sound, the dipping of their paddles. In what seemed an instant, the launch site fell behind. Drifting swirls randomly creased the water's surface. The smell of dry earth rising from the surrounds blended with the water's soft scent, derived from the merging of its many mountain-fed tributaries. Casey felt the current pulling her boat much stronger than farther downstream by Hood River, where between the Bonneville and The Dalles Dams, the flow of the water is regulated.

Rex stroked up alongside Casey. "Think ya spooked them?"

"Hopefully, I reminded them about what's going on out here. Buddy up with me, and let's 'observe' together. I'm curious about underground plumes. You know, like, is it a myth or what?"

"What do you think we should be looking for?"

"I'm not sure. Something tells me we'll know it when we see it. Maybe a wet spot on the bank? Some sort of discoloration at the shoreline?" She adjusted her course with her paddle and drawled over her shoulder, "Maybe there's a sign posted like: 'Beware of poisonous seep.'"

"Yeah, right."

A gravel bar showed through thin water towards

the bank on the reactor side. Casey stroked towards it. Rex followed. Silver and green flashed in the sunlight. A small school of salmon fry flitted across the bar and away from their kayaks, colors brightly seen when they turned broadside to the light and current. A pleasurable riffle passed through her. The baby fish pleased her. Amazing that life existed in the place of death after all. She remembered the view from the overlook. Pointing at the fish, she caught Rex's attention. He came close to share the experience with her. She drifted, engrossed in the little fish. "Poor little guys have to grow up in this environment. Didn't the A-Bomb makers even think about it?"

Rex watched the sunlight reflecting off of the water quake upon Casey's face, pleased by her lightening up. "I doubt it mattered to them, even though this part of the river has been a major spawning ground forever. The place has been imprinted in the fish DNA. Plenty of gravel and the islands break up the strong current. This stretch is the last place where fall Chinook spawn in the river."

They floated along through the wild corridor. Scattered shrubs rooted hungrily into the rocky dry ground on top of the banks. Fed by the mists rising off of the water, a trim of green plants edged the shoreline. Sagebrush, the dominant plant, trailed off into the surrounding desolation of Hanford until it vanished altogether. Across from them, the more interesting Oregon side enchanted. The hilly preserve sprawled into the distant, bleak, but life inhabited wilderness. Ahead, kayakers pointed towards the bank where a coyote drank from the only water around. His thirst quenched, he warily trotted over the rise, returning to the backcountry with his tongue hanging in satisfaction.

They came upon a small cluster of driftwood encrusted islands where a colony of the spoken of white pelicans sprang white-feathered to the skies. She stuck her paddle flat against the current to slow her momentum, gaining time to absorb wildlife activity while they floated through the islands. An eagle screeched. Casey turned her head to see the great bald head dive. It plunged onto unsuspecting little ducks that swam in the lee of a dot of an island. Reacting fast, the ducks dove deep, escaping at the last moment from the raptor's talons trimming the water. The eagle lifted and circled. It prepared for another assault while the little ducks popped up their heads for a breath of air. Enthralled by Nature's drama, Casey sat silently watching the diving and dunking survival ritual go on.

The Reach held life despite everything. Carrying on like it always had. Wildlife fed and reproduced off of and within the contaminated waters. The creatures didn't know. They belonged to the River. What were they to do but live as they always had? Just like the native peoples who still ate the fish from these waters as they had for millenniums. The people and the creatures all survived one way or another, paying the price with their health; some mutating, some contracting fatal disease. Casey's insights irritated her. Not fair, this unknown pollution. Not the natural part of the circle of life but the radioactive polluting. Man's disruptive hand.

They paddled farther but saw no signs of seeping. In Casey's heart, if it were there, she'd find it. Her mind arched on a tangent. She imagined making an assault, beaching her boat, crawling up the bank, and then skulking across the barren waste with nowhere to take cover and going to where? Intent upon doing what, to whom?

The thought fizzled out, and she returned to scouting the shoreline. All the studies said the seeps existed. Even RiverKeepers knew of them. The dumping in trenches, the leaking tanks, gravity carrying the toxicity underground to the low-lying River collaborated facts, not fake news. She had to see for herself.

The abandoned reactor sites came into view. They loomed much taller from the water than from the far perspective the overlook had provided. Julie signaled the group to follow her to the Oregon side of the River, where a safe, legal beach gave a place to rest and gaze across at the ruins.

Landed and pleased to stand and stretch, the kayakers slowly made their way to sit on the warm, dry sand. Humanity's outstanding achievement of atomic meddling and the creation of undying nuclear waste glared directly at them from the Washington side of the river. For some, the sight triggered old memories of the Cold War and further back to when the unleashing of the atom's awesome power lifted the human species from top predator to a God-like position. A position that held the fate of the world in its hands, literally having the trigger in its finger, the button on the desk, poised to end life as known. Blow everything to smithereens. Evolution completed.

Most of the group, die-hard environmentalists, sat with anguish on their faces, absorbing the window into history, crumbling into the dirt in the distance. But one of the women held a different perspective. With her chin held high and arms proudly crossed on her chest, a sense of righteousness exuded from witnessing the source of power in the western world. Casey imagined the possibility of a government agent infiltrating the group, while, at the same time, Julie pointed out the B-reactor, where the plutonium for the atomic bombs dropped on Japan in World War Two got made.

Energy bars, a sandwich, fruit, and water consumed, they went back upon the water. Soon, the tattered ruins of Hanford Town stood to the north. Like the tribal members whose village had been nearby, all of the townspeople got moving orders when the nuclear project proceeded. Casey pointed towards the ruins to Rex. "Let's swing over by old Hanford Town."

They paddled towards the far shore where the battered high school still stood. Aged and decayed, it could have been a bombed-out, European World War Two relic.

Avoiding a sandbar, they swung into a backwater eddy. Spooked ducks sprang into flight in front of them. Gliding, they studied the depth of the water, avoiding the chance of running aground. Some sickly grasses stuck out from the bank. Was this it? She brought her kayak closer, excitement rising. Pointing to a spot upon the bank, she called to Rex, "See that? See that? Is that water trickling out of the ground over there?"

He removed his sunglasses and squinted. "You're right. I see a wet spot."

Straggly, yellowed grasses drooped away from the seep edge. They moved their boats to get a better viewing angle. A foam rose from the trickle of liquid and spread to a nasty orange and pink gunk smeared over exposed rocks. "I see it!" Rex cried out, a jolt of fear zapping through him. "Radioactivity!" He quickly backstroked. "You've got your evidence. Let's get out of here. I don't want to be anywhere near that stuff."

"Okay, okay. Take it easy," Casey said while joining Rex in retreat. She had her proof. Toxicity still flowed into the river. How many other places existed? Perhaps beneath the water, much worse. Nobody doing anything about it other than talk. Untouchable Hanford getting away with whatever they wanted. But what could she do about it? Launching an attack from the shoreline seemed hopeless. Attack what? Attack whom? Her taking on security a ridiculous notion. Frustration wrenched her nerves. Something needed doing, but what? Not only for Charley but for the birds, the fish, and all the little creatures suffering at the hand of man's dereliction of duty. Suddenly, she knew what she must do.

The rest of the expedition floated a long way ahead. "Let's cruise and enjoy the ride. It won't matter if we're a little behind," Rex said. They sat back and let the River carry them, using their paddles like rudders. The sun burned hot. The water flowed cool. The air, off the water, soft and sweet on a delightful summer day.

Rounding a bend, they fell outside the lee of the point of land that had sheltered them. A gust of wind bellowed in upon them. It suddenly raised their bows and turned their boats sideways. Instinctively, they stuck their paddles and gained control of their kayaks only to continue to be assaulted by stiff headwinds from the west. The three o'clock blows had arrived, traveling inland from the Pacific Ocean a couple of hundred miles or so away. The big river and the ocean were all tied together in the Northwest circle of watery life.

Upstream wind and downstream current offset each other, and they traded the drift that they had enjoyed for the light chop that lifted upon the water. Without a keel, river kayaks are not well suited for wind. They suffer the danger of being pushed sideways. On top of that, the Columbia was no ordinary river. Powerful and wide, like a lake in places, it could kick up like a shallow sea with tightly formed peaked waves.

They worked their way over to the cliff edge, seeking protection and calmer water. Next to the far bank, they found temporary respite from the wind. Enjoying the momentary loll, they knew that a battle remained to make way towards their final destination.

Finding their stride, they gained upon the group, who haggardly struggled against the wind. Many were older and not powerful paddlers. Casey saw them puffing hard with heads bent. Exhaustion hung on their faces. Desperately, they stroked towards a landing they wished to please be not too far away.

A white-haired woman had fallen behind. Visibly straining, she began to lose ground to the wind. Casey went towards her but refrained from making contact. She evaluated the woman's state of mind while pulling within a couple of boat lengths. "Need some help?"

"Yes, if you can," the woman answered breathlessly.

"Can you stay calm? No jerky movements?"

The woman gave a thumbs up. It reassured Casey. She did not want herself or the other woman falling into the water. Kayaks are a tippy business. The cold water treacherous. If someone panicked in the water, they could drown. The current was next to impossible to swim against, the shore far, and the water temperature in the forties.

She noticed a line attached to the other boat's bow and brought her boat alongside, calling out to the woman against the wind. "Don't stop paddling, no matter what. Stay balanced and calm. I'm going to try and hook up."

"Okay," the frightened woman said.

Casey reached and took hold of the line. It spooled out enough to give clearance between the two boats. The boats jerked and rocked when the rope snapped taut. The white-haired woman's mouth gaped wide open in shock while she wisely slapped her paddle side to side against the water, fighting to hold her balance. Casey worked her boat forward until she could get a short glide. She quickly tied off the tag line into a slot behind her seat. Hooked up, she bore down with a strong and steady rhythm. "Better?" Casey shouted over her shoulder. The woman heaved a breath and flashed an encouraging smile.

The joyful sight of the expedition's trucks, standing and waiting for their arrival, gave an inspired push to the finish line. A cheer went up when their hulls scraped the gravel of the beach. Onshore, the towed woman vigorously hugged Casey. "Thanks so much! I was really in trouble. I didn't know I was so out of shape." Her ruddy face glowed from the wind, and her white-blonde hair flew about in a tangled mop. Grabbing for her sun hat, which hung flapping on her back by a cord, she said, "I'm Lidia from Portland."

"Casey from Bingen. Glad I could give you a lift. That wind was a surprise."

"Makes you realize how much the water needs respect," Lidia said.

Wearily they loaded up. The drivers assisted. Stripping out of wetsuits, they washed hands and climbed into the van, eager to be free of the wind, done with adventure, and returning to civilization: a hot shower and a meal pictured in their minds.

Lidia sat next to Casey. The van chugged up from the river bank and onto the flat of shrub-steppe. Pointing out of the window, Lydia said, "Reminds me of back home out there."

"Oh yeah. Where is that?"

"Texas. I moved up to Portland last year. I was able to pull some strings and transfer to the Intel office for my last couple of years. I wanted to live in a green world where the air was fresh and clean and get into all the big nature out here. The water especially. Coming from Texas, you can understand why."

"I've never been there, but I can imagine how up here is different."

"Different, all right. Like night and day on the liberal factor. Anyway, I got a kayak and started exploring. Then I read an article about Hanford's accidents and was shocked and surprised that I knew nothing about the place. Didn't even know it existed. When I found out how much nuclear waste remained, the history, and how it continued to leak into the water, I wanted to see for myself. It's unbelievable that more isn't done to keep things safe."

"My brother got killed in one of those accidents. That's why I made the trip. To find out more about the place."

"I'm so sorry, Casey. It must have been hard being close to where your brother got killed. Something needs doing. Hanford is out of control. People getting hurt and all. I think of those poor birds eating poisoned food and the fish getting born in those waters. My God, it's awful. I'm not eating fish out of there. What is our government doing?"

A woman sitting behind them interjected. "They're doing the best they can with a challenging situation."

"They should do something better, and soon. All the stockpiled oozing waste is unforgivable."

"It was necessary to win the cold war. If we hadn't made those warheads, we could all be speaking Russian."

Casey recognized the proud woman from the observation point. "What a load of crap. Like Russia was going to invade us. The government is not doing what they're supposed to do because they don't have the will to spend the money. They're just buying time to cover it up. Passing the buck. Using workers as expendables." The woman sat back in retreat. "You're not a RiverKeeper, are you?" Casey demanded.

"No, just curious to see that stretch of the river."

"Probably a spy," Casey sneered.

Julie, hearing their heated conversation, turned from the front seat. She spoke in a firm voice, like a consoling mother on a road trip. "Come on, you two. Let's settle down. We have a long trip ahead. I, for one, don't want to hear any bickering."

"There's a spy among us," Casey shouted out.

"Everyone has a right to an opinion," Julie countered.

Casey frowned. Would the camp songs start?

The convoy pulled off of the Interstate and into a truck stop for a meal. "Join me at the counter, Casey?" Rex asked. Glad to distance herself from the group, she sat with him. Rex asked, "What was going on back in the van?"

"A difference of opinion offered by a spy. My gut tells me that nuclear proud woman was on the trip to watch us."

"Could be. It's a known trip sponsored by a group that is adversarial to Hanford, which is an extension of the government."

The waitress came. Rex ordered. "Chicken fried steak, eggs over medium, hash browns, rye toast, and coffee."

"That sounds really good. I'm super hungry. I'll have the same but make my eggs over easy," Casey said.

Rex took a sip of coffee and faced Casey. "Good work helping out that woman on the river."

"She's nice. She moved up from Texas and supports me in believing something needs to be done about Hanford. I need that. Most of the time, I feel like the Lone Ranger."

"We all believe something should get done."

Casey leaned her head towards him and bored with her eyes. "Not good enough, Rex. We've seen the seeps, and I have a dead brother."

His lips turned down, his head bobbing in acknowledgment.

Chapter 10

Light from Jett's basement lab spilled through the upstairs cracked door leading into the kitchen. Frank opened the door and peeked down the illuminated stairwell and heard the fans spinning loudly. He knocked hard and called down into the lab. "Okay to enter, Jett?"

"Come on down," sounded from below.

Frank bounded down the stairs, taking them two at a time. When he reached the bottom, the top of his head nearly popped off from the astringent scent. He staggered to a stop. The air reeked with the clinging smell of solvent even though Jett had fans extracting and refreshing. Jett stood dressed in a lab coat with his hands on his hips. He sported a three-day-old beard that seemed never to get shaved or grow out. Jett pushed up his protective goggles onto his forehead and wondered what could be up with Frank? Odd, the way he descended the stairs. His visit into the lab a rarity.

Frank sniffed around the room, warily. "Shit man, I always get paranoid when I come down here. Wonder when my house is going to blow up."

"Come on, Frank. I know what I'm doing. Didn't go to college for nothing."

"You hear the stories all the time about blasters getting blown up."

"Amateurs."

Frank shifted side to side, his eyes sparkling. He

rubbed on his chin and launched into his pitch. "Something amazing has happened. You have to listen to this. I just got a call from my cousin, Tony, in Chicago, and his people want to back a lab in Oregon." Up on his toes, his face electrified, Frank practically screamed the words— "And they want to do it with us! You know, cash in on the green rush of legalized weed. The lab could be huge for us. Casey too."

Jett cocked his head sideways. "Cousin Tony's people?"

"Tony is my older cousin on my mother's side. He and my uncles are into business investments and stuff, and they see the legal weed opportunity as a bonanza. Knowing me, they figure I would be a fit to represent them out here."

"Okay, go on."

"Tony has done some research and knows that Oregon doesn't require residency to apply for a license. They'll hire a savvy attorney to set up the company and submit all the forms and fees. It's only $4,750 for a processor license, but getting the building and lab setup will be big bucks. The deal is they put up the money, and we run the show. You know, like a silent partner. You supervise the lab, and I'll make the sales. I've been getting bored lately, you know, same old—same old. It would be fun hooking up with all the dispensaries and meeting new people. Hey, Casey could get on board, too. She might like running a grow room or helping me with sales. These guys have deep pockets, man. Anything can happen. They trust me. I'm family."

"Your family wants to go into the weed business?"

"My uncle and my cousin. They're entrepreneurs of sorts. Got their fingers in many pots."

"You never told me about this."

"Never was a need to. I've been kind of hiding out from all of them. A family drop-out. Off doing my own thing. You know, since my dad died."

"You think you could run a business? What's the split?"

"We'd have to negotiate the split. Business management we can buy if needed."

Jett allowed Frank's news to percolate and got on with his clean up. Entrepreneurs huh? Jett kept Frank jogging in place until it all sank in then responded with, "Yeah, yeah, yeah, it all sounds great. Weird to be jumping in with who knows who to cash in on the weed gold rush. This whole thing has been about consciousness for me, not how much money I can make."

"So. You could spread more consciousness, dude. The legal road is paved. Why not us instead of somebody else going for the ride? The big guys are already moving in. They smell the money. There's no stopping it."

He had a point. "I'll think about it."

****

Casey's feet plodded along the pathway leading to the door of her home. Her backpack hung loosely over one shoulder. She had to keep bumping the pack up as she walked. She couldn't be bothered to put it on properly after the windy day on the River and all that traveling. She went straight to the refrigerator in the kitchen for a cold drink. Voices lifted up the stairwell from down in the basement. That was unusual. "What's going on down there?" she yelled into the stairs.

Jett answered. "Hey, Casey. We'll be up in a

second. Welcome home."

Casey sipped on her beer as clomping footsteps on the wooden stairway announced Frank and Jett. "How'd it go out on the Reach?" Jett asked as soon as he came into the kitchen.

His interest perked her up. "Rex and I saw a suspicious seep flowing into the river. I can't prove it, but it sure looked like nasty, toxic liquid oozing out of the ground. Something like colorful, stinking scum."

"Damn. It's true then?"

"I believe so. What else could it be? Otherwise, the plant and wildlife were pretty cool along the water and on the Oregon side's high desert. What a contrast to the nuclear site. I searched for a possible opening, but I saw no way of doing anything to Hanford. Same observation as on the cliff. Lots of dirt and concrete."

Frank scowled. "Hope you didn't get too close to that seeping glop. You know, spreading radiation stuff around."

She made a grab for him, and he about jumped out of his skin and laughed a nervous laugh. "So, you hung with Rex mostly?"

"He was the only person I knew, and I get along with him. There was this spy bitch there too."

"Doing like what?" Frank asked.

"Watching, listening, and later standing up for the government when I said something negative. Anyway, I went. I saw it, and I've played with the RiverKeepers. Right now, I'm worn out and still have no answers. There doesn't seem to be any way of getting back at that damn Hanford." She threw up her hands and shrugged. "I remain fucking clueless." She drained her beer. "What you guys up to?"

Frank stepped under his spotlight. "Oh, explaining to Jett about an offer to set up a honey lab and a commercial grow from some family of mine. The whole deal financed and we run the show. There could be a place for you in it, too."

She scrutinized Frank in disbelief. He got defensive. "What do you think? Maybe get you to forget about all that vengeful thinking going on in your head. Pull you away from working at the saloon and into something where you can make some serious bucks."

"Damn, Frank didn't realize you had such a low opinion of me."

Frank's face sank. "Sorry, Casey, sometimes I say things that come out wrong. I simply meant that the deal could be a good thing for you and everybody. What's wrong with you people? Can't you see it? How exciting this is?"

"The idea sounds interesting, I'll have to admit, but I'm not giving up on getting payback for Charley, Frank. He didn't die for nothing!" She puffed herself up, like a tea kettle ready to blow. "Damn it! I'm so frustrated. If I can't get at the site, then maybe I'll have to settle for getting at them!"

Frank and Jett arched back like she'd slapped them with a wet fish. A flash exploded inside her head while listening to her own words spilling loosely off of the top of her tired mind. Had she found the answer? Getting at people is a lot easier than trying to take down a nuclear facility fortress. But, getting people is up close and personal. A lot different hurting somebody than something. She wondered if she had the guts to do that and do it to whom. That little prick and his slick, air speaking cohort immediately jumped to mind. The two of them represented Hanford's evil face to her. They protected their interests at all costs, the hell with anybody else, the environment, or the safety of workers. Lying, cheating, manipulating, doing anything to cover their asses, and proliferating alternative facts.

Jett's right eyebrow played Spock. "Interesting conclusion, Casey. We'll have to explore that thought when you're more rested."

Frank turned his back on her words. He didn't want to hear thoughts like that. Frank began to leave the room but changed course and spun back to face them. He raised his voice. "So what about the lab, guys? Let's move on from Hanford. How about it?"

Jett leveled him. " Charley's death isn't going away, Frank. It's not over. You should be helping us figure something out, not shutting it down."

Frank lifted his hands in dismay. "I don't want any part of it. You guys are crazy plotting against the government or whatever. You can't win against those guys because they're it, man. They're the law. They control everything," his voice scaling octaves. "I know you don't like hearing it, but get over it. Move on!"

Casey threw her beer can into the empty beer can bin. "Welcome home, Casey. Let's go sell out to corporate interests and forget about all this Hanford nonsense. No thanks, guys. I've had enough for today. Goodnight!" She turned and walked towards her bedroom.

Jett grabbed Frank by the arm. "Coming down on Casey doesn't help her, you know."

"Somebody has to give you two a reality check. Going after those big guys is bat shit crazy."

Jett kept silent, but in his mind, he agreed simultaneously with both Frank and Casey. Yes, contemplating revenge on Hanford seemed insane, but he'd done crazy things before. "I'm going to call it a day, too, Frank. Look, set up a meeting with your cousin or whoever, and let's see what's what. I know you mean well, and the deal might be a cool thing. So, you know, let's keep our options open." He gave Frank a bro-hug and a slap on the back. "See you in the morning, my brother."

Casey lit the candle on her dresser and held the picture of Charley. She needed to get close to him before falling asleep. The long day on the water flowed onward in the recess of her mind. She closed her eyes and conjured her brother's face. The handsome one that she hung on the wall of her inner room. She touched the necklace she found at his apartment. It lay around the candle, joined by the big tree's happy picture of the two of them, providing an altar and a channel for them to stay connected. She shared with him how she had witnessed the oozing seep.

Knowing what she now knew about Hanford's apocalyptic legacy raised the stakes. She thought of the Fukushima disaster, for it glared as an example of gone wrong nuclear and then put a question to herself. What if an earthquake, an explosion, or some crazy terrorist thing happened out there at Hanford? Toasted Northwest and worse. An alarm must be sounded. Something more than journalistic outrage. Could it be an attack on Hanford's leadership? Perhaps it had come to that.

Forgiveness found no home in her heart. She couldn't bear to think of innocent Charley swept away as if just another foot soldier laid in his grave by nuclear age garbage. She feared no end to future catastrophes was in sight. Nothing existed to stop the brewing, leaking threat that waited to unleash into some unknown disaster. She turned the burner down. The day for her had been long—time to rest.

Tiger, the cat, lay curled, on his side of the bed. She snuggled herself beside him and stroked his soft fur. He perked his ears and stretched, arching his back, paws reaching long out in front of him, and then settled back down to tuck into her stomach. She stroked him gently, and he purred, forming a ball of loving comfort. " So, Tiger boy, where do I go from here? Hanford is a giant. I feel like a lonely ant trying to move an apple."

She softly kneaded his tummy and relaxed with her eyes closed. Maybe she should be a RiverKeeper. Join the group and not get so carried away. Find fellowship. Perhaps not be such a loner, taking on the world by herself. In a way, the idea sounded inviting; finding peace through belonging. That would be something new for her. She had always stood apart from the crowd. What do you think, Charley?

She waited for his answer, talking to him, keeping him and the dialogue alive. Going deep into the tunnel, she waited for him. He came towards her. Their hearts and minds met. He showed no disfigurement, emanating a warmth out of what seemed a chilling space. She gave her unspoken love to him and wordlessly told of her frustration at not finding a way to avenge what had happened to him—until now. The face acknowledged her disappointment, and then his chin lifted and fell in encouragement.

She cleared with Charley, and the smart ass little

man jerked back into her mind. Vengeance became tangible. She knew not how, but the idea seemed so much more approachable, deviously pleasurable, and held a sense of potential satisfaction. She caught herself reveling in that satisfaction. A guilty flush startled her. Could she be so wicked as to seek harm to another human being? She'd never been like that before. She always shunned anything to do with hurting anybody or any living things. Could she be an avenging angel? Or was that a devil? Where did vengeance for being wronged stand on moral ground?

She awoke in the morning feeling thick and heavy, unsettled, her dreaming unfinished. She got up to use the toilet, her thoughts hazy. Returning to bed, with the dream sensation clinging, she rolled over and fell back asleep. Mid-morning, she groggily rolled out of bed and hunted down some coffee. Frank had gone windsurfing and Jett remained behind, surfing on his laptop at the kitchen table. "Morning, Casey. Rested up?"

She grunted and walked straight to the still-warm coffee pot, ignoring his question. Half a cup down, she yawned, stretched, and passed her hand through her uncombed hair, attempting to clear the cobwebs. "Sorry, Jett. Miserable night. I would have thought I'd have slept like a log after being on the water in the wind and everything. Dreams, man, crazy dreams kept running through my head."

"What dreams? Remember anything?" Jett asked, his eyes remaining on his screen.

"All I remember is that ass hole DOE guy was in them, and we were battling."

Jett looked up interested. "You win?"

"I don't know. It's all vague in my head.

Unresolved."

"Sounds like real life. Nothing about Charley is resolved."

"He likes the idea of getting back at those people."

"He tells you that?"

"In his way," she leaked out. "Nothing specific. When I thought about getting somebody, those two DOE guys, Richard Shorter and Bill Glibson jumped right into my mind. Like meant to be."

"If going after people associated with Charley's death is what you've decided on, those two seem like reasonable choices. But even though you don't like them and they may act like assholes, they're still people, probably with families and everything. To them, they're just doing their job."

"I don't care who they think they are. They're doing wrong, and they need to be held responsible. Being an 'upstanding citizen' doesn't give anyone a free ride. Anyway, I haven't decided anything for sure. The idea just started bouncing around. But I sure am beginning to think hard about it, considering how good it would feel hurting them, somehow. Knock them off of their high horses and get people's attention. Show them that they are at risk too. It's sickening how everything out there just stays the same, untouchable, getting worse all the time with nobody doing anything. It's a strange thought, I have to admit. You know, doing something to them. I've never been into hurting people on purpose before. I will have to be sure before I choose that direction."

"Same here. Don't think I've ever hurt anything other than a mosquito deliberately, but you may be right. Doing something radical could be the only way to get attention. Nothing else seems to have done anything. How about Frank's cousin putting a hit on them or something?"

Casey bent her head back. "You think Frank's 'people' are those type of guys?"

"I'm not sure. I've got a hunch that maybe they are. They aren't going to come out and tell you now, are they?"

"You interested in going into business with them?"

"I'm looking at it just for kicks."

"Anyway, their doing something wouldn't do. Any acts against Charley's killers are personal for me. I gotta have a hand in whatever goes down."

"You are serious about this."

"I think so, yeah. Dangerous crossing over to the dark side, like being a hitman or something, but right now, it seems the only way. Don't ask me what I have in mind. Just shooting them like dogs seems too everyday. Something more dramatic and meaningful is what's called for."

"How about blowing up their cars or their houses or something? I could make a butane bomb. I use the stuff in my blasting," Jett said.

"Yeah, with them in it."

Jett drew back his chair from the table. He looked her square in the eye. "That's a whole different ballgame, Casey. You're talking about killing people now?"

"Yeah, like the whole eye for an eye thing. It's welling up inside of me right now, just talking about it. I believe I definitely could do something to them. I'm burning inside and mad enough. I know it sounds horrible, but I don't know what else to do, Jett. Their smug faces hang in my head, mocking me. I can't stand the thought of them getting away with not protecting Charley and everyone else for that matter. So, I'm throwing this idea out there. Running with it. See where it goes." She shifted, placing a hand on hip." Got any clues on how we could find out more about them? Like where they live or what they like to do?" Her hands splayed outwards. "Don't suppose they do Facebook?"

Jett let out a snort. "You never know. I'll do some searches. See what I can discover. I want to help you, Casey, but I may need to draw the line on how far I go. Let's keep this talk to ourselves, okay? Not a word to Frank. What you are suggesting could put us all in great danger."

Chapter 11

Lolly paced around backstage while waiting for her gig to begin at the Waterside Lounge. The club was located in the small town of Umatilla, Oregon, on a frontage road near to one end of a bridge over the Columbia River that connected Tri-Cities, Washington to Oregon. The only titty bar, as the locals called it, for miles around, and just off of the Interstate 84, it drew customers from a wide swath of desert and beyond. Searching for a wild night out, men from the Tri-Cities migrated down to more progressive Oregon to catch a show. Adding to the Hanford guys were a slew of government contract workers stationed around the region, involved in projects like the hydro-dams or nearby weapons storage facilities. The men, mostly from out of town, holed up in motels, miles away from home, lonely and with money to spend, offered a perfect set up for Lolly's act. Well worth the drive out from the city of Portland.

The DJ pitched high, and then dropping low, he vibrated his voice suggestively into the PA system. "And now, let's have a warm welcome for L O L L Y, the girl you'd love to lick." She checked her face and hair in the mirror, the music came up, and she strolled out of the dim bar light and onto the soft-lit stage. A silvery shaft thrust upward from the center of the circular platform. A low railing rimmed the ring, holding the herd at bay. Grasping the central pole, she spun a slow inviting turn; her sequined, fringed bikini top and short skirt sparkling off of the light of the colored neon beer signs hanging on the wall. The stage spots glossed a sheen upon her satiny skin.

Unwinding from the pole, she strutted in her platform heels once around the ring to the sound of Bad Company's "Ready for Love." Her honey—vanilla scent trailed behind. Nostrils and primal urges flared. Urged on by what the men saw, they edged closer to the rail for what would come. With dollar bills floating onto the stage, her body began to grind and sway to the music.

She slowly rolled her top over her shoulders. Anticipating eyes stayed glued as her breasts sprang free, firm, and arched upwards like a semi-truck mudflap girl. Her top fell to the floor. She kicked it away naughtily while massaging and stiffening her garnet, baby bottle nipples. Returning to the pole, she rubbed seductively against it, then tossed her hair wildly about and sinuously wound down the rod to her knees. Taking to the floor, she slinked low across the stage like a panther, her mouth open, wanting.

Bill Glibson had just thrown down double. She paid him his due by leaning over the rail and wrapping her hair and scent around him. He leaned into her closeness and dug his nose within her hair while clutching the seat of his chair with both hands, fighting off the urge to grab her and bring her near.

Everyone knew the rules of the game. Around the ring, the players anteed up wanting some of that personal attention, if not this song, then the next.

Staying with Bad Company, Burning Sky opened for act two. Money swept into a pile at the base of the pole; she monkeyed up it and ripped off her tight little skirt, then circled down legs wide open, nothing hidden. Leaning with her hands on the pole, she bent forward, arching her ass into the air. With cheeks rotating side to side to the music, she gave the boys a full rear view of her womanhood.

Glibson elbowed Shorter and cupped his mouth to Richard's ear. "I told you she was hot. Would you look at that ass? Sweet Jesus!" Shorter sat entranced, red-faced, and with mouth parted as if ready to drool.

She worked naked around the circle, teasing the men with half shots of her trimmed pussy. She rubbed her breasts and, slapping her buttocks, randomly bent over and wiggled her cheeks. Song over, she leaned to gather the money, smiling at her customers upside down through her spread legs. Feel Like Making Love announced the last dance. She opened with another open-legged descent on the pole then took to the floor, mixing it up between sideways leg lifts, open leg scissors, and on her hands and knees ass rolls. She gave the men what they had come for. Money spurted out of the men's hands like an ATM. All the boys were eager to catch her eye for a personal, up close, money shot. Glibson threw a fiver, nudging Shorter, who did the same. She crawled their direction, following the scent of money. After posing for a nearby patron, she rolled onto her back and placed her ass nearly against the rail in front of Bill and Richard. Lifting her knees, she clicked the heels of her red shoes and wantonly spread her legs. There it protruded, crowned by the gleaming red, hood piercing jewel. Beneath it, the pink centered, black-lipped orchid that lived in Glibson's wet dream. The sharp slap together of her stacked heel shoes broke

Bill's trance. She returned to rolling and slithering her way around the ring, offering her charms to other men eagerly awaiting on the edge of their seats before parading herself around one last time, building lasting desire for her next set.

Dressed in a flowing silky robe, Lolly glided towards the bar. She passed close to Glibson. Watching his eyes follow her, she thought to work the high rollers for a private dance. Her finger gave the come hither sign. "Buy me a drink?" she asked.

Glibson swiveled out of his chair in a flash. Pleased by his readiness, she took his arm and lead to the bar while the next dancer came onto the stage. Shorter leered enviously. Lolly handed her money bag to the bartender and asked for a Manhattan. Bill found his voice. "Make it two."

"So, you liked the show?" she asked.

"Loved it," he said huskily.

She squeezed his arm. "How'd you like a special, private dance?"

Charmed, he answered, "I'd like that." They sipped their drinks, all the while making flirting eye contact. She put her napkin over her glass, and he took a long pull on his. The skin headed, tattoo armed bartender nodded. She motioned to Glibson towards the back room. Taking him by the hand, she strolled to the private dance area. He'd been there before but never with her. The bodyguard sat inside by the entrance.

"You can give forty dollars to the guy," she said, and Bill handed over the money. A sofa sat against the back wall. The room smelled of musk and perfume. She brought him by the hand to sit on the couch and stood in front of him. She loosened her robe and then seductively slid into a straddle upon him. Leaning over, she tented him with her long, auburn hair, creating a private world for him, close and warm, intimately scented. She pressed her breasts up into him and ground slowly on his lap. He stiffened and fell under her spell. She felt his rise. Maybe a big tip in the works. She undid his top shirt button, stroked his chest, and felt the fine cotton of his dress shirt. "You're a well-dressed man. What's your name?" she asked while continuing to work him over.

"Bill."

She held power and knew she could pop him off any time if she wanted to. Holding the edge, making them want more, the essence of the game. She went fishing, thinking of Casey. "You must work in management somewhere."

"Public relations."

"Oh, wow. Maybe you could do me a favor?" she said, nuzzling in close.

"Name it."

"I have a friend wanting to get hired on at Hanford. You know somebody?"

"Can't help you there. The Department of Energy isn't involved in hiring."

"Oh Bill, Department of Energy. Don't worry; I'll keep it a secret," she hushed into his ear as he nuzzled, drunk on his paid pleasure.

The meter ran out. Slowly extracting herself, she gave him a minute then offered a hand up. "We'll have to do this again," she said, taking his arm and leading him woozily back to the bar. Their drinks waited. She took a sip and asked, "Maybe your friend would like a special dance too?"

Bill grinned, a private dance might be just what his uptight buddy needed to shake loose. "I'll ask him.

"Lolly, I'd like you to meet my friend Richard Shorter, Director of Operations."

He blushed shyly when Lolly placed a warm hand upon the back of his neck. "I'm impressed, Richard. Pleased to meet you. Enjoying the show?"

"Yes, you are a great dancer." He gulped on his drink. Feeling challenged, his sense of pride took hold. He lifted his head to measure her fully and to show his appreciation as a man.

"That's sweet. Thank you, Richard." Her move to make, she rubbed gently on his shoulder. "Would you like to have a private dance with me like your friend Bill?"

Without hesitation, Richard gallantly offered his arm. He pursed his mouth at Bill like a man with something to prove and one in complete control.

She brought him to the backroom and banked another forty. Not surprisingly, she discovered that Richard, like many men of his stature, was a breast man when her cleavage matched perfectly to his face. She rode away on him, thinking all the while how she couldn't wait to tell Casey of her fortunate encounter.

Lolly led a flushed Richard back to the bar. In her heels, she stood a head taller. Bill welcomed with an 'atta boy' pat. She finished her drink and said, " Time for my next set. You boys going to watch?" They smiled like enamored schoolboys and watched her move away, her flimsy robe sinking into the crease between her swiveling cheeks, the anticipation of another glimpse of what lay within pictured in their minds.

****

Out in the parking lot, Lolly gathered herself in her pearl white pickup. She sipped a large coffee from the bar and got her head together for the long drive down the Interstate to Portland. A passing train clattered alongside the river. The air conditioning kicked in. She called Casey.

"Hey, babe. How are you?"

"Lolly! Hey. I'm getting ready to shut down the bar. How are you? You coming by?"

"They want me in Portland, and I'm running a little behind, so going to have to wave from the freeway. We'll catch up on the way back. Sorry."

"Me too."

"Hey, you're going to love this. I had a couple of guys related to Hanford hot for me tonight. Said they were DOE. Big shots, I think. Bill something and his twerky buddy Richard Shorter."

"Oh my God, Lolly! Those are the guys I've been dealing with."

"Seemed pretty innocent to me. Could have had the boys barking on a leash."

"They're dogs, all right. Don't be fooled. They're devious little shits. This lead is amazing news. Stay close with them. We may need to use them somehow. Crazy how I've been thinking about those two. Spirit works in mysterious ways."

"Since when have you been a philosopher?"

"Guess Jett is rubbing off on me. Think they'll be back?"

"Oh yeah. The boys are in love."

As she pulled out of the club's gravel lot, a streetlight reflected off of a sticker on her truck's rear window.

'GIRLS RULE AND MEN DROOL.'

Chapter 12

The Honda's tires hummed on the metal grated Hood River Bridge. The vibrations ran through the car and traveled up the back of Casey's neck. Dead ahead, Mt. Hood shone scarlet syrupy, drenched in the evening sun like an inverted snow cone. Even in summer, the sleeping volcano stood smothered in deep layers of glacial snow. Its presence formed a majestic backdrop behind the boutiquey town that rose from the Columbia River's banks. Midway across the bridge, a cool, western wind blew up the Gorge and passed through Casey's window. The soft breeze held the summery, algae scent of the river and brought relief from the lingering heat of the day.

On her way to work as a bartender at a saloon that sometimes showcased live music, Casey ruminated about how fate had placed her doing the same kind of job as her mother. She winced at the ironic twist. With nothing more than a high school diploma, hard-earned for all the trouble she endured socially in school, and the need to keep her days free for the outdoor sports that provided the excitement and interaction with nature she thrived on, what else could she do in a small town? At least she hadn't found anything she'd like better.

Her conversation with Jett about her thoughts on hurting the DOE guys snuck into her mind. Someone else who had lent an ear most likely would have blown her off. Jett listened. Always there for her when she needed an ear or some help. Lolly is good for that, too, sometimes. Lately, her summer schedule kept her running. She wasn't around much, which left a gap that Jett filled as far as sharing thoughts and feelings.

Few people in her history fit into the caring category. Her father left her when she was an infant. Her mother neglected her. Her few other kinfolks wanted nothing to do with them, and her number of childhood friends counted upon half a hand of fingers. She loved Jett like a brother, all the while knowing that secretly he wanted her in another way. But that wasn't going to happen. Not her type. Besides, good friends are hard to come by, and she did not want to jeopardize the stable relationship that she treasured. She hoped that he'd come up with a way to avenge Charley.

Getting closer to the saloon, she realized her teeth were grinding. Too many thoughts were tossing like greens in her mind's salad bowl. So much to consider and no clear answers. Tense and brittle as a kale chip, she couldn't lose the edge. If only Lolly were there to hold. To take in her arms and make love in the way that always worked. Casey imagined the release and how she needed it—waiting for it the hardest part.

No band planned to play that night. Throughout the place a murmur of conversation edged in front of the soundtrack seeping from hidden recesses in the saloon. Only a few regulars lined the long wooden bar, along with the occasional tourist wanting a liquor drink in the microbrewery and winery soaked town. The quiet customers sat mulling their thoughts, snatching occasional glances of themselves amid the reflections of colorful liquor bottles in the antique mirror that served as a backdrop behind her.

Her shift wound down, and her edge still clung a stubborn, aching cramp. When she heard the Harley rev out on the street through the bar door propped open on a warm night, she wet her lips. Leather vested and panted, the rider strode through the door. He ran his fingers through his windswept, black hair, biceps bunching. His head turned side to side as he walked, wary as a tiger, towards the bar where he straddled the stool in front of Casey. "Hey Sam," she greeted, with a glimmer in her eye.

He softened and smiled. "How's my wild child doing?" he said, then ordered in a thick voice. "Rye whiskey and a beer."

"Could be doing better," she called back, turning away to make his drink. His eyes followed her. They took in her rolled up at the waist plaid shirt, ponytail, and cutoff jeans—a regular Dolly Mae. She brought him his drinks and leaned forward on the bar with her nipples pushed up towards his face. "Maybe you could help me out?" she said.

"Just might be able to do that, sweetheart. Always ready for a taste of you." Reaching out and gently cupping her chin, he brought her forward into a kiss. The smell of leather and musky sweat coiled around her, and that was all it took.

"Stick around, Sam. I'll be done soon."

Chapter 13

Back at the saloon, Casey put in another days work, her mind stretched thin over infertile plans for revenge. It was a slow afternoon shift. Little Bear lumbered in and plunked down at the bar. His big ass buried the bar stool. He wore a well-worn size XXL cut-off sleeves T-shirt with bald eagles flying around on it and a Yamaha baseball cap. His hair hung straight and black. " Hey Woody," he greeted, calling attention to her reddish hair.

"Hey, you old bear. How's it going?" She liked Bear's sense of humor and gave him a warm smile.

"Going good and catching a lot of fish in my nets. I'll take a pint of Rainier."

"You got it. Fish are running strong?"

"Pretty good in the big river. Haven't gone up into the streams yet to spawn."

"I was up in the Reach the other day. You ever work there?"

"Sometimes, but I don't like it up there much. Bad vibes. Too much reminder of wicked things from the past."

"You hear about my brother?"

"No, what?"

"He was working at Hanford and got killed by some radiation explosion."

Little Bear's eyes beaded dark as coffee grounds. "I'm sorry to hear that, Casey. Bad place up there. First, they took away our village, and then they made their nuclear things. They've been slowly killing us off ever since. Poisoning us through the fish." He raised his palms and twisted them in the air. "Look. See my glow? I eat so much fish. All us Yakama do."

She looked him over. "Come to think of it, you do look a little red."

Little Bear waggled his thick finger at Casey, his deep eye lines creasing in good humor. "Pretty sharp beak there, Woodpecker." He drained his beer and sat back, appearing to think. She never could read his mind. He came straight ahead out of wherever it roamed. She observed his presence while he quietly sat. His neck was thick like a bull's, and his back and arms broad and stout like a bear's. He sat solid, like a boulder that had rolled down a cliff and lodged into the earth. He pointed to his glass.

She brought him another beer and leaned into him. "Can you keep a secret?" He scowled incredulously. "I want to get back at them for Charley."

"Me too," he whispered. "I'd like to repay them for what they've done to my people and to the Mother. When I'm on the River, I think of what it must have been. I listen to her. She tells me how she once felt, so clean and alive that she sang with beauty. My heart gets sad thinking about the poison that runs in her. I am sorry for the fish, animals, and birds that depend on the River, as my people do. We are one with them. I will think about it. I am your brother in this," he said, placing his massive hand onto her arm. She felt his strength and the collected spirits of his tribe gathered upon his leathery face. She believed him and nodded so.

Sam came into the bar. "Hey, you moving in on my girl, Horney Bear," Sam said, slapping him on the back and offering a hand.

"Just might be. I like this one."

"We got something in common there. Hey, Casey, looking good."

She stood with her hand on her arched hip. "I'm always looking good to you, Hungry Dog."

"Ha! Horney Bear and Hungry Dog. You better keep your legs crossed. Shot and a beer, please, my darling—and a shot for the Bear."

Little Bear waved over the bar. "Not today, Sam."

"What, you get religion or something?"

"Hey, don't poke the bear, or we play Cowboys and Indians."

Sam slapped the bar and huffed. Not many gave him a run for it. "Offer the man a drink, and he gets all growly."

Little Bear growled, then burst into a booming laugh and shouldered Sam with a thunk. Bear downed the remainder of his beer in one gulp and got up from the barstool. "See you. Pulling nets in the morning." Catching Casey's eye, he laid a finger on the side of his nose.

"Been thinking about you, Casey," Sam said.

"Can't imagine what about," she said, leaning into the bar.

"You know what I'm talking about. I'm getting hot just looking at you."

She pulled away and serviced some customers down the long wooden bar. He watched her move, and she knew it. Hers for the taking if she wanted. She liked the grip she held over a powerful man. He made her feel desirable, and she liked that. He needed sex, and so did she—best of all, with no strings attached—different than with Lolly. Although her mate, Lolly worked her route and lately, was hardly around. They had an unspoken agreement that what happened when they were apart didn't come between them. Sam offered something Lolly didn't supply.

They lay in her bed propped against pillows allowing the sweat to dry. A cigarette moment if they smoked. Sam shifted, rested his head on her chest, and cupped her breast. Perhaps wanting to go again. He never spent the night, and she didn't mind. It kept things non-committal. She trusted him in a peculiar way. Believing that ex-cons had some sense of loyalty, like gang stuff. "Sam, could you do something for me?"

"Name it," he said, kissing his way down her belly. She pulled him up and spoke directly. "I might need your help in doing something dangerous."

His face scrunched. "Like what?"

"I'm not sure yet. Something to do with getting even for Charley." She brought her finger across her lips. " You can't tell anybody. You promise?"

He zippered his lips. "My lips are sealed. You need somebody roughed up, scared silly?"

"Something like that."

"Hey, whatever. You're my girl."

She kneaded the hair at the back of his neck and nudged him down. "Good man. I needed to hear that."

Chapter 14

The fusion formed particles were trapped in a dank, metal chamber, reeking of deadly, rancid odors. There, the molecules of forced cohabitation wormed in strained confinement. Strontium 90 reluctantly embraced Tritium. Chromium and Carbon Tetrachloride roiled in the Uranium sludge laced with Iodine-129. Dancing all together in a forced measure, they pressed and gnawed at their walls, longing to escape captivity. Mixed and consolidated, the Frankenstein born conglomerate hungered for the juice of the living. Hungering to leech upon and erode life, acting out its natural dark nature—to poison and destroy. Thick with the residue of its original ungodly mandate, it had stewed into its own Hanford house brand of 'Toxic Soup.'

Etching against the steel walls, radiated fingers of linked molecular electrical charges moved in random directions like unseen deep-sea creatures. They could sense the life filled River, across the dry sand desert, flowing vulnerably only five miles away. The proximity drove it mad, causing it to claw downwards relentlessly. A gap cracked at last. Seeping in trickles, gravity pulling, it wound down through the sands to ink into the River, merging with the oceans of the living world.

Bubbles squirmed. Gleefully celebrating, they amoebaed within the sludge—hydrogen gases filling with laughter. The noxious Alka Seltzer rose.

"Burrrrp!" … Ahh… What a relief it was as they gassed through the crust of confinement, airborne and into the living world.

Chapter 15

Casey passed Jett on the way to the coffee pot. "Morning, Jett." His eyes held fast on his computer screen as he begrudgingly responded, an edge remaining from a restless night. Casey's room sat above his space, and whenever Sam came over, he knew. He didn't like Sam and all his swagger and sure didn't want him to know about downstairs. Jett made Casey promise never to tell. What Casey did with him was her business, but he wished she did it with him instead.

She poured a cup, drank, and searched for some bread to put into the toaster. She nearly banged her head on the cabinet door when Jett shouted," Casey, you've got to look at this!" She turned. He pointed to his computer screen.

"What's happening?"

"Something is going on at Hanford."

On the screen, a King 5 reporter readied for an interview. Richard Shorter and Bill Glibson stood in the background, talking into each other's ears. "Damn! It's them."

The newsman glumly faced the camera. A barren desert sprawled brown behind him. "This is Bob Olson with breaking news from King 5. There's been an eruption in the nuclear waste tanks at the Hanford Site. I'm referring to the one hundred and seventy-seven tanks that hold fifty million gallons of toxic waste left over from the plutonium reactors of the Cold War," he informed, grimacing, his words spilling out in pained disbelief.

Casey gasped and held her face with two hands. "Seven workers have been exposed to toxic vapors and taken to the HPMC Hanford Site medical facility for evaluation. I'm here with Mr. Shaw, an officer for the UA Local 598 union. Sir, what can you say about this tragic event?"

"Thank you, Bob. Horrible and disgusting that it's happened again," he said, head lowered, shaking side to side with his lips pursed. He lifted his saddened eyes to face the camera. "First, let me say that we extend our sympathies to the injured worker's families. We are appalled that these injuries continue to occur despite our requests and warnings to the DOE. Only recently there was a man killed. The company cannot use missing deadlines as an excuse for not taking care of the worker's safety. People are not disposable items. We have been demanding the use of supplied air inside the tank farm area. Despite our requests, they continue to do business as usual, denying the supplied air systems and monitors to protect workers from being exposed to chemical vapors. Our people matter."

"Do you know the extent of the workers injuries?"

"That is being determined at this moment. But remember that in many instances, the symptoms take time to manifest, proven by the cases of lung disease, cancers, and brain damages recorded throughout the years."

"How dreadful. Let's hope that the injured are soon on the road to recovery," Bob said to Shaw and motioned to the Hanford representatives who separated themselves from the Union men.

Richard and Bill, holding serious faces, walked towards Bob, the reporter. Casey hissed, "Watch the bastards try and wiggle out of it."

"With me now is DOE public relations man, Bill Glibson. Bill, can you tell us what has happened here."

"Yes, Bob. What's happened here is just part of what has been happening for a while now. Hydrogen builds up in the tanks and needs to release itself. We can't predict when it will happen, and there isn't anything we can do about it other than continuing with our plan of containment."

"But, the tanks are leaking."

"Yes, that is troubling. We are addressing the situation the best we can. If I may, Bob, I'd like to offer our sympathies to the workers and their families over this incident. Our thoughts and prayers are with them. Be assured that they will receive proper screening and treatment at our facility."

"And standing beside Mr. Glibson is Richard Shorter, Director of Operations for the Site. Mr. Shorter, what do you have to say about Local 598's claims of ignoring their requests for supplied air inside of the zone?"

"It's a simple matter of economics. It would cost millions of dollars to provide this, and the odor releases are sporadic. They do not happen all of the time. Besides, it would drastically slow the work down, and we wouldn't want that, would we? We'll see what we can do. I think more studies of the situation need doing."

"Odor releases! That what you call it? Studies! You've been studying since 1992, and nothing has changed," Mr. Shaw screamed, stepping into the microphone, waving his fist in the air.

Richard recoiled and said in a flat voice, "We're done." He stepped away, motioning to Glibson to follow, muttering, "Fucking Unions."

"This is Bob Olson from King 5 News reporting live from one of the most dangerous cleanups occurring on the planet—a place where injury has struck once again."

Casey pounded on the refrigerator. "Did you hear that fucker! It just keeps going on out there! Nothing has changed. People are still getting hurt, and the DOE carries on doing their thing. Deny-deny-deny. Did you see the smug look on that little prick's face? I'd like to stuff his face in a bucket of that waste glop and brush his teeth with it—See how he likes that," she said, with bared teeth. Jett snickered and scuffed his chair away from her, appraising her menacing face. " Yeah, you heard me, Jett. Sounds good, doesn't it? It would feel good, too. I can feel his head in my hands. They can't keep getting away with this shit."

"I've found their addresses."

"Good. Let's get the motherfuckers."

"What do you want to do?"

"I don't know! Check it out, I guess. Do some Recon. See if we can get at them and then do something. Maybe your bomb idea. Something come to us." She paced. "I can't just sit here." She leaned upon the back of his chair and calmed down." I'm no military person or anything. All I know is what I've seen in the movies."

"So, let's make like it's our movie. You know, make it up and see where it goes. You want to take a drive out there and scope it out?"

"Shit yeah! I've got nothing going today. There is no time like the present. Let's make a couple of sandwiches and hit the road. They live close to each other?"

"Yep. It's a housing development south of Richland. Probably one of those big-box types we passed on the way to see Charley. I've got some binoculars, and our phones can take pictures. Remember, we're not doing anything other than trying to locate them and see the layout."

She hugged Jett. "This is good. It feels like moving forward. We're doing something other than scratching our heads with our thumbs up our asses."

****

Off of the highway, shy of Richland, they turned west towards a visible cluster of new houses filling a lazy, rolling valley. The homes sheltered below a rock outcropped hillside, that would cast an evening shadow over the otherwise baking in the sun subdivision. They approached the Hillsdale sign, elegantly painted in black and gold, and supported aesthetically by well-placed rocks, trees, and plants. The open gate invited them into the perfectly paved and curbed avenue that welcomed into the community of homes. Manicured lawns, bright green from irrigation and chemical fertilizer, displayed the marvels of man's ingenuity at creating such a setting in the middle of nowhere, dry scrubland. Southern plantation colonial pillars graced the front of some of the homes, purveying a sense of aristocracy. Casey pulled over and idled while Jett studied the layout on Google Maps. "So, up three blocks and turn left, then wind around a big curve and keep going until you reach Vista Ave then left again.

That should get us close to Shorter."

"Maybe he's home, and we can say hi," Casey said dryly.

"More than likely, he's at work."

They slow cruised around the big curve. Suddenly, the whoop of a siren squealed from behind. "Pull over," barked from a loudspeaker.

"Oh shit," sprang from Casey's lips. She tightened on the steering wheel.

"Be cool. Let me do the talking. Remember, we're not doing anything wrong."

The officer approached their car. The late-year model with windsurfing decals appeared out of place for the neighborhood. Casey kept her head pointed straight ahead, hands fixed on the wheel. Jett observed the patch on the man's shoulder. Only a security guard. "Can I help you with something?" The officer asked. "You look a bit lost. This neighborhood is a private area."

Jett leaned across Casey towards the guard peering through the window. "Hi. We were just trying to track down a lost aunt of mine at 62 Vista. I think the road is not far up ahead."

"That would be the Benders. Don't think any auntie types are living there. What's your aunt's name?"

Jett laughed. "Well, it's sure not Bender. I had a hunch this might be a wild goose chase but had to try. Thanks, officer, for the help. I guess we'd better go home and get the story straightened out."

"You should. You are in a closed neighborhood. You can turn around in that drive."

Casey put it in gear and maneuvered carefully,

going out the way they came. The security guard shadowed to the gated entrance.

"So much for that plan," Jett said down the road.

"Think he took my plate numbers?" Casey asked.

"Maybe. I'd say the car is made to be on the safe side. But at the worst, something possibly noted to do with somebody searching for an old auntie. How'd you like my story? Pretty ingenious, huh?"

"Handled like a PI in the movies, man. You know, I think we're paranoid. I know I am. I have to remember that nobody knows what I'm thinking. Even so, after this, there's no way we'll be able to get to them at their houses unless we become a lot more clever. Like pretending to be plumbers or something."

"Pretty cliche. Seen that one on TV a few times. Slap a bushy red mustache on you and dress me in a pair of coveralls." They laughed off the tension. "It didn't even cross my mind to consider security messing with us while doing a drive-by. Goes to show how you have to think about everything, you know, think plans through. Then, of course, there's always the unpredictable—the famous fickle finger of fate." Jett let that one drop and struck a 'thinking man' pose. After a spell, something came to him. "We know they ride from here to the Site and back. How about an ambush?"

Casey shrugged. "Maybe. I don't know. Okay. Let's drive the route and keep our eyes open for possibilities."

Not encouraged by what she saw, a straight highway through a dry, barren stretch of dirt and scrub, her face soured and she said to Jett, "Let's get out of here. I don't see it. We'll have to try something else."

Chapter 16

In the lobby of the Best Western Hotel, Hood River, Oregon, Frank paced in circles impatiently while Casey and Jett casually leaned against the wall, arms crossed, waiting for the mysterious Tony to appear. Questions squirreled around in Jett's brain. What was this family business Frank spoke of? What kind of person could they possibly be jumping into bed with?

The elevator doors opened, and Frank immediately recognized Tony. Ten years had passed since they last saw each other, but Frank could never forget that meaty face and his crooked grin. That big cheeked mug that teased the heck out of him in his childhood. The guy who dangled worms over his face until he cried when a little kid and the guy who later showed him the glossy pictures inside his Penthouse magazines. Frank walked towards the big guy with arms open. They gripped each other in a back-slapping embrace. With hands resting on each other's arms, they took stock of one another. "It's been a long time, Frankie. You've filled out," Tony said, squeezing a bicep. "And look at that hair. Got that surfer boy look going on."

"Thanks, Tony. You've filled out yourself."

"Hey."

"How's Uncle Lou and Aunt Adele?"

"You know Lou. He's still the boneheaded boss, but he's playing a lot of golf, so life's a little easier for me. Mom's doing yoga now. Can you believe that?

Always after us about what we eat. By the way, she sends her love." Tony motioned to the suited, sandpaper faced man by his side. "This is my associate, Enzo. Enzo, my cousin Frankie."

"Hey, Enzo. Just Frank, okay?"

Enzo rocked his head. " Sure, sure, Frank. Good to meet you," he said, taking Frank's offered hand in his rock hard grip.

"Tony, Enzo, meet my friends. This is Jett, the chemist, and Casey, who works in distribution."

Casey's nostrils flared at Frank's deception but bared her teeth in an accommodating smile.

"So. I checked this place out earlier. There are some booths in the bar, more private for a meeting than the dining room. Let's get some lunch. I'm on Chicago time," Tony said.

They ordered food. Tony rolled up the sleeves of his collared dress shirt. "So. How about this legal weed thing? Big deal, huh?"

Jett answered. "Right, Tony. It's been a long battle to get here, and many good people have had to do time along the way. It's a big deal for everyone; users, makers, retailers, and government gets a fat payoff right off the top."

Tony's mouth spread wide. "Now, how about that? They don't even get payola. So, you know what you're doing, Jett?"

"I do. People like my stuff. I've been making oils and butter since before they got popular, working underground for years. I have a college degree in chemical engineering, too. But my little lab isn't legal even though the stuff is basically legal. I haven't wanted the problems and expense of getting involved with the government."

"What's changed your mind?"

"From what Frank's told me, you guys are going to take all that hassle out of the game, and all I have to do is be creative."

"Something like that. What about you, Frankie? You ready to stop being a flake and get with the program? You know, do something with your life besides living off of that trust fund?"

Frank deflated and pinched his brows. "Give me a break, Tony. There's a time for everything. Don't worry, I'm ready to do some business. Legal weed business is cool."

"Lou has his doubts about you, but we need a face, and we'd rather it be family. Know what I mean? Are we going to see your show, Jett?"

"After lunch, we can go over to the house."

The orders came with a round of iced teas. Casey and Enzo concentrated on their lunch. He checked her over between bites of his grilled salmon. She didn't mind. She wondered about him, too.

They filed in through the back door of the small house in Bingen. "Pretty funky setup, Frankie."

"You're in the country, dude, close to all the outdoor activities. You ought to come out on the river with me. Do some windsurfing."

"I'll stick to speed boats."

They tromped down the wooden stairway to the crowded, low ceiling basement. Tony rocked his head side to side, unimpressed. "I know it doesn't look like much, but with the right equipment, I could crank out a lot of product. The market in Oregon is only so big anyway."

"Jett, this is bigger than Oregon. Oregon is the legal place where you can make this shit. Where it might go, nobody knows. Get what I mean? Can't say much for your operation, but maybe your stuff is good. Give Enzo a taste, see what he thinks."

Jett selected a vial and loaded the pipe. "There's a lot of variety in this, and there are different kinds of products for different needs. Take a sip on this, and we can try a couple more," Jett said, passing the pipe to Tony.

He waved it away. "I don't touch the stuff. Muddies my head. Give it to Enzo. He knows good and bad dope."

Enzo lit it and took a draw, exhaling smoothly. "Nice taste."

"Yeah, but what about the kick?" Tony said.

Enzo took another pull on the pipe, holding the smoke longer this time while Jett prepared another pipe. "Try the Velvet Sky."

Enzo sucked, lifting his chin as he drew in. His eyes brightened, and his face tingled as the flowery pollen hit the back of his head. He exhaled blissfully. The pipe went around. The vapor drifted up Tony's nose, like it or not. He fidgeted uncomfortably from his changing headspace—a guy who liked to maintain control. "Enzo. What do you think?"

Enzo's head swelled into a bubble. "I'll tell you what, Tony," he said with a cough. "There's nothing like this shit in Chicago."

"That's what I wanted to hear. Let's get outta this dungeon and talk some business."

Upstairs in the lounge, Frank passed around some beers. Enzo went out for a cigarette. Casey followed.

He went by the house's side and leaned against the wall, checking out all the sporting gear. Casey came over, and he offered her a smoke. "No, thanks. Catch a buzz?" she said.

He floated behind his sunglasses for a moment. "What do you think? … I see you guys are really crazy for all this outdoorsy stuff, aren't you?" He said, waving his hand over the yard full of gear.

"Lots of fun playing in Nature around here. Different than where you're from, I bet. You travel much?"

"I go where Tony goes. Mostly business and mostly big cities." He shifted his weight towards her, leaning in. "So Casey, if we get something going out here, we could get to be friends, huh?"

She stepped back, smiled, then lifted her head flirtatiously while giving him a once over. His dark, bottomless eyes appealed to her. "Maybe we could. I like dangerous guys. That you?"

"Sometimes," he said, his lips spreading and his eyes digging deep into her. He fluffed his jacket and rearranged himself closer to her against the wall.

She brushed her shoulder against him. "Let me ask the mean guy a question? I got a problem I need to take care of."

"Lay it on me."

"Hypothetically, if you had to get rid of somebody around here, how would you do it?"

Enzo's forehead creased in surprise as he measured Casey. "You're getting more interesting all the time, sweetheart."

She gave her hair a flick and returned. "Seriously, what would you do?"

Enzo checked over his shoulder, pulled on his cigarette, and lowering his eyes, dropped his voice secretively. "First, I'd grab the guy with nobody seeing or suspecting. You know, throw him into the backseat of a car or a van and bring him someplace out of the way." He made a pistol with his finger. "Off the guy and sink him with some concrete blocks in that big old river of yours and let the fish eat him." With that image dangling, he searched her for a response.

Casey's voice went low and sultry. "I like it, Enzo. I like the fish-eating part."

"Enzo curled his mouth and leaned back in. "You got it bad for the guy, don't you?"

The back screen door flapped shut. Frank, Jett, and Tony come onto the drive, words flying. Enzo and Casey caught up to them on the way to Tony's rental sedan. "So, we'll see you in the morning at the hotel, and we'll check out some buildings," Tony said with the car door open.

"Sounds like a plan, cousin. See you tomorrow," Frank said.

The sedan pulled away. Casey turned to Jett. "How'd it go?"

"All right, I guess. They liked the stuff. I'm not sure I trust these guys, but for now, I'm playing along."

"What do ya mean, not trusting?" Frank said.

"The trial period before the contract sounds sketchy. We could get it all set up and be left with nothing."

"They wouldn't do that to me. I'm family."

"Okay, Frankie."

Chapter 17

Escaping from the urban sludge of late afternoon Portland traffic, Lolly crossed the Sandy River eastbound on the I-84. She tapped Casey's number, making the call before the mountains of the gorge interfered with reception. "Hey, babe. I'm heading your way."

"Fantastic. It's been too long."

"Let me take you out for a burger and a beer at Everybodys. I'm going to be hungry by the time I get there."

"Me too, but not for that."

"You naughty girl... . I've missed you, too. I'm so horny I might have to rub one off while I'm driving. Don't think I'm immune to getting turned on doing what I do."

"I can imagine. Wait for me."

Casey never mentioned her occasional fling with Sam. When together with Lolly, what they shared, was all that mattered.

An hour and a half later, clothes scattered on the floor, they writhed like mating eels upon the bed. Tongues and fingers probing, hearts pounding, their breaths panting. The loving was worth the wait.

Connection restored, their want for food returned. "Let's head to the Pub. Everybody's okay?" Lolly said.

"A burger sounds good."

They sat at a table off to the side, and their waitress

came with waters. "We know what we want," Casey said. "I'll have a burger on ciabatta, medium-well."

"I'll have the same but hold the onion. Sweet potato fries, too."

With an air of comical disbelief, Casey filled Lolly in on big Tony and the cannabis oil lab while they waited for the food to come. "They're looking at properties today."

Lolly shrugged. "Hey, you never know. The lab could be a lucky break if you all can work with those guys."

"I'm staying out of it. Frank and Jett can decide what they want to do about any lab. I've got other things on my mind. Know what I mean? Getting back for Charley hasn't changed. The feelings are dug in. If I can't get at Hanford, maybe I can get to somebody at the top." Her eyes darkened. "Like those two guys you met."

Ah-ha lit across Lolly's face. "Don't ask me how or when I'll get them, but the hate — there, I've said it, festers inside me. It's taking over Lolly, and I can't stop the burning of it inside of me. It keeps me awake at night. I'm thinking about doing things I never would have thought about doing before. I'm thinking about hurting people, and you know what … it feels good." She dropped her head and peered sheepishly up at her lover. "Am I a bad person?"

Lolly embraced the raw depths of Casey's emotions. "Look at me. You're not bad. You're human, and humans can hate too. Been hating and killing each other for thousands of years. Hanford's been killing for decades, and no one has done anything to punish them. Absolutely nothing. You and Charley have been done wrong. His life was stolen from him. You're rightfully angry, and you want to do something about it. Look at it this way. What are your choices? Sob and say, oh well, that's the way it was meant to be, poor Charley. Or—nothing could have saved him, and nothing can be done. Nobody can go up against this monster. It's too powerful. Go religious and forgive them? Or fight back. Try and shift things. Don't let these people get away with it. Let them know that they can't. They count on fear and helplessness. That's their ace. People being intimidated by them, feeling hopeless, and allowing themselves to be bullied." Lolly reached across the table for Casey's hand. "I'm with you, Babe. I'll help. Come up with a plan."

Casey's eyes watered. "I'm trying," she said, squeezing Lolly's hand. A flush of hope ran through her. Lolly's support meant everything. She told Lolly how Jett had found where Bill and Richard lived and how they had an idea about sneaking upon them in their houses and how silly that turned out to be.

"Thought you could do a drive-by, huh?"

Casey gave a shy laugh.

"Maybe if you had a better cover, you could get them, but the getaway seems risky."

"Here's another idea." Casey talked about her meeting and conversation with Enzo. Lolly considered. "Makes sense to abduct the guys. You get total control. What he described sounds like the classic hit. You like it?" Lolly asked.

Casey's voice hushed as the waitress approached with their plates. When she moved away, the conversation resumed. "Grabbing the guys discreetly makes sense, but shooting seems too good for them,"

Casey said, reaching for a french fry. "Think they'll be back to see you at the club?"

"Can't guarantee it. The guys are probably married and have meetings, responsibilities, and whatnot. I could tell that they'd been in the club before, but I couldn't say if they were regulars. The Bill guy seemed familiar. He knew the ropes. They're probably sneaking out on their wives, you know, getting all hot and bothered and going back to have sex with them. Win, win for everyone, I guess. Long as the wives are into it. When they return, if they do, I'll get my hooks deeper into them. Maybe we can set something up. Keep that in mind as an option as you work on your plan."

Casey's phone pinged. She quickly texted back their position to Jett. "Looks like we'll have some company."

"Wonder how the meeting went?"

"Soon find out."

The burgers tasted good.

Entering the Pub, Frank and Jett went straight to the bar. "Two Logger Lagers," Frank called out. Beers in hand, they came to the table. "How are you doing for drinks?" Frank asked the women.

"Waiting for you. I'll take a stout," Casey said.

"Glass of white wine for me. Thanks, Frank," Lolly said.

Frank went for the drinks. "How'd it go with Don Antonio?" Casey said to Jett.

"Hey, he's all right. He is a straight-ahead guy with a great sense of business. Whether he's putting the smooth on me, I don't know, but he is family with Frank, and there is something to that. If nothing else, Frank could be a local figurehead." Jett leaned toward

Casey. "That might actually suit him better than trying to run the business."

"Talking about me behind my back?" Frank placed the glasses on the table and plunked down into a chair.

"You gonna rough us up, Frankie?" Casey said.

"Get out of here. Give me a break. Now you know why I never said anything about my family. It changes things."

"So, what's up?"

"Looked at some places and started getting a feel for what's out there. They want to go big, and I got to admit it's scary jumping into something like this from scratch. What do you say, Jett?"

"Tony is a pretty aggressive guy. They have to understand that organizing something like this takes some planning, and we need a little time to work things out."

"When they want something, they go after it."

"What's next?" Casey asked.

"We meet for dinner, and they fly back, leaving us to figure out what the lab needs. They'll handle the legal stuff."

"You sign a contract? Is it going ahead?"

"We'll see later tonight."

****

The temperature swelled in the late afternoon summer day. Casey and Lolly returned to the house, seeking some shade, and hoped for a breeze from the river through the bedroom window. Lolly's dancing routine kept their visits spread out and short, which impassioned their time together but left them unsettled by the lack of a normal co-existence. Content to spend time laying upon the bed, resting and being close, they took refuge from their worlds, listening to whatever bubbled up from out of their hearts.

Lolly loosely gestured towards the chest of drawers against the wall, past the end of the bed. "I see that Charley's altar hasn't moved," she said.

"No, it hasn't. Charley is going to stay with me until we have a plan. He's sad to have left the world so soon and angry that he wasn't better protected from the tanks. He's still confused and disorientated. It all happened so violently and unexpectedly. He feels used, like his life didn't matter. Like he was dispensable."

"You're getting all that from having an altar? Seems a little far out. You know, talking with the dead like that."

"Charley and I are still connected. He's staying with me until we make a plan." Lolly stared curiously at the altar. Casey squeezed the sheet and placed her head on Lolly's breast. She closed her eyes and drifted into the ethereal. Charley came close. His gauzy spirit loomed like an anguished genie, befuddled and searching for resolution. Casey had none yet to give. Peace for him would have to wait.

Chapter 18

Charley's ghost and Casey's undying attachment shadowed Lolly as she drove to her gig out in Umatilla. She worried about Casey's state of mind. What was with those conversations with Charley? Her hanging out with him in the bedroom, pretty far out there. Had Casey cracked?

The barren summer brown landscape did little to distract. With nothing but blank miles of road ahead, she had plenty of time to mull over what Casey had told her and what she had said in return. She chewed her cheek, a nasty habit she engaged in when nervous or concerned. She meandered into what revenge meant and found it a foreign thought. What were the consequences? People don't always get away with that shit, and often in the process, get dragged down into the sickness that they sought justice from. Doubting, second thoughts circled her mind. Many things could go wrong. Red flags flapped, caution lights flashed— "Wait a minute." Make sure the plan is sound. Study her role well, if any, before jumping in. She loved Casey and wanted to help her get what she needed and deserved, but kidnapping?—Possibly a lifetime of jail? Not a hot prospect. Suffering a weak moment, she wondered if she had allowed her emotions to charge into a commitment too soon.

****

Bill and Richard walked side by side down the hall

after a weekly briefing with George. Coming to a halt outside of his office, Bill turned to Richard and "Grouchoed" his eyebrows.

"Ready to have a night out?"

Richard perked like a bush rabbit. "She's back?"

Bill's mouth warped devilishly. "Yes, indeed, my man. "I checked the club posting, and she's dancing this weekend."

"I wouldn't mind having another look at that," Richard croaked light-heartedly. "In fact, I'd like to have more than a look. How about we proposition her?" he said while playing pocket pool in his slacks' loose pockets.

Bill's mouth made a wow, and then he leaned in and gave a subtle elbow nudge saying, "Hey, nothing ventured, nothing gained. You doing the asking?"

Richard's imagination stretched way more extensive than his reality. He shuddered at the thought of coming right out and asking her. His shoulders slumped. "You're better at that kind of thing than me."

"Tell you what. I'll ask her for you. That way, if she gets pissed, I'll still be in the clear."

"I don't think so, buddy boy," Richard snapped back. " We're in this together."

"All right, amigo. We'll work it out. Pick you up at seven for that card game with the boys," Bill said with a wink.

****

From backstage, she heard her musical cue. The MC made his pitch. She pinched her nipples, threw back her hair, and slinked like a sultry cat onto the stage. She twirled on the pole. Through the dimmed lights, anonymous bodies ringed the raised dancing platform. Her inner cash register chimed. Her body responded, turned on by the arena of lust and desire focused upon her, she swirled down the pole, shook her tits, and spread her legs. That's what they came for. Working her way around the ring, she noticed her marks had returned. They must have checked her schedule. Game on. As she neared, they threw their money down, leaning expectantly forward in their seats.

She had them back.

After finishing her act, she slid in next to them. She gave a sexy rub to Richard's shoulder and winked at Bill. "Hey, guys. Nice to see you. Want to go to the back room?"

"Of course," Bill said, sounding familiar. Her closeness and honey—vanilla scent triggered memories and expectations. Her breasts, hanging half out of her robe, taunted.

"Sweet that you care for me," she whispered, her hands pawing their shoulders. "Before we go, how about a drink? Dancing makes me thirsty."

"I've got it," Richard said, on top of his jangling nerves. They ordered Manhattans and made small talk or tried to while the impending proposition cotton wadded Bill's head.

Lolly got on with business. Remembering his name, she squeezed Bill's hand. "Ready, Bill?" As Bill led her away, she trailed her free hand smoothly down Richard's back. "I haven't forgotten you, Richie." He didn't mind Bill going first, trusting him to make the pitch.

Inside the barely lit private dance room, she straddled Bill and pressed her bosom into his face. He nuzzled into the breasts he longed for, inhaling her scent of sweaty musk and sweet lotion that awakened his urge for sex. She ground hard on him, and he responded. She needed him to want her … for Casey. Have him in the palm of her hand, ready if needed. Bill moaned as if he might come, causing her to ease her position. He needed to want that but not get it. She pulled her ass back towards his knees. "Getting a little excited there, Bill," she said, running her fingers across his scalp. "I like it that you want me."

Bill exhaled into her ear. She had him on the edge. His dick throbbed. "I do, and so does Richard. I dream of you at night. We'll pay anything you want. Meet us in a room somewhere."

She hugged him. "Sweet that you want me, honey, but I don't do things like that. I'm a dancer."

"I know, and be sure that we respect you. But we're both crazy about you. Don't say no. Make it just one time. Think about it. Name your price," he said, irresistibly placing his hands on her ass and bringing her back on to him.

She held back his hands. "Can't do that, Bill. We'll get in trouble." The hulking bouncer eyed from the doorway—damn rules.

Richard, waiting at the bar, downed his second drink. She held out her hand to him, and he floated off his chair. The alcohol had transported him out of his self-absorption. She led the way back. Wasting no time, she straddled him and laid on her charms. He wondered about the prospect of a rendezvous. Had Bill asked her? She arranged his face into her cleavage. She remembered him a breast man. Her breasts cuddled his head. He nuzzled them. Her body glided back and forth upon him. "You like me, Richard?" She said softly.

He rubbed his head up and down. The men, passive participants. The women doing what they liked to please while the men endured their restraints like in bondage, a more desirable sensation to some men than to others. His words spilled out, "God, yes, I can't get you out of my mind. I want you bad."

"Poor Richard, suffering so," she said, arms holding him while she slid on his lap. His head fell back, drunk on her steamy closeness. "I'll think about it, baby. Maybe we can work something out."

She brought Richard back to the bar. Sandwiching herself between them, she leaned into Bill's ear. "Give me your phone numbers." Euphoria sprung across Bill's face. He whipped out a pen and obliged on a cocktail napkin. "Thanks for the dance, guys. I'll think about what you said." She gave them the look. "Stick around for the next set."

In the dressing room, she banked the napkin in her handbag with a smirk. She brushed danger aside and sent a mental nudge to her lover. Okay, girl, come up with a plan.

Chapter 19

Richard Shorter glided his black Lexus ES into the tidy, two-car garage. Barking from his Jack Russell Terrier exploded from the chain link dog run outside. His yips and wails penetrated the garage walls and were heard a block away. Despite the racket, Skip would have to wait. A man of routine, Richard had his unwinding ritual. Extracting his tie en-route, he went straight to the bedroom, shed his suit uniform, and put on some shorts and tennis shoes. So what if neighbors a block away could hear the little fellow? They could wait too.

In the kitchen, he threw down a glass of orange juice and made peanut butter toast. With a leash in one hand, some dog treats and a ball in his pocket, and his toast hanging from his mouth, he went out the back door to the dog run. Skipper sprang up and down like a kangaroo, banging against the fence. Dropping the leash and stuffing the remainder of toast into his mouth, Richard garbled lovingly to the dog. "How's my good boy? Glad to see your dad?"

Opening the gate, Skipper scratched up onto him, yipping while his tail whipped excitedly. Down on one knee, Richard patted his dog. The stress of the day ran off his fingers. Skipper licked his face as an appetizer before munching down or rather gobbling down the dog treats. "Ready for a walk, boy?" Richard said, clipping on the leash to the dog's body harness. Skip knew the routine and led the way out of the gate and up the street, making his mandatory sniffs and leg lifts as they proceeded.

Humming a song, Richard cast his eyes back and forth as he walked the street. He smelled the fresh-cut grass of his neighbor's lawn. What a nice neighborhood. Neat and tidy, everything in its place. For the most part, residents looked like him, had a similar social status, and voted for the same political party. No one ever questioned his being alone; no Mrs. Shorter and all that. No one giving him a hard time. Nothing upsetting. No hard decisions to make.

His comfortable neighborhood was a significant improvement over the South Carolina Savanah River Site he transferred from. More prestige came with his elevated, new position. He thought he'd die if he had to endure that southern drawl a month longer. Far from his native Ohio, his green, oasis neighborhood, with manicured lawns, surrounded by hills and scrubby desert, suited him just fine.

Skip pulled harder on the leash. He knew the community park lay just ahead. His tongue hung wet, thinking of sniffing dogs, scratching in the wood chips, and running and playing ball retrieval with his master.

The park, and most notably inside the dog area, was where Richard's scanty social life existed. The dogs' interaction brought about offhand conversations—dog lovers to dog lovers conversing about nothing too deep. Their dogs, proxies of themselves, made friendly investigations while Richard safely rubbed shoulders within his closed community. Doing so allowed him to feel a part of the human race, something he deeply needed.

His work had him in opposition to so many people. Being a demanding boss required a firm, steady hand and strict attention to detail. That, and his sharp tongue didn't endear him to many. Negative feelings followed him wherever he went on site. 'Here comes the little bitch' and such muttered under breaths. In response, Richard raised a self-protecting veneer, an armor that shielded his vulnerability and, ultimately, his loneliness. In the park, he lowered his shield, which occasionally allowed a disturbing thought to creep in. Invariably, there was always that someone or something that managed to get under his thickened skin. Despite having his mind on the park, a memory of that surly Long woman calling him a weasel glared in his mind. He hated that word and the implied association. The unsavory recollection unnerved and twisted into him just long enough to prod his ulcer before he moved it on. Therapy sessions had provided him with defensive skills. The sting got neatly tucked away.

The Hanford related people at the park did their best to leave work behind. With managing nuclear slop their occupation, they had to protect their denial. Pride in their service to their country carried them over and kept their heads raised. They remained believers. Pleasant, non-offending chit-chat deflected the horrible reality of the substance and the consequences of that paid their bills.

People liked Richard's dog. Skip, an extension of Richard; short, chesty, proud, and assertive. Maybe, kinda cute. Through Skipper, Richard got his pats. When people liked his dog, he felt appreciated in turn.

After plenty of sniffs and scratching around, dog and master moved into the highlight of the visit, throwing and retrieving the ball. Richard lobbed the ball upwards, and Skip launched with Richard's arm's movement, leaping and snatching the ball in mid-air. Onlookers applauded and cheered. Richard shone with pride.

Settling into the evening, most days, Richard sat in front of the TV, eating off a TV table. Fox News gave filtered reports. He cursed when the liberal sound bites spliced in out of context and cheered at his president's outlandish remarks. The crazier, the better. Skip lay by his side quietly waiting for plate licking.

Thoughts of tomorrow's impending meeting with George Marshall began to spin in his brain. Unending and unsolvable problems remained. The issues of nuclear waste storage not going anywhere, a management style limping along without a solution. He wondered about the prospects of a solution ever occurring during his watch.

However, he had persevered, his career notching up to Director. Nothing to dismiss lightly. He gave himself a pat. Although getting stuck with nuclear garbage management rather than power or weapons development as a career, he ranked at the top in his field, guaranteed a fat pension and superb health care for life. The safeguarding of the stash of nuclear waste by-product a vital position. If only they could get rid of it some way.

No one or no place wanted it. Nevada had seemed a viable prospect, but the people resisted, unswayed even by the promises of 'compensation.' Why couldn't they just accept the benefits of its placement and get on with things? Help their country. New Mexico became a bizarre flop. It seemed like a good idea, dumping the waste down into ancient salt beds, figuring the area would collapse and seal the canisters. But science goofed. Imagine the ridiculousness of packing waste canisters with kitty litter to soak up the liquid, only to have the chemical reaction cause an explosion that blew off the lids, spewing the contents in all directions and contaminating the site for eons to come. Mounds of white radioactive foam blasting upwards and out like a shaken Coke bottle, ruining the air and the mine. His additional 24,000 temporaries of above-ground storage canisters remained in a holding pattern. Because of that mistake, going nowhere. A management nightmare. His nightmare; to safely contain a toxic, potentially disastrous, and threatening stockpile of immovable gunk. He longed for the days when they chucked it in the river. Over and done with. Flushed by the tides into mankind's great toilet.

****

The three men gathered in George Marshall's office. George spread his hands and smirked. "You'll never guess what, guys? I've gotten word that we need to prepare for another shipment of portable waste canisters. " Mouths dropped in dismay. "Richard, get WRPS to prepare another concrete slab. In fact, make it two. Forget about relief. There's no end in sight to our stockpiled mess. There is no news about a dump coming online." He sat back in his chair, the impotent Czar. "First New Mexico blowing up and now Nevada flaking out because of a bunch of concerned citizens. Holy Jesus! What are we supposed to do with this stuff? For all I care, we could shoot it to the moon."

Bill cleared his throat." Wouldn't that be nice? But it's not going to happen, is it, George? I'm afraid we're stuck with continuing to give the appearance that all is well. Believe me, I share your frustration."

George fiddled with his pencil as if he could snap it at any time. Years of being up to his ears in never-ending problems had taken its toll. Fortunately, the golden handshake would soon come. "How are the inspections working on our temporary canisters, Richard?" George asked.

"Royal pain in the ass, that's how—such regulations. Inspecting them every week requires a whole lot of time and manpower. Columbia Generating Station keeps producing a by-product that really should be going to the dump. Instead, we add another drum. Meanwhile, the big tanks continue to leak. We fix one, and another one goes bad. We're struggling to hang on." Richard adjusted his glasses. "In my opinion, we need to can Bechtel and find a company that can get the Vitrification Plant running. Get the stuff into the glass. They've been dicking us around for decades, lining their pockets and pushing way out into the future. The damn pipes will be corroded by the time they complete in 2039 and the installed equipment obsolete."

George muttered into his desk. "I can include your suggestion in my report." He locked his fingers together and rested his hands on the desk. Weariness was deeply etched in dark smudges under his eyes. "I wish there was a ray of optimism here, but it appears that keeping the ship afloat is our mandate." He cleared his throat while lifting his chin and giving a smile. "Hopefully, our big babies will lay off the 'burping' for a while," he said, attempting to inject some lightness into their quagmire. "Are the unions satisfied with the supplied air?"

"For the time being. The 200-foot vapor control zone is being enforced. If the union gets the injunction to make it permanent, our budget will be screwed. If they don't, we'll revert to the old ways."

"What about the sister of the deceased man? A follow-up call would be in order."

"Will do," Bill said and wondered why. He knew how she felt.

George slapped his hands on the desk. "Anything else?" The room went silent. He sat back in his chair and swiveled. "No mistakes. Let's keep this operation on track. We can't afford any more accidents."

Bill and Richard walked in silence down the hall. If George didn't have the answers, then who did?

Chapter 20

Casey stormed into the kitchen. Jett sat with notebooks and papers sprawled in front of him. "Can you fucking believe it! I just got a call from Bill Glibson's office asking me how I was doing."

"No, shit? What did you say?"

"I said, 'FUCK OFF! You people killed my brother,' and hung up."

"Bet they liked that."

"Tough. Like I give a shit. You come up with anything? You know, plan?"

"Sorry. I've been working on the lab details. How about you?"

"Maybe an abduction with Lolly's help."

"What you going to do with them?"

"I don't know. I'm racking my brain."

"Be a lot easier to blow it off, Casey. You sure about doing something?"

"Fuck, yeah! This is bigger than Charley. Dealing with Hanford is something that has come to me. Like one of those 'missions from God.' I have a purpose. I am somebody. I'm not going to pass. You get it? This is bigger than me. What about you? You still in?"

"I'm in, but it's gotta be good. I don't want to get caught, and neither should you. We're talking federal offenses here. Kidnapping alone is some serious trouble."

"Where's the outlaw in you?"

"Behind survival."

"Guess we feel different about bringing down that reeking monster out there. You're all right with the status quo?"

"What are you talking about? Hell, no! Just don't want to spend the rest of life breaking rocks on the chain gang. Let's get a solid plan, and I'll help."

"So, it's all on me?"

"You're the leader. I'm open to an idea when it comes, but nothing has come to me yet."

"Try harder."

"I'm buried in this lab plan."

"No wonder you can't think of anything. That's just great," Casey said, turning her back, her arms crossed in front of her chest. She turned around. "So, are you getting anywhere?"

Jett scuffed back his chair, glad to change the subject. "I've determined that we don't need a huge warehouse space unless we'll be growing. You interested in that?"

"What a stupid question."

"Anyway, researching the lab has got me excited about upping my game. Getting into CBDs. Maybe making RSO. Creating the cleanest and best product."

"Frank down on that?"

"Frank doesn't care about details. You know Frank. He wants it all to fall in his lap."

"Pretty much has. … You're still good on keeping our talks to ourselves, right?"

"Of course. I'm not stupid. Frank or anybody else doesn't need to know anything. Whatever you are planning has to be a closed circle, or I'm out. Who have you told so far?"

"You, me, and Lolly." She lied.

The screen door from the back entry flapped, and in came Frank fresh from the river, more pumped than usual. "Sweet out on the river this morning, Casey. You should have been there."

"Thanks, Frank, but you know where I'm at."

"Yeah, PARANOID," he yelled, pronouncing every syllable in her face.

She held back at the last minute from punching his lights out. Instead, she folded her arms protectively across her chest like she did with Jett. Frank's rudeness hurt. Sensitized by her dilemma, it didn't take much to send her spiraling. Besides, it was hard enough for her to give up the windsurfing she loved without him digging it in.

"Asshole!"

Frank shifted his tone. "All right, all right. I'm sorry." His face dropped. Obviously, something else bugged him. Tentatively, he laid his hand on Jett's shoulder and blew air. "Had an interesting talk with Tony on my way home. Brace yourself, Jett."

"Now what?"

"Sorry, buddy. They've changed the deal. They want their own management team running things with us working under them as employees. We'd get fat salaries and basically be running the action but under an umbrella."

Casey inhaled in disbelief and then spouted out, "Surprise, surprise." Holding back from further insult, she turned away. But on her way out of the door, unable to control her lingering anger over Frank's last attack, she took a hard swing. " I knew it was too good to be true, Frankie."

Jett cleared from his initial shock. "Those fuckers. That's not the deal we talked about. What happened to our piece of the action? So, now it's just like … a job? I don't know if I can do that, Frank. Go back and tell them we want in or no deal."

"It's still a good deal, Jett. The salary will be way more than what you're making now. Think about it."

"If I wanted a job, I could have gone to work for a chemical company out of college. They're moving in on my turf and offering a job? What a fucking rip off."

"It's the way this weed business is going. Big money smells big profits, and they want in. I could live with it. You know, doing the fun stuff, letting them worry about the business, and bringing down some good dough. You could delegate, man. Be a boss."

"Do I look like the management type? Get your head out of your ass. Where is the art? Where is the culture? Lost to the corporate world or the mobster world in our case."

"Hey, careful."

"Why? The truth is that the counter culture has kept the fight going for legalization all these years. Grassroots, man. People going to prison. People losing everything. Me, risking my ass all this time only to be offered a job in a mob take over? No thanks. I'd rather stick to my game and make it better. My people would stay loyal. Fuck corporate dope. It's as bad as the Mexican cartels. What's the difference?"

"You could still get busted, and my house would be at risk. It already is. Ever think about that?"

Jett glared, not believing his ears. "So that's where it's at—Frankie?"

The room fell silent. Frank's big foot was in his

mouth again. But, he needed to get the truth about how he felt off his chest while the sticky window was open. The lab had always bugged him, even though he enjoyed the free product. He had Jett backed into a corner.

Jett let the house business slide. There were too many raw emotions to untangle. He stuck to the deal gone wrong. "Go back to them and tell them we deserve some ownership, or I'm out. We do have some leverage. They don't know anything about the business or this area. True, they could find and hire some other people, but this business is not like the traditional job market. They have to find people they can trust and be able to work with, especially with the dodgy distribution idea they've hinted at." Frank put his chin in his hand. Jett resumed. "They already have trust in us. That has value, man. Don't just roll over. They're making a move, muscling in like these kinds of people do, figuring they can dupe some country bumpkins … and you know, that attitude really pisses me off. It's souring the whole deal for me. Making me not want anything to do with these guys. Some family you got."

****

Casey wandered outside to clear her head. The old shed in the back yard called to her—a dark, away from it all closed space. She didn't question why. She just went. Inside the shed, eyes unadjusted, she stepped onto a misplaced rake. The handle lurched and whacked her. She had to laugh even though it hurt. She wanted a shaking up, and she got it. She found the light switch against the wall, which set off a stuttering fluorescent light that eventually blinked on. The jumpy light revealed a jumble of tools, unfinished projects, and junk haphazardly strewn about the dirt floor, all encased in spiderwebs. She pawed loosely through the mess lying on the workbench. A dusty satchel hung high on the wall. What's in there? She reached for it, her movement disturbing a sleepy fleet of wasps from a tucked-away nest. She couldn't seem to lose trouble. The wasps hovered then settled around the rafters, calming down, meaning no harm. Her phone rang. She slipped out of the shed and took the call. Lolly. "Hey, girlfriend. Have I got some news for you!"

"Good news, I hope. I just nearly got stung by a swarm of wasps. What's up?"

"You're going to like this. I have Bill and Richard's phone numbers, and they're moaning for me to meet them in some motel room for some extracurricular activities. How's that for setting the bait?"

"You and your magic ass. Fantastic! Can they wait?"

"A few weeks at most, I'd guess. Get a plan together. I can't keep them waiting forever."

"Right. You have the setup. Now I have to figure out what to do with the bastards. Got any ideas?"

"Grab them out of the lot like your guy said."

"Have they got TV cameras out back in the lot?"

"Only by the doors, I believe. I'll check it out. You'll need some muscle."

"I'm working on it."

"So, what's new on your end?"

"Looks like the cannabis lab deal might be falling apart."

"Figured that was a long shot. What's wrong?"

"The boys from Chicago don't want to share

ownership. They want Frank and Jett to work on salary."

"That must have gone over big with Jett. Frank—he's easy. What about you. You want in?"

"I've got too much on my mind. Know what I mean?"

"Should be passing through within a week. After Portland, okay?"

"I'll get a plan together, somehow. Good work. See you soon. Love ya."

"Love ya, too."

Casey thought of those DOE guys moaning for Lolly's ass and laughed. No matter how high and mighty, when it came to wanton desire, a jackass lived within every man, braying to escape his penned up existence.

Chapter 21

Casey checked the fluid levels of the liquor bottles placed decoratively across the shelf behind the bar. She arranged the picture to her liking while listening to the bar's soundtrack throbbing in the background. The music sounded louder than usual in the empty, voiceless saloon.

Breaking the afternoon lull, Little Bear walked through the doorway. He suspiciously scoped out the place like Sam always did. What was with these guys, always looking over their shoulders? Someone, sometime, must have got to them. She couldn't imagine anyone wanting to jump the Bear.

He came towards her and sat, leaning on his forearms and staring straight ahead as if in a trance. Casey thought it strange. Something appeared not quite right. He was not his joking, engaging self. Fond of the big man and the cheeky rapport they shared, she propped her head on her hand and waved in front of his gaze. "What's up, Bear? You look like you're ready to scalp somebody," she joked.

Little Bear huffed. "Maybe so, Woodpecker. Maybe I'll help you to take a scalp."

Casey straightened and took a step back. "What do you mean by that?" He lifted his head and brought his deep brown eyes to meet hers. "Bring me a Rainier, and I'll tell you."

She brought the beer and waited petulantly for the

words to come. Little Bear curled his forefinger in and out. She put her face alongside his. The thick mass of his head radiated warmth and smelled like a mix of river and fir sap. She gave him her ear. "I have been thinking about what you said, you know, about getting payback for Charley. You may not be able to take down the tree, but you could weaken its roots." She pulled back and screwed her face, then moved her ear in close and waited. "An idea came to me. It makes me feel good. A way to get at some of those Hanford people." He paused, and her interest hung on the cliff of her patience until he let it drop. "Give them a taste of their own medicine," he breathed into her ear like the wind rustling leaves in a tree. He backed away to watch her face as his words tumbled non-sensibly in her head.

Confused, she sought his eyes. Within them, a doorway to understanding opened. "Taste of their own medicine," she mouthed to herself, and then it dawned. She raised her hand to her mouth. "Wow! How? Where? You know, I came to the same conclusion. No way could I get at Hanford, but I could get at the operators of the beast." She clutched his arm and pressed her words to his ear," Tell me more."

"I know a place where the poison flows out of the earth into the river. I've seen it when fishing in the Reach. I could take you there, and you could gather some."

She remembered what she had found up in the Reach on her kayaking trip, the dreadful smell, and look of it. Yes! A taste of their own medicine! "Then what?" she said keenly.

"Capture them and make them drink. Have the poisoners share communion with that which they have put into so many lives. My people, your brother, the river, the fish, and all the wild creatures that have suffered so." Menace spread across his face. "A fitting gift for their treachery, heh?"

A thrill sizzled through her as she imagined the horrible method of retribution—a suitable payback for Charley. Indeed an eye for an eye of biblical proportions. Her fierce anger co-mingled with Bear's long endured hatred of the deeds done to his people and what continued to leech into the natural system that he loved and respected—Deep Nature—The Mother. The holiness of the natural world. The shared hatred took root and grew inside of her. She squeezed his arm. "Yes!" she hissed like a serpent. "It's a fitting plan." She sprung up and over the bar forcing him to grab his glass. She gripped him in thanks and celebration, then slid back across the bar planting her feet back onto the floor. "Thank you for the answer to my prayers, Bear."

Now that they engaged in a plan of vengeance, she surrendered her full trust. She described to Bear the possible abduction of the two DOE men with the help of Lolly. "I know how to get them, but I don't know where to bring them."

His eyes brightened. "I do," he said like a sly fox. "I've already thought about that part but couldn't figure out how to grab them. Together, we make the plan. You and me, Red, settling the score. The place I have in mind for them is a fitting place for their end. A tribute to my people and to the River Spirit. That part matter to you?"

"Only if it does for you. I haven't been able to think of anywhere where nobody would see, and I could have a clean getaway. If it's a meaningful place to give them justice for you and your people, works for me all the better."

"I'll show you the location, and you can decide if you agree." He checked if they still had the bar to themselves. "Taking them at the club seems like a good idea, far from the security of their homes and Hanford. They most likely are sneaking off to go there so nobody would know where to look for them right away after they are discovered missing. Buys time."

She took hold of his two hands. "Let's do it!"

He shook affirmation, and then his tone of voice came sonorous. It rumbled into Casey's core. "There is danger in what we do. We will have to be careful and think through all the steps. There is also a price upon our souls. Are you prepared for that?"

She had already wrestled with that very question and pinned it down. She had navigated a path between her two mountains, allowing her heart to cross the moral bridge of willfully doing harm. She stood ready for any judgment to come from the great whatever, wherever. Here and now, all she cared about. Charley mattered. The environment mattered. All the damaged lives of the past mattered. She answered, "Yes, I'm ready."

"Good. Step one. Get the poison. You'll need a couple quart mason jars and lids, some kind of gloves, a backpack, and maybe a mask. There is a risk to gathering the stuff. It shouldn't be touched. I don't know how much it can hurt you just being near to it but without the poison water, no plan. Day after tomorrow, meet me down at the harbor at 5am. I'll have my boat hooked up to my truck, and we'll ride out to the Reach and launch like we're making a fishing trip. Bring your kayak. You'll need it to go ashore. Bring a headlamp too, just in case."

Two men came into the bar. Little Bear turned, took the last swallow of his beer, and walked to the door.

****

The last stars of night faintly glimmered in the brightening sky. The blue-yellow of first light fanned from the eastern horizon's edge, upriver where their quest awaited. Casey found Little Bear harbor side. His boat hooked to his truck, he sat with his diesel engine idling. Casey untied her kayak from the rack on her car and placed it into the boat, lashing it down to a cleat, securing it from the highway's wind. After parking her car, she climbed into the truck cab and placed her backpack between her legs. "Good morning, friend," she said.

"Morning. It's a good day for fishing, don't you think? Let's go." Truck and boat chugged up the incline, out of the marina. At the stop sign, Starbucks across the highway called. "Want coffee?"

"Sure, it's a long ride."

Eastbound on the freeway, the sun rose into their eyes, and the forested mountains of the Cascades changed to the templed buttes of the high prairie. They passed the Dalles in short time, observing the river tumbling through the dam while they silently sipped coffee, digesting the closeness of the cab. Little Bear ruffled open and reached into a giant bag of M&M's parked at his side and grabbed a handful. "Want some?"

"Don't mind if I do." Although they were pledged to fulfilling their objective, they were strangers in many ways, having only bar banter as a base of friendship. He knew she was committed to revenge for her brother, and she became more aware of the grievance that Little Bear carried in his heart. Awkward glances passed between them. Dips into the M&M's bag tied in the time between being lost in their own thoughts. Conversation would come. They had always liked each other, their personalities naturally finding playfulness in their interaction. But today involved serious business. Little Bear pointed to the roadside sign showing Celilo Village up ahead. "You know what that is?" he asked.

"That's where the falls used to be," she answered.

"The falls where for more than thirteen thousand years, my people had a trading village and caught fish. A sacred place now buried beneath the water. Dam the water and damn the tribes. Herded them up and called them a Confederation. Look towards the river as we pass, and you will see a wayside park given in remembrance. All that is left is a memory, and that fades with each passing year. There is a fancy plaque with a story on it and a boat launch, and a special area for native people. Some seasonal trailers are placed there by fishermen. In one of them, we can put the poisoners."

"Are you sure about that? If the guys are found, it will point the finger at Native persons."

"Point all they want. If there is no proof, there is only suspicion, and there would be suspicion anyway. Who else would authorities point the finger at?"

"Maybe at me for all I know or someone from a long list of Hanford victims. No telling what kind of personal shit those creeps have got themselves into?"

"Even if anyone saw something, no one would ever say anything. Some would not like violence, but our people stick together. I believe most, especially those who work on the river, could care less about a couple of DOE guys who got themselves in trouble. Anyway, I don't think anyone will see, and I feel strongly about this spot. From Umatilla to here is a straight freeway shot. No stops, no towns. Scoot off the freeway and back on—low chance of anything going wrong. If you can think of somewhere else, let me know. I'm open."

"I'm working my head around it. Seems like a strong plan except for the possible link to you when the bodies are found. I'd like to check out the site closer."

"Don't worry about that. Could be anyone that put the guys there. After you are done, maybe they could disappear? No proof, no victim, no case. No matter what, we have to be careful not to leave evidence. No fingerprints—nothing. Putting them in the trailer could work smoothly for you. You said you were concerned about escape? You could leave downriver in a kayak. Have your car parked up downstream. How about that? No trace. No other vehicles in or out."

"What about the abduction vehicle? It can't be traced to anyone."

"A van of some kind would be best. Grab them, throw them inside, tie and gag them, and bring them to you waiting at the trailer. You are the one to give them the drink."

Casey swallowed hard. Of course, she would be the one to poison them. She had always envisioned payback by her own hand—a personal touch from Charley. Seeing it clearly laid before her, she felt the weight of it all. "So a van. Maybe a rental or a stolen one. Lolly says there are no cameras in the back lot, only ones by the doors."

"No cameras at Celilo either. If anyone is there, they'd most likely be kicking back at night. Maybe get a van rental from a third party? We'll need three people to pull off the abduction. A driver and two grab guys. Nobody has to know anything more than we're grabbing these guys and bringing them somewhere. The medicine for them is between you and me. Our secret that no one else will know. It's got to be that way. You okay with that?"

She didn't need to think long. The fewer knowing, the better. Besides, for her and Bear, it was personal. "I promise." She put out her fist. They bumped.

They rode quietly digesting their thoughts until Casey broke the silence. "Sam said he would do me a favor when I needed him."

"Sam? You trust that guy?"

She decided to go all-in with Bear. Although unsure how far she could trust Sam, something inside her believed in the big man beside her. "Enough to help grab these guys. He's my lover sometimes, so I've got something over him."

Bear's eyes went wide, and he broke into a grin. He made like he was going for the candy bag but poked a gentle tickle in her ribs like he would to a little sister. "You and Sam, huh?"

She squeezed her arm down on his fat finger. "Don't, I'm ticklish," she said, hoping to laugh it off. "It's only a rare shot in the dark, him and me. Anyway, he's a badass and grabbing a guy might be fun for him. He's not a stranger to down and dirty. He'd keep his mouth shut."

Little Bear grunted approval. "Thought maybe something was going on between you two."

"Nothing more than a roll in the hay once in a while."

"How about that, me and Sam being bag guys together. I guess why not? He's loyal to you, and we get along in a sorta way. Between the two of us, handling these guys will be no problem. What about the driver?"

"My housemate, Jett. He's been with me on this from the start. He knows all my thoughts. I trust him completely. He's my best friend, other than Lolly."

"He doesn't know about the medicine, does he?"

"No. As you said, nobody but you and I will know about that. Not even Lolly."

"So, me, Sam, Jett, and Lolly in on this. Anybody else?"

"Nope."

"Keep it that way."

They launched the boat into the river and motored upstream. The sun burned down on the cold river. Bear passed her a baseball cap. "We need to look like a couple Indians fishing. Cover your hair with this cap and keep your hood up. We'll go upstream and set a net." She put on the baseball cap and thought about her hair. The dark red was a sure-fire identifying factor. She will need to dye her hair. All the loose ends to take care of suddenly flooded her mind, now that a plan formed. It dawned upon her that afterward, she needed to disappear. Leave her town, leave the state and possibly the country. Leave all that had become so dear to her. Lolly had to go too. She reined her horses. One step at a time. First, the dirty water.

Up above the small islands she had kayaked around on her river trip, they set a net by throwing an orange buoy, then playing out the net and placing another buoy at the far end. Little Bear kept a close eye on the boat position. The ever flowing river quickly drifted them down without the thrust of the engine. The old nuclear ruins on the Washington side of the river came into view. The Oregon side, sprawled brushy wild, rambling off into the distance. Bear pointed the bow downstream. "You ready for action, Casey?"

"Ready as I'm going to be." She pointed out to Bear the place she and Rex found the plume leaking from the bank. He acknowledged her and said, "We're going farther down by old Hanford Town. You'll see the ruin of the high school." The familiar to her battered building came into view. Bear turned the boat cross current and brought the engine down, drifting sideways. He throttled slowly towards the edge of the river. The boat hung in the slackened water near shore, holding safe from running aground. Casey untied her kayak line, making ready for what she wasn't sure. Perhaps something like what she experienced with Rex. Her pack had the jars and gloves but only a bandana for a mask. She bent to take up the kayak.

A barking voice from a loudspeaker jerked them out of their socks. "Move away from this side of the river. This is a restricted area. Go to the other side of the river."

Little Bear bumped the throttle. The boat lurched, causing Casey to make a desperate lunge for the side of the windscreen. She tugged at her disguising hood. Bear turned the wheel hard over, bringing the bow around, then backed off the engine and slowly moved away towards the other side as instructed. "Damn!" Bear cried out. "They must have been watching when we set the net. We won't be going ashore today."

He set a course upstream and across to the Oregon side. Idling down in the lee of a point of land, Bear got out on the bow and threw the anchor. They waited for the anchor to catch and for the boat to come around and hang on the hook. Bear hopped onto the rear deck, where Casey sat glumly, gathering herself from the shock of the interruption of their plan. "Wow! That scared the shit out of me, that booming voice out of nowhere. So much for the gathering idea. Big Brother is watching."

"Don't worry. Probably think we're just some dumb Indians thinking we could anchor up over there. They can see we've corrected ourselves and are on the right side of the river. We'll come back another time to get what we want. A night run, I think. How about some lunch? Gotta wait a while before we can pull the net."

Food was hardly on her mind. She fidgeted on the bench while the boat swung with the current. "There's a timeline on this setup. Lolly can only keep those guys waiting for so long."

"How long you figure?"

"Maybe three weeks max." Little Bear acknowledged her thought and pulled a sandwich and some smoked fish out of his pack. The smell of the sweet and salty, alder wood smoked salmon watered her mouth. She reached for her food rations in her backpack. Some trail mix, an apple, and a cheese sandwich were all that she had. Despite her jangled nerves, she found her appetite.

Eating and sitting for a while, she watched birds going about their hunter-gathering activities as the wide river steadily flowed by. The nuclear ghosts reflected the sun on the far shore. Circling back to the plan, she spoke to Bear. "I guess organizing the van and the abduction should be my focus. Once we get the stuff, the plan can go into action, right?"

"Those are the pieces; poison, grab the guys, drop them off, do the deed, and escape. Have you thought about that? The escape? Best, you disappear."

"Haven't really thought it through, but yeah, disappear, leave this life behind and start over somewhere new. Lolly too." The sun got hot in the sheltered bay. "Wish I could take my hoody off."

"Don't, they may be watching. Got nothing better to do. You should change your hair. Brown would be a good choice. Blend in. Look like most everybody."

"So much to think about. I've been a wise-ass but never a criminal before," she said, defiantly jutting out her chin.

"Think of yourself as a brave warrior for good. No ordinary person would risk doing this, giving them some of their own medicine. Making them know firsthand how they've allowed others to suffer. Show them that everyone is in danger. Nobody is safe. Want some smoked fish?"

It smelled great. Casey's paranoid mind said no, but her mouth said yes. "What the hell. Hasn't killed you yet?"

"Not yet."

They motored upstream and pulled the net. In it were some flapping steelhead. Bear checked the fins determining hatchery or native fish, begrudgingly releasing the native as mandated. Hatchery-raised fish, what the river had come to. He filled the long cooler with them. "Help pay for gas," he said as he turned the bow downstream, returning to the launch ramp.

Bear brought the truck and trailer down to the water, and they quickly winched the aluminum boat on to the trailer and lashed everything down. Casey, drenched with sweat inside her sweatshirt from the late afternoon sun, bounded for the cab of the truck. Inside, she tore off her sweatshirt and cap and gulped down some water. Bear came to the window. "Keep your hair covered until we get on the highway, okay?" She wrapped her head in an old towel, and they drove away.

In a reverse of the morning ride eastward into the sun, the low, western sun glared into their faces. Bear put the air conditioning on. Bugs splattered steadily against the windshield, rising in swarms off of the river in the summer evening.

After seventy-five miles or so, they exited near Celilo in the lingering glow of sunset. At the far end of the launch area, many well-worn trailers sat near the river. Off of the pavement, parked on dirt, surrounded by scrub brush and thin-leafed, wind-whipped willow trees, the far trailer blended into the landscape. They climbed out of the cab and stretched their legs by walking down to the edge of the river. The air smelled fresh and clean. The river ran oxygen-rich—enriched by the clean flowing tributaries entering from deep inside the mountain ranges. Broad and deep the big river pushed onwards. Steady and waveless, it moved by with only occasional swirls of current marking the surface. Casey pointed to the riverbank. "Look, there's a hidden cove over there with sand for beaching a kayak and some brush to tie up. I could bring my kayak in here from upstream and go down the river to make an escape."

"That you could. Let's have a scout inside this old trailer." Little Bear gestured towards the metal box. Rusty decay ate at its seams. The relic's color was long bleached away by sun and wind. Bear muscled the door. It gave way with a creaky groan. A damp, moldy flush of hot air surrounded their faces. Sun-streaked curtains that covered the few dusty windows fluttered lazily. A cluster of unwashed dishes lay on the counter. They spilled over into the sink, and a sack of cans and plastic sat on the floor. The odor of aged garbage wrinkled their noses. A torn couch, with a blue, stained sheet cover and rumpled blankets, filled the remaining space before them.

"Got any lights?" Casey asked, trying to push past Bear and poke her head inside. Little Bear motioned her away from the entrance, and his bulk filled the doorway as he went inside. He opened a cabinet beneath the sink, pulled out a kerosene lantern, pushed aside some dishes with one hand, placed it on the counter, and removed the glass mantle. Finding some box matches, he lit the wick. A dim light spread through the trailer. A vision of her victims bound and gagged, sitting on the sofa like doomed witches waiting for the cleansing fire, leaped into her mind. She imagined their fear, blindly waiting in a dank dungeon smelling place for their fate to come. A dark satisfaction kindled inside of her, and she fed into it, allowing her suppressed hatred to surface and glower in the lamplight. "This place will work just fine, Bear."

"Thought so. Think of anything that needs to be added?"

She thought about it. "Is there enough oil in the

lamp?"

He checked under the cabinet and brought out a gallon can with some kerosene in it. "I'll go over the place before you come and make sure the lamp is full. Anything else?"

"Can't think of anything right now. You drop the guys off, I dose them, then split. Simple, as that."

Chapter 22

Harbor lights mirrored off of the dark glassy waters inside the marina—the docks floating, devoid of people. Hulls rocked quietly in their slips. Bear swung the truck and boat around in the wide launch area and came to a halt near Casey's parked car. It had been a long and emotional day for Casey. Despite failing to capture the 'water,' much got accomplished. A plan had been devised and placed into motion. The bond between Casey and Little Bear became deepened by their commitment to each other and to the plan.

Bear placed Casey's kayak onto her car rack. She tossed her gear into the back seat of her car and tied down her boat. "Let's plan on another trip in about a week. I'll let you know. See how many of those loose ends you can tie up before then," he said. "Don't worry about today. We'll get what we need next time."

"I'm counting on that, Bear."

"Nighttime will be better."

"Right. I'll work on pulling my pieces together."

"I'm sure you will. We'll be in touch."

She hugged him hard and went to her car.

Casey's body rocked as if still floating on the river. Her mind wired instead of being tired from the long day. She scrolled her contacts and poked Sam. "Hey, it's me. What you up to?"

"Miss me, huh?"

"Maybe a little … Could you meet me down by the

marina? There's something I need to talk to you about."

"How about at the Trillium? I could use a drink."

A drink sounded good. It could help to knock her edge down. "Half an hour?"

"You got it. See you."

Casey waited in a booth along the sidewall of the 'shotgun' bar/restaurant, tequila and tonic in front of her. Sam came into the bar. Heads turned. His veiny, tattooed arms bulged out of his cut off sleeves shirt. His scowly bandito mustache and hawkish face caused people to instinctually turn away, afraid they might look at him the wrong way—especially people who knew him. Drink in hand, Sam came to the booth. He planted a kiss on Casey's cheek and slid in beside her like any other dude looking for some pussy. "What's going on, girlfriend? You got some sun today. Been out on the river?"

"No, just hanging by the river thinking. Must have caught some reflection."

"So, what do you want to talk about?"

She took a pull on her drink, and he followed suit. "Remember when I asked you about doing something dangerous for me?"

"Yeah, what about it?" he slurred out of the side of his mouth.

"It's getting close to the time."

"Well … don't keep me in suspense. What's the gig? What's the plan?"

"I'd feel better talking outside."

"Sounds serious," he said, eyes shifting about.

They downed their drinks and went outside. Against a building on a side street, Sam grabbed her and pinned her to the wall with his body. "Gotcha my

157

little rabbit—So what's this all about?"

His hard body pressing against her felt good. It grounded her, and he wasn't hurting. She searched his face for assurance of her trust. She found it in his eyes. "I want you to abduct these two guys from outside a bar out in Umatilla with the help of Jett and Little Bear."

"That all?" Then it hit him. "Little Bear? Me and Little Bear partners in crime?" He said with a mad smile. "Now, ain't that something?" He stepped back and posed cockily before her. His mouth twisted. "Damn. I like it. What you want these guys for?"

"It's a kind of personal payback."

He shifted, his eyes lighting up. "We gonna do something to them?"

"Not this time. They'll be pissing themselves as is. You and Little Bear are the grab men, and Jett is the driver. You'll wear some kind of ski mask or something, so they don't make you. You'll tape and gag them and drop them off someplace, and that's it. What do you think? Will you do it?"

"Think I'll wear one of those spooky nylon stocking masks." The notion turned him on, and he moved closer and slid his knee between her thighs. "Piece of cake, sweetheart. You got the place staked out?"

She squeezed his knee, then pushed it out and got serious. "There are no cameras, but it has to happen fast. No one can see. And there's one other thing. Can you find some plates to switch out on the van? It will be a rental, but just in case, the false plates will give us cover."

"Smart thinking. No problem. Figure it handled. That all?"

"That's all. Nobody can know."

"I figured that. When's it going down?"

"Not sure, exactly. Within a couple of weeks. I'll tell you as soon as I know."

"Going to tell me what it's all about?"

"Believe me, it's better that you don't know."

"It's gonna be like that, huh? What are you getting into, girl?"

"Like I said, better you don't know. Can you leave it at that? Just do me this favor, no questions asked."

"Sure. Whatever." Gripping her shoulders, he kissed her hard, and she yielded. He nibbled her ear and spoke into it. "You're on my side of the river. Why don't you come on over to my place and cozy up with me?"

How quickly it turned to sex with him. She dampened him down gently by shifting her body away and placing her hands on his chest. "That's a nice thought, Sam, but not tonight. I'm tired and have too much going on in my head."

"I could make you feel better. Come on home with me."

She lifted her chin, gave him a quick peck on the lips, and pulled back fast. "You're sweet, Sam, but not tonight," she said, back stepping on the sidewalk. "I'll call you."

****

Casey returned to her house to find the living room filled with a circle of Frank's friends. A cloud of cannabis hung in the air. She considered sneaking by and going straight to her room, but she went into the lounge to say hi despite being exhausted. Maybe some herb would ease her mind. "Casey!" Frank shouted.

"Where you been hiding?"

Jett passed her an oil pen, and she took a deep pull. "I went up on the Deschutes today. Floated my boat. Got some space. It's all good," she said, then took another pull and handed the pipe back to Jett. She figured that her boat tied onto her car rack would cover her story.

"Hey, the bars open, and we've got beers," Frank slurred, his eyes droopy under his broad Roman brow.

"You celebrating something?"

"Another day of living," he said with a shit-faced grin. Everyone laughed. "I'm serious, Casey. Come out windsurfing with us. Get over it."

"Well, tomorrow's another day. You never know. I'll see what it brings." Resting her hand on Jett's shoulder, she gave him a rub and swept her free hand in a wave to the others in the room. "Night all. It's been a long day."

She got into bed and snugged the sheet around her, not for the cold but for comfort. The pulling of the sheets disturbed Tiger, who lay curled in a ball at the foot of the bed. Irritated by her intrusion on his space, he jumped down to go lie in an open window. Her legs could now stretch freely, and she found her sleeping position. The cannabis high floated her mind. She drifted past the day's events on the river and through the sparkly dark behind her eyes.

Channeling, she journeyed to reach the ghost of Charley. Her mental fingers parting her way through the cosmic layers. Floating into another dimension, she merged into the field of her youth, where the sharing of their hearts opened true, and the joys of life beckoned before them. Through the fog of her imagination, he swirled towards her to conjoin with her thoughts. His image cleared, and she wordlessly spoke to him. We have a plan, Charley. It won't be long now until we have our revenge for you and for many others. She revealed the plan, sharing Little Bear's connection to the justice that they sought. Charley listened, his eyes a pained, hollow stare. His lost eyes dug into her. His soul called to her. "When will I be released? When will I go home?"

She felt his plea. A tear formed. Yes, Charley, it is time for you to go home.

****

Frank occupied the one bathroom In the small house. Casey knocked on the door. "I'm waiting," she sang through the door.

"Nature is taking its course. Hold on. I'll be out soon."

She turned away, took several deep breaths, and swirled her hand on her stomach until the cramp passed. To distract her mind, she returned to her room to make the bed. She hummed a made-up tune while she worked. The toilet flushed, and the door opened to Frank grimacing and waving his hands. "Sorry, alcohol bombs. The window's open."

"Sweet inspiration," she said, fanning as she entered and shut the door.

She gathered her thoughts while she sat on the toilet. Most of her plans seemed to be formulated. Loosely assembled but seeming to be credible. Bringing Jett on board and finding the van remained undone. And then there was the disappearing act. She placed that on the back burner and stayed with her present tasks. Today, she would have a word with Jett. She had to wait for the date before booking a vehicle, but she could research it and be ready. Everything hinged on getting possession of the stuff. She placed her faith in Little Bear.

In the kitchen, she buttered and jammed her toast. She called out to Frank and Jett over her shoulder. "So what's the latest on the lab, guys? Heard back from cousin Tony?"

"Nothing yet," Frank said under his breath.

"Right," she said and waited for Jett to blast off.

Jett took his cue as expected. "I'm not budging. My work and knowledge have value. I'm not falling into this 1% gets the cake, and the worker gets the crumbs deal."

"They're sweating you guys. A classic case of working one against the other," Casey said.

"Hey, what they're offering is a good deal. Better than what we got now."

"Speak for yourself," Jett said.

"Whatever. It's up to you guys. I'm out of it." Casey changed the subject. "What you doing today, Frank?"

"Not sure. See if the wind picks up this afternoon, I guess." He watched out of the window for movement in the trees. His eyes suddenly lit up. "Hey, you guys, I've got an idea. Let's all go float around on the Klickitat. It's gonna be hot, the river is cool and not so crazy fast. Come on. We haven't done anything together for a while. You know, lighten up. Give ourselves a break. Remember how it used to be?"

Casey wasn't sure about Frank's proposition. She wanted to work on her to-do list and mull over all that she had on her mind. She paused and reconsidered.

Going to the river could allow her to get what she needed from Frank and Jett, the river offering a private place to make her solicitations. Besides, there may not be many more times to hang out with her friends. Sad thinking that way because, after all, the rivers and the playing on them were what had brought them together in the first place. "I'm in, but I have to be back in the afternoon. Got work tonight."

"All right, Casey! How about it, bud?" Frank said to Jett, giving his arm that irritating bro slug.

"Okay. I'm down. I'll ride with you, Frank. Casey, you take your car to make sure you get back on time in case Frank and I get adventurous."

"Like checking out the girls at the swimming hole up on the commune?"

"Not a bad idea, Casey," Frank said with a wicked smile.

They carried their boats down to a flat area where they could launch below the series of falls where Native Americans dip netted salmon during the autumn run. On the calm, deep pooled section of the river, they relaxed, drifting in the revitalizing air coming off of the river. The Klickitat was a more significant river than their local White Salmon, but it flowed from the same source—glacier-capped Mt. Adams or Patoh as the Yakama called it. The mountain was sacred to the tribe. The snow melts fed the springs, streams, and rivers that sustained their communities and the greater region. 'Water is life,' they said. If only Hanford and the polluting industries could agree.

The Klickitat River ran ice cold. To swim in it burned the skin. Even so, the air coming off of the water cooled and refreshed as Frank had suggested.

Frank paddled over to the shady, far side to glide along the steep walls of basalt lining the river canyon while Casey and Jett drifted, lost in the peacefulness of the moment. A wide-winged osprey swooped in front of them. It circled and perched on a bare tree limb.

Jett broke the silence. "Good idea coming out here. Time to reflect and time to be with you, Casey. Seems like we've been caught up in a whirlwind between Charley and the lab happening. Frank sometimes does have some good ideas."

"He loves playing on the water. I've been so overwhelmed I've forgotten how much I love it too. I'll miss this when I'm gone."

Jett stiffened. "When you're gone? Casey, what are you talking about?"

"Things are falling in place, Jett. The plan is going to happen."

"Do I have to guess, or are you going to fill me in?"

"I'll give you the details soon. You up for a ride to Spokane with me?"

"What's happening up there? When?"

"Maybe tomorrow? I've decided that it's time to put Charley to rest. Have a ceremony that feels real. I have the necklace as a physical symbol to offer, but it's his spirit that needs peace. Back up there in Spokane is the only place that makes sense for him to be. You know, at our special spot."

Jett drew a breath and exhaled slowly. "I'm glad you're coming to your senses. I'll be happy to go with you. No problem."

"I don't know about coming to my senses, but the way is becoming clearer." She stuck her paddle and pulled away. "I'm going to catch up with Frank. There's something I need to talk to him about in private. I'll be back." She stroked hard and slid in alongside Frank. "Good idea coming out here," she said.

"I've got a few, you know."

"Yeah, you do. Sorry if I make you feel otherwise." She gathered herself. " Listen, I have something serious to ask of you. Please do me this important favor and don't ask me questions."

"I smell trouble. You're not getting me involved in that crazy revenge scheme of yours, are you?"

"Not really, but it is related. I will have to leave town and go away, and I need some help with a new identity. I figure your cousin Tony might be able to fix me up with that. Could you ask him?"

Frank threw his head back and yelled into the air. "Holy shit, Casey. You are going to do something stupid over Charley, aren't you? You don't listen to anything I say, do you? I can't believe that you're willing to throw your life away over something you can't really do anything about. What a waste. You're turning into a real nutbag."

Casey laughed. "I guess you could say that, but I still need just a tiny bit of help from my friends. I'm not getting you involved in my plan. I just need a new identity. I've made up my mind to do something for Charley and for everybody and everything that has been fucked over by that God awful place and those God awful people running it, and you can't change my mind. Sorry."

He gazed off into the distance, then turned towards her. "I'll miss you. Where are you gonna go?"

"Okay, this is where I have to trust you, and you have to forget that I ever told you. Can you promise me that?"

"All right already. Where?"

"I need a contact in Las Vegas for the new identity. Where I go from there, I don't know. Lolly will need a new identity too."

"You two love birds flying into the sunset. Seems fitting. I could ask, but he's kinda pissed at me right now over a hard time with the lab contract. No guarantees, Casey."

They drifted, bobbing like fishing floats. "Fantastic, Frank. Contact him is all I ask. If he says no, I'll find another way."

"Determined, aren't you?"

"Absolutely …" Her face shrank. "One other thing. It could be a going-away present. That's up to you. An uninvolved way of helping me with my quest. I need some money. I could give you my boat and my windsurfing gear. All these changes are going to cost, and you know I don't make much at the bar." She waited for him to freak out.

He mulled over her request. "You know, this whole thing is so sad. You could have let things go. I thought we were all happy here, living a good life, having fun, catching a ride." He lowered his head, and reaching with his paddle, he stroked away. She followed. When she caught up with him, he shrugged and said, "I'll call Tony and see where we go from there. All right? You may still have a change of heart. If not, I'll buy your boat and stuff."

"Thanks, Frank. It means a lot for you to help me out. Come float with Jett and me. Let's be silent with the river and enjoy the moment here together." He followed her lead upstream where Jett idled in the shadow of a cliff.

A fish broke water ahead of them, it's residual ring spreading before them. Frank stroked his boat, aiming to glide alongside Casey's. He sat back in his seat, his momentum carrying him forward until he drifted in next to her. Turning his head to face her, his words came with a deep exhale. "Ah, Casey, life could be so easy." She raised her head skyward and wished it true.

Chapter 23

Frank looked at his watch and saw that it was a good time to call Chicago. His promise to call and ask a favor for Casey had weighed heavily on his mind. He hated the idea of asking for a favor from his disadvantaged position. The unclosed deal had him climbing the walls. But what the hell.—She's a friend. He iced his nerves and poked Tony's number. "Morning, Tony."

"How you doing, Frankie? Got some good news? Got your buddy straightened out yet?"

"I'm working on it."

"Work harder. I'm tired of waiting. We want to get moving on this deal, and there are other guys around who would jump at the shot. If you weren't family, you'd be in the trash can by now. You get that? Make up his mind soon, or you're out."

"Give me just a little more time, and I'll bring him around. Any way you can sweeten the deal. Cut him a small piece of the pie?"

"You kidding. It's a sweet deal already. You guys got nothing."

Frank held his tongue. He wanted to fire back about Jett's knowledge and his product's level but couldn't get it up to take on Tony. It was now or never for Casey. "So Tony, I know this is a bad time to ask a favor, but something has come up. You remember my friend Casey? She's got a big problem. She and a friend got into some trouble, and they need new identities. Somebody to set her up in Vegas. Think you could help out?"

"It'll cost you."

"Whatever. Casey's desperate, and she's like family to me."

"I'll think about it. You think about what I said. The clock is ticking."

"Thanks, Tony. Don't worry. He'll come around."

Casey's request off his chest, and with the weight of his impending showdown with Jett still hanging over him, Frank headed out for a sail on the big river.

****

"Are you up for joining me for a ride to Spokane? You know, to bury Charley? I'm going today," Casey said to Jett in the kitchen.

"Oh yeah. Sure. No problem. I'm glad that you've decided to finally do it. Charley has to be more than ready to be put to rest. You leaving right now?"

"After breakfast. I'm hungry this morning. Don't ask me why."

"Probably because it's a long road trip ahead."

" I could make some eggs—Jethro? Sound good?"

"Go for it. I'll try your cooking for a change."

"Are you insinuating something?"

"You know me better than that. Make mine with that pumpernickel in the fridge and semi runny in the middle, would you, Cooky."

"Don't worry, Fuss Pot. That's the way I like it too. Crispy cut-outs as well?"

Jett clicked on a breaking news story. He scanned it quickly and jerked back in his chair. "You've got to hear this! It's an article from King 5 News. The headline reads; Hanford Lab Ordered To Stop Work. 'A laboratory leader was suspended, and his security badge taken away for calling a Stop Work Order at Hanford Lab due to dangerous conditions.' Can you believe it? According to the article, he stopped work because of 'inadequate ventilation for hazardous fumes and lack of protection from toxic oil on lab equipment.' His attorney states, 'If Hanford continues to punish workers who raise concerns, the message is clear—look the other way and say nothing if you want to keep your job.' "

Casey bashed the spatula on the edge of the cast-iron skillet. "Those rotten bastards!"

"That's not the end of the article. A senator says, 'It's clear that DOE contractors are going to great lengths to signal that when employees blow the whistle, it signals the end of their career' and, listen to this piece of work, 'that the DOE pays the legal expenses of contractors who engage in retaliation against whistleblowers.' Unbelievable!" Jett screamed before slapping down the screen of his computer.

Casey's face shadowed. Her voice dropped low. "It continues going on, doesn't it. They keep having their evil way, hurting people, endangering more, and no one does anything. Talk, talk, talk. They hide behind their lawyers, lie and get away with it. I know that it sounds like I'm repeating myself, but you see why I've got to do something. Make the bastards and their families feel the pain. Make them pay like all their victims have. Experience what it's like. Maybe then something will change," she said from the stove. She slung the plates of food on the table and stared disgustedly out of the kitchen window.

****

Charley's necklace, all wrapped and tied in a blue cloth, sat like a third passenger on the back seat. Thoughts about the upsetting article stuck like dry blood on a scab as they began the ride north to Spokane. Silence kept them company for most of an hour. Jett offered a Band-Aid. "This is good, bringing Charley to be buried."

"I guess so." She sighed heavily. "Charley's tired and ready to find peace. He knows there is a plan in place, and that's a comfort for him. This time the burial will be real. It's up to me to carry on now."

"Burying him will be an end and a beginning. Are you going to tell me about the plan?"

Her features softened. "I'll tell you about your part. Some of the plans are best for you not to know for your own good. You'll most likely learn about it after I'm gone but better that you didn't hear it from me."

"That sounds heavy. I'm not to be trusted, huh?"

"It's not that. I'm looking out for you, man."

"So lay it on me. The part you think I should know."

"You, Sam, and Little Bear are going to abduct a couple of guys up in Umatilla and drop them off. That's the simple gist of it. You will be the driver, and they'll be the grab guys. There's just one extra thing, I need you to rent the van. I'll give you some money, so don't worry about that."

"I'm not worried about the money. It's my name on the account that freaks me."

"Got ya covered there. Sam will 'borrow' some plates for the night and swap them out, just in case. There are no cameras at either end, so should be no problems. Surgical grab, a ride down the freeway, a quick drop, and you're done. Can you handle it?"

"You know I'd do almost anything for you," he replied. "So, Sam is in on it. I guess you trust that guy. I don't like him at all, but I suppose that doesn't really matter."

"You'd be surprised. Sam's got a good heart under that tough skin."

"I wouldn't know … Little Bear, that's that big Native fisherman, right? He's probably got a good reason to want revenge. You know him? Trust him?"

"Getting to know him better. He's the one who gave me the idea for the plan. In fact, he's key to the plan. I trust him completely."

" When is it going to happen?"

"There are some details to work out but within a few weeks."

"I'll miss you terribly, you know."

She squeezed his arm, and her hand slid down to hold his tenderly. "I'll miss you too. You've been my loyal friend. I'll never forget that."

Watery marshes and small lakes announced the outskirts of Spokane. Passing the city center, they exited and made their way through a rundown suburbia made up of dated ranch houses cluttered with wrecked vehicles, boats, and noticeably unkempt yards. She slowed as they passed in front of a trailer park. "This is it. My happy home," she said facetiously. A short way farther, she parked in a pullover next to a stand of pines that broke up the neighborhood. A marsh wove through it, the only thing protecting nature from further development. She turned to the back seat. "Well, Charley, this is it. Back to our old spot."

She popped the trunk, pulled out a shovel, handed it to Jett, put Charley into the crook of her arm, and led into the woods. "It seemed so much bigger when we were kids. This was our world away from the trailer. A sweet spot with critters, birds, and butterflies. A place to dream of another life. Charley was seeking that. Working at Hanford was only a way to try and get a step ahead. He would have made it."

Crows squawked as the woods darkened beneath thickening narrow pines, and then, in a clearing, it stood, the massive pine of the picture. A lone survivor from a past logging venture in the days when no wetland rules existed and the forests appeared endless. Chunky, red bark encased, the fat old pine ruled the copse. They sat underneath in the bark and needles that encircled the tree's base, leaning against the old one, listening to the small sounds found beneath the stillness: a chipmunk skittering and hunching on a neighboring fallen log, a creaking of little frogs in the marsh, a bird fluffing on a limb.

Nature enveloped them. Her body rested against his. Past and present converged in the sacred place of her childhood. He placed his arm around her and tenderly held her, only imagining what she must be feeling. She drifted, memories streaming on a strand of moving time. Arcs of loss and destiny mingled, leaving tears dripping down her face. She trembled like an injured bird. He lovingly stroked her in silence. She snuggled deeper into his chest and then raised her face to search his whiskey brown eyes. In them, she found his true heart, the one always there for her. She opened to him for the first time. Her heart throbbed in her chest as she pulled him down to meet her upturned lips.

Blood spiked his veins, responding with his all to the unexpected, long-awaited moment.

They held in sweet silence for a while longer, but the world turned as it always does. Casey gathered herself, unashamed of the kiss that lingered still on her lips and in her heart. Her eyes dry, she pulled Jett up by his hand, saying in a steady voice, "Guess we better do what we came for." She stepped away from the tree and slowly walked around it, searching for a sign to show where to lay Charley to rest. Two thick, armed roots reached, forming a cove against the trunk. There he could lie, held in the motherly nook of the tree where a sword fern decorated in the lee. She pointed. "See if you can get a hole in there."

Jett chopped around on the surface, feeling the ground with the point of the shovel. He felt a soft area, flicked away a small stone, set the blade, and pressed with his foot. The yielding ground encouraged him to jump down on the shovel. The blade sank to the top. Loamy with only feeder roots, he took the hole down to where it turned to clay. He rested, leaning on the shovel handle. "What do you think?" he asked.

"I think it will do fine. Charley will be happy to be here." She picked up the necklace wrapped in blue. "Want to say good-bye?"

"Sure." He held the small bundle awkwardly, then lifted it and reverently said a silent prayer. He passed Charley back to her. "He wants you."

She cuddled the symbol of him like a baby, rocking him in her arms, humming a childhood memory. "Okay, Charley, time to go home," she said, placing him at the bottom of the hole. "Rest in Peace." With the grave covered, she searched around for rocks. Jett understood what she was doing and joined her in making a burial mound. They gathered scattered wildflowers and greens from the shaded forest and sprinkled them over the rocks for the last touch.

A blurred movement in the forest shadowed past the corner of her eye. Raising her head from the mound, she saw what appeared at first glance to be a big dog. Large, with a long snout, it sat staring into her with fire in its eyes. It's gums lifted, revealing sharp teeth. And then it was gone. She grabbed her chest in shock. Jett followed her troubled gaze into the forest. "What is it, Casey? What is wrong?"

"There was a wolf over there in those trees." Jett saw nothing, but taking a big stick in his hand, he warily stalked to where she had pointed. Scanning the woods, they found nothing. Not even tracks. The Wolf's face remained imprinted in Casey's mind. Strangely, it left no fear. Confused, she said, "I swear I saw it, but it doesn't make sense. I must be overtired."

"You've been through a lot. I can only imagine what being back in this wood must be like. Have you seen it here before?"

"No. I don't think so," Casey said with creased brows.

They returned to the tree and sat. "It's a long drive back. Let's rest our eyes for a little while." They held each other with eyes closed. Behind her closed lids, the Wolf sat by her side.

Chapter 24

Tony's name lit up on Frank's telephone screen. The music played. It surprised him to hear back so soon since only that morning he had made his special request. He paced around, alone in the kitchen, the phone ringing in his hand. Something must be up. Tony might be calling the whole deal off. He only called when he had something on his mind. Frank swiped his hand down his face, exhaled a deep breath, and answered the call. "What took so long? Catch you jerking off or something?" Tony barked.

"The phone was stuck in my pocket. Ever happen to you?" Popcorn popped in his stomach. What was up with Tony?

Tony's voice dug into a serious tone. "So here's the deal, Frankie. If you want a favor from me, who's already offering you a big favor, you gotta give me something in return. I'll give the girl the set up in Vegas if Jett signs on with the team, and we get the show rolling. We want the lab guy. No more fooling around. You got that?"

It stung to know they wanted Jett more than him. "Yeah, yeah, I got it. I'll tell them the good news. I'm sure he'll just love getting guilt-tripped into signing.

"He cares about the girl, right? So, he gets to be the hero, and she gets what she needs. Convince him. You want to be a salesman, prove it. Let's get this show moving. Come on. You got a day. I've been letting you jerk me around long enough."

"I'll talk to him as soon as I see him. I'll call you."

"Don't bother calling if you can't tell me what I want to hear. Get it done. This is your shot."

Frank heard the back door open. Jett and Casey poked their heads into the lounge where he sat waiting. Frank sprang like toast from his comfortable chair. His excited voice broke into a high pitch. " Where the hell you guys been? I've been waiting for you."

"Since when were you mother hen?" Casey slashed.

"Since I talked to Tony and got the answer to our little problemo," he said directly to Casey. "Where did you go, anyway?"

"We buried Charley," Jett said. "Way the fuck up in Spokane. I'm tired. What's so important that it can't wait?"

"Decision time, brother." Jett Spocked his eyebrow while Frank said to Casey, " I'm glad for Charley that he's at rest at last."

"Thanks, Frank, I appreciate your concern. So, what's the big news from Tony?" With no patience for his stuttering stall, she flagged him on with her hands.

Frank took a big breath and laid it on the line. "Tony says he'll connect you up with the right people in Las Vegas, Casey— if Jett agrees to the contract and comes on board." The news cut like a double-edged sword. Casey, leaping up and down—Jett, turning away dashed, fists clenched.

"What the fuck!" Jett shouted, staring into Frank's face. "That's extortion! What's this all about, Casey?"

"I asked Frank to ask Tony if he could hook me up in Vegas with a new identity. I figured he'd have those kinds of connections, and I need help." She shifted her feet uncomfortably, guilt and embarrassment worrying her face. She searched Jett for forgiveness. Her hands went down and out by her side. " I had no idea he would tie you into this, Jett. Please understand and forgive me. I'm sorry. You don't have to do it. I can find another way."

Jett held his head and spun away. He searched his heart for an answer while he paced the small room, a dark cloud hanging over him. Abruptly, a calm descended upon him. His aura cleared like the air after a summer rain. He moved to stand in front of her and, taking hold of her shoulders, sought her eyes. "It's not your fault, Casey." He swung his body towards Frank. His voice rose loud and bitter. "Cousin Tony just knows how to use people—doesn't he?" He let his words dig into Frank. He half laughed at his predicament. "Damned if I do and damned if I don't. Good old Tony has got me by the balls."

Frank shirked. "Hey, don't look at me. I didn't come up with the idea. What am I going to say to him? He wants to know by tomorrow, or everything is off the table."

Jett squeezed his fists, staring down Frank. His words streamed out in sarcasm. "What do you think I'm going to do? Save Casey or throw her under the bus? There is no choice, is there? I'd sell my soul to the devil for her," he said, a lump rising in his throat. She felt a lump too. Hearing those words, she came to him. Holding him, tears beaded in the corners of her eyes. She understood his sacrifice. He rested his head upon hers, recapturing the big pine. Frank's lips hung open, silently observing the closeness between them.

"Jett, I can't let them get over on you like this. I'll have to find another way," she offered.

He slid his hands to hold hers and stood solid in his resolve. His face brightened. His path became clear. "You will take his help, and I will make the lab work for me. It's our destiny. What else could it be? Let this be my parting gift to you. Don't worry about me. I'll be fine." He dropped her hands and stalked towards Frank, who stepped back warily. An awkward silence gripped the room. Jett grinned like a shark. "We'll be just fine. Won't we, Frankie? In fact, we'll be making a whole lot more money than we are now. Right partner?" He said, slapping Frank's shoulder soundly, letting the irony of Frank's earlier pitch sink in. "Isn't that what you've been telling me? Besides, No legal hassles either. And, we can leverage them for more when it all gets up and running. So the cookie crumbles. Think of Casey's deal as a signing bonus."

****

Early the next morning, still dreamy from the night, Casey lay awake and let her thoughts wander. A sweet breeze off of the river, blew through the open bedroom window. Lilac leaves against the edge of the window frame lightly rustled. A happy bird song chirped away. The giant pine came to mind, and then his kiss met her lips again—the kiss, gentle but arousing. Jett had moved her. Surprising but true. The awareness stirred her. In her heart, she felt the genuineness of what had happened. Always close with him, sharing easily, another layer awakened in her world. Softness with a man. How different from her other male experiences. She let the thought hang, knowing that her plan was to leave and be with Lolly, her girlfriend and lover. Could she love two? What would it be like to lay with him? Most likely, she'd never know.

Charley was gone from the dresser top. His company missing from the room. Unresolved vengeance remained in his place. Leaving entered her mind. Scanning, she took note of the stuff to leave behind and what to bring. She didn't own much—clothes, some old furniture, and some artwork she didn't need. She decided a day hike backpack will be all that is necessary. Start clean, travel light, the rest of the stuff could go to Goodwill, or just stay put. Let Frank sort it out. Her car, her boat, and her windsurfing gear were her significant possessions.

She observed the room with a nostalgic eye while thinking about leaving. The room had been a safe space. A place to have her own thoughts and to share when and with whom she wanted. The reality of leaving it all worried and unsettled her. The unknown future spooked her. She tried to imagine her life in Vegas or wherever she and Lolly might finally land. Will they be happy together? Their part-time relationship worked well. Maybe it went that way because of being part-time. Fluffing her pillow behind her head, she continued her mental ramble, her ongoing moral thread now holding court. Would her deeds haunt her forever? Will she be good again, and will the world be glad and forgive her? Will she regain her free-spirited lightness? Will Lolly still love her? She crossed her hands over her chest and returned to the open window where the lilac leaves still rustled.

****

Hot water passed through the coffee grounds; its

trickling broke the silence of the kitchen. The computer screen was open, a front for Jett's traveling mind. A portal into a zone of euphoria where his lips pressed on hers, and they breathed the same air. By the tree, she gave him a sliver of the love that he longed for—if only for a twinkle of time. Could she have been overcome with emotion about Charley, or mixed up by being there at their special place? He hoped not but could understand if it were connected to all those feelings. He waited for her morning arrival, longing for another chance to hold her heart again.

Frank called Tony from the privacy of his room. "Maybe you're a salesman, after all, Frankie. Well done. Listen, the paperwork is at the lawyer's office in Hood River. Go sign so we can close the deal. You remember where?"

"Of course, I do! You ever gonna stop busting my balls?"

"Comes with the territory, Junior. Lou still busts my balls like crazy. Welcome back to the family."

"What about the contact for Casey?"

"Sign the contract, and you'll get it. Don't worry about it. Give the lawyer a call. Don't just pop in."

Frank clomped into the kitchen like everything was cool. "Anything good happening in the world?" He fired at Jett.

"If there was, we wouldn't know about it."

"I called Tony. We gotta go over to the lawyers and sign the contract this morning. I made an appointment. You okay with that?"

"He wants it signed in blood?"

"Get outta here."

"He give you the set up for Casey?"

"We gotta sign first, so the deal is closed."

"What happened to good faith and trust?"

"It's business. That's all."

****

Little Bear hunched over his beer at the age-darkened bar top when Casey came in for her shift. She ran the palm of her hand along his back as she passed by. Her reflection followed in the mirror behind. Greeting the day man, he discreetly pointed towards a couple of guys at the far end, celebrating an afternoon drunk. Their booming voices shouted over the rock and roll thread running in the background. "Don't worry, Matt. I can handle them," she said, moving matronly down the bar. "You're in a good mood, Randy. What's going on?"

Randy tugged down his two-toned baseball cap, brought his hands together to megaphone his mouth, and leaned across the bar. "Troy's forty," he drawled and made a clown face.

"Wow, that's a big one! Shit, Troy, I never would have guessed." Troy tipped his hat off of his receding hairline in acknowledgment. She placed two new shot glasses in front of them. "What'll you have? This one is on me. Happy birthday."

"Maker's Mark," they slurred and threw them back as soon as she poured.

"Bring us two cans of PBR and hit us again, Casey," Randy called. She poured again and brought the cans of beer, leaving the good old boys celebrating. Let them have their fun—they'll run out of gas soon enough.

The bar under control, she approached stoic Little Bear and leaned in. "What's up?"

"I see you still got your red hair."

She angled her head and frowned. "I've been busy. I buried Charley."

He kept his head directed down at the bar and muttered without moving his lips. "How about tomorrow?"

She jerked to attention. "Let me make a call." She rang Sandy, another bartender. With a kid to support, she will take all the hours she can get. Her mother is always happy to play with her granddaughter. The conversation didn't last long. Sandy agreed to stand in for her. Casey came back to Bear. The party boys had moved on to the next bar. "I'm covered. What time?"

"Let's say at three o'clock at the meeting place. Bring the same stuff." He laid some money down, cinched up his pants, and walked into a cloud of dust particles hanging in the air captured by the afternoon sun streaming through the bar-room door.

"See you," she called to his back, wiping down the bar while her mind flew ahead. She pictured herself at the river, the jars in her hand, fearlessly filling them with toxic water. A memory of her dead brother in the sack flashed darkly into her thoughts. Her face flushed as the hate surged, and the Wolf bounded into the front of her mind. Its fierce eyes became hers. Hunger for the kill rose within her. At once, she found herself far from the bar, lunging, ripping at a throat, blood on her tongue, knowing the power and taste of the kill.

Chapter 25

Casey took up her ready backpack and left the house with a determined heart. The jars sat securely within her bag, alongside of her gloves and bandana. She wore shorts and a T-shirt and carried her grey hooded sweatshirt in her free hand. After placing her backpack next to her wetsuit in her car's back seat, she went for the kayak. Noticing the bright orange of her usual boat, she decided to swap it out for a less obtrusive dark purple one that would meld into the dark of night. She had her phone plus one for Little Bear. Food, packed in her bag. Hard to think of now, but she'd need fuel for later when taking on the river. She paused behind the wheel, set her intention, and left for the marina. No false start this time. Nothing must get in the way.

The late afternoon sun baked down on Bear's truck like a potato in an oven. Blazing relentlessly, it followed from behind as they drove eastward. Little Bear's air conditioning happened to be on the blink, so the hot air blow-dried in a steady roar with the windows down. Flowing alongside the highway, the broad river's blue coolness offered visual comfort from the steaming road. On the other side, the parched country visually wobbled in the heat waves steaming off the rocky surfaces. They passed Celilo, and Casey pointed. Bear grunted and gave an enthusiastic thumbs up. Casey said, "You never told me if you have any family out here?"

"You never asked. I have one sister who lives on the Reservation up at White Swan. My Granny, who lives with me at the river camp, plus some cousins scattered around."

"You live with your grandmother?"

"She has nowhere to go. It's okay. We get along."

"Mother?"

"Nope. No mother, no father. Both dead from cancer. Mom had Hodgkins and Dad had a bad stomach. Ate too much river fish, I figure."

"Your granny, okay?"

"Too stubborn to die. Granny is wise in the old ways."

"I'm sorry about your Mom and Dad. You still became a fisherman anyway?"

"I was always a fisherman. From the time I was a boy, I fished on the river with my father and uncle. I learned from my father and him from his. It's our way of life, and I like it. The river is part of me even as it is, and I like catching fish and eating them, too. My blood is half fish oil, you know." With a straight face, he stuck out his arm for her to feel. She pushed it back and laughed. He glanced his dark eyes towards her, lifted his chin, and continued his story. "Fishing is a good life. Nobody tells you what to do. You are close with all of nature. Once I was happier with it, but now, the river talks to me." She saw his eyes become troubled. "I have bad dreams. I dream of the poison in the tanks escaping and killing the river for good."

"I know that horrible thought. I saw the same vision when I stood on the bluff overlooking the Reach. It's not so far- fetched. It could happen. Somebody has to make them care enough to make a change. Somebody like us."

"Me and you," he confirmed, offering a meaty fist to bounce.

"Bear, I am going to trust you with something going on inside of me. I need to tell someone. It's pretty strange, but somehow, I think you might understand … I have a Wolf spirit that comes to me. I think it's a she, and she is angry and fierce."

"Like you." He rocked his head in understanding, not appearing to think it odd at all. "It is a good sign. The spirits are with us. I spoke to old Granny about my dreams, and she said she would journey to the spirit world and ask for an answer."

"You told her about our plan?"

"Not everything. Only that I wanted to do something for the river. I am glad for your She-Wolf. She is a cunning, protective, and lethal ally. Maybe Granny met her in the spirit world? Anyway, the wicked ones have gotten away with their poisoning for too long. Wolf has come to help us. You will need her strength to do what must be done. Don't be afraid. Allow her."

"I'll try. Seems strange, but I can use all the help I can get." She reached into her bag, pulled out a flip-phone, and set it upon the seat. "I got you a phone, Bear. I'll get one for each of us to use then throw away. We'll have our own little network."

A couple of empty boat trailers and their trucks sat in the launch parking lot on a Sunday afternoon. Casey faced Little Bear with worried eyes. "Don't be concerned about them. It is a big river out there. They won't get in our way. Anyway, they will be returning

186

soon. I have a plan. Trust me?"

She met his eyes. "All right, partner. Let's get what we need!"

They launched Bear's boat off of his trailer. Casey tended the bowline while Bear parked up the empty trailer. They climbed on board and motored slowly upstream. They had time to kill before nightfall. Casey had her hood up over her baseball cap and kept her face away from the Hanford site. Her nerves tightened. She knew this time had to be it—no more rehearsals.

The bugs off of the water thickened as the sun eased into the western horizon. In the distance, the Cascade mountain range sketched a wavy, purple outline across the sky. The air hushed and lay still. A fish broke water and rippled the reflection of the sunset on the smooth river. Bear spoke. "We'll go up to where we were last time and mess around like we're fishing or getting ready to fish, and when we lose the sun, we'll fall back to where we were anchored on the Oregon side. We'll act like normal fisherman spending the night there, just in case someone is watching. It will be safer to launch your kayak in the dark, out of the mainstream of the river."

Apprehension squeezed her face. "So, I'll cross the river and go to the spot in the dark?"

"That's the idea. Can you do it?"

She lifted her hand to the air, felt the lack of breeze, and scanned the river. No waves to be seen, only strong current running, but nothing she hadn't experienced before. "I can do it, Bear. I'll have to."

"No light on until you reach the shore and then, keep your head below the bank," Bear said.

They went upstream and dropped some lines until

the sun began to sink. In the nightfall, Bear pulled the anchor and swung out into the middle of the river. Downstream, he subtly pointed to the spot they failed to reach before. "Mark the signs of the spot in your mind. You'll have to find them in the dark." He slowed the boat and pointed towards the location of the plume. Following his point, she committed the shoreline to memory as best she could. From the distant position, she strained in the dimmed light to get a few markers to guide her way.

Away from the river's main flow, the spot lay in a small cove with a point of land jutting out on the upstream side. The bank had eroded in high water, leaving a massive boulder perched at the peninsula's edge. She marked the boulder in her mind and lifted her eyes to a stand of willows clustered on top of the bank. Their tops rose higher than their surroundings, but nonetheless, they looked like all the other willows that lined the river's banks. "Take a mark now, and don't take your eye off of it while I drive the boat to the far side," Bear said.

"Aye, Captain." As the boat moved farther away, she kept a close watch on the big rock until her squinting eyes filled with water. She glanced upwards to catch an awakening star. The new reference point fortified her faith in being able to make the perilous journey. She knew full well that the current would surely do it's best to drag her off course and planned accordingly. "I'll aim high," she said to Bear. "That way, I can drift down on it if I need to. Don't want to fight upstream on the shoreline, trying to find the mark. I might not have the strength, and I might attract attention."

"Good plan. Gather yourself. The river is strong."

"I know her well. She's the strong, silent type. She does what and how she wants."

"So true, Casey. In case you are wondering, you will launch your kayak on the shadowy land side."

Loving respect for her friend welled up inside of her. Without him, where would the plan be?

The viscous flow of the river steadily surged by. Deceptive in its power, it appeared sluggish but was a body of tremendous force. She laid out her wetsuit and arranged her backpack with still no sign of watchers. No lights to be seen on the far side either. Bear dropped the anchor, and they swung to, her markers remaining barely visible in the darkening sky of the early night. The star brightened. It was a long way to the far side.

"Better eat," he said. "If they are watching, let them see us settle down. On high alert, Casey felt as if she'd drank a whole pot of coffee, but heeding Bear's words, she ate handfuls of trail mix, two bananas, and an energy bar to give her strength. She had another bar in her pack for the return. In the darkness, she dropped her shorts and hung her bottom over the rail and peed a long stream after drinking nearly a quart of water. She slipped into her wetsuit, lifting the hood up over her head. Little Bear sat down beside her and faced towards land. He held a coke can, and some fisherman snips in the other. He cut off the ends of the can and handed it to her. "Put this in your pack."

She rolled it around in her hands curiously then put it to her face like a telescope. "Can't see any better with this. What is it for?"

Bear snorted a laugh. "A funnel. When you find the stream, stick this into the mud and catch the water off of the spout lip."

A wave of doubt swamped her. "Will I find it okay? You know, the seep?"

"It's big enough to see, and it smells horrible. Look for discoloration around it if you can or follow your nose. It works in the dark."

She remembered what she and Rex encountered on their day time foray with RiverKeepers. Trying to find the seep in the dark, possibly covered by brush and tall grasses, a different story. "You sure I'll find it okay? I can't see shit in the dark."

"Your headlamp will show the slimy, nasty gunk when it passes over it. Don't worry. You will smell it."

She took a deep breath and worked on being calm. She knew the rules of being out on the water—fear and panic were enemies of survival. While her nerves shot waves of anxiety up and down her chest and arms, she searched Little Bear's face for support and confidence. He gave her a firm hug and a reassuring rub on the back and motioned towards the kayak.

She squeezed his arm, put on her backpack, and lowered her boat over the side. The river immediately wanted to carry it away, even by the edge of land. She held tightly to the tugging line and passed it to Bear. "Trickier than you might think to get into a kayak from a boat," she joked, hoping that making light would calm her nerves.

"You're braver than me. I'll hold the kayak steady for you. You ready?" He leaned far out over the side and firmly grasped the rail of the boat. She took a last look at her bearings, found her star, and lined up a silhouetted peak in the distance. Hanging her legs over the rail, she placed her feet into the tippy kayak. The hull wobbled and shifted, forcing her to restrain her weight until she felt secure. Very carefully, she lowered into a squat and put her paddle in hand. Little Bear gave her the line. She tucked it into the cockpit. Silently, she fell back from Bear's boat like a shuttle launch in space. The consuming river pulled her downstream. She stared, stunned for the moment, into the deep, dark water, then stuck her paddle and stroked furiously to shift the momentum from falling back to moving forward.

She beat her way upstream and over, always on the brink of loss against the downriver flood. Any pause would yield hard-won territory. With the fear of failure driving her on, she managed to water bug her way into the midstream of the mighty Columbia. The Columbia River being so powerful that it surges the electrical current of gigantic hydroelectric dams like the Bonneville and floated grain loaded teams of tugs and barges and paddle-wheeling old-timey excursion boats. Tonight, the water, a smooth, black plane of pushing force. Her arms burned from her tireless stroking. She longed to rest for just a minute but doing so would cost her hard-won currency.

Focusing on her star, she furiously dug her two-sided paddle back and forth, fighting her way farther across the big river, toward her mark on the far shore. Making way, the dark edge of the shoreline came into sight. Closer to the bank, the current somewhat slacked, but the river poured on. Nowhere to rest until her hull wedged into the sandy bank.

She came in high on the point and crashed into the beach. Landed, at last, she hunched forward, her breath coming in heaves. The edge of the river lapped her hull.

After a much-needed pause, she pushed off and carefully glided downstream, staying tight to the shoreline. The big stone appeared, and she aimed her bow into the rocky beach that lay behind in the sheltered cove. Shaking, she stood beside her grounded boat and realigned her thoughts. Wobbling from exertion and spooked by making landfall on Hanford's shores, she stumbled on loose rocks, collapsing to her knees. Collecting herself, she remembered that staying low was the plan. She panted from exertion and rising fear while she waited for her land legs to return and her eyes to adjust to the blackness found on the beach. Crashing into the seep in the dark—a dreadful thought.

She dug out her headlamp from a side pocket of the backpack and slid it over her head. Sidewinding forward, she stealthily kept below the bank's crest and, when feeling safe, flicked the headlamp on.

The sound of a trickling stream of water tinkled in her ears. Following her nose, she skulked towards it, hunting her prey. In her headlamp beam, a chemical sheen reflected off a small pool. A swirl of red-brown-orange-yellow-white-pink crusty scum spread dry where the level of the seep had risen and fallen. She angled her light up from the pool, to where the fluid oozed out of the ground from a collapsed bank section and into a slot of neon green slime. The colorful array might have been considered pretty to a detached mind, but for the deathly smell of putrefaction and sulfur. She coughed, covered her mouth, and backed off repulsively. Steadying herself, she studied the whole situation emotionally detached and sought to visualize her access. She pushed open some dry brush and crouched at the edge of the seep, knowing that she must not go in it or get any of the fluid on her. Somehow, she had to get the poison water safely and get out quickly. The colored gunky stuff, the stinking water, all frightened her, but this was her shot so she carried on.

Laying down the pack, she took out the mason jars, the cut Coke can, her bandana, and gloves. She tied the bandana behind her head, covered her mouth and nose, and slipping on the gloves, stepped gingerly, heel and toe towards the trickling seep. In whatever way she gathered the poison, without protective eyewear, she damn well better not splash. She squinted her eyes moving forward.

By the light of her headlamp, she searched for a place to make the lip with the Coke can. She found a spot where enough water dribbled out of the earth, and pushed the Coke can into the flow, angling the lip to form a ledge. She withdrew her hand fast as possible. The water muddied behind the disturbance but then cleared and flowed off of the lip well enough to capture in a jar.

"Gotcha," she said and reached for a jar.

Holding her arm steady, the trickle filled the jar. She screwed on the lid and twisted her body to set it down. On uneven ground, she momentarily lost her balance, casting her hand out to catch her fall. She pulled her wet glove out of the muck. A shock bolted through her. Desperate to get away, out of there, the flight instinct filled her chest. Her breath accelerated. Her mind raced fearfully. She grit her teeth and desperately wiped her hand in the grass, off to the side, away from the seep. Hotblooded, she returned to the can—funnel and filled the second jar. She calmly set it down then yanked the funnel out of the stream and tossed it into the bushes. After checking the lids security, she placed the jars in the backpack along with the mask and gloves.

The beam of her light splayed low on the ground as she slunk back towards the boat. It would have been so much easier to have done the deed at least under the light of the moon, but on further thought, moonlight would have made it easier to be discovered. Wise Bear must have taken that into consideration when he chose the date. Her purple hull glinted in the headlamp light, so she switched it off and allowed her eyes to adjust, feeling safer in the darkness.

She launched her kayak. A heady, triumphant sensation swelled within her as she silently set course towards the mainstream of the river. The now starlit sky guided her. She had the goods in the bag—time to bring them home. She stuck her paddle and worked hard across the deep black waters. Somewhat easier going downstream, a lateral course still had to be made. If she gave in to the downriver pull that sought to seduce her, a backbreaking fight to return to Bear's boat awaited her.

The boat came into view. She rallied what strength she had left. With her arms burning and breath puffing, she brought her kayak to the inside of the awaiting vessel. When the kayak clunked against the boats hull, Bear was there to grab her bowline and secure her alongside. She wearily handed him the heavy backpack. The weight told him she'd been successful. He gave her a heroic grin.

With strained effort she rolled herself over the boat rail, flopping onto the deck like a landed sturgeon. Bear gave her a hand up and began to bring the kayak aboard. Casey grabbed the stern. Boat on board, shaking from exertion, she staggered into Little Bear. He hugged and rocked with her. Her mind reeling shock began to peel away. He spoke to the side of her head as he held her dear. "No small thing what you have done. You didn't give up. You fought and won the river crossing. I'm proud of you, brave warrior woman. Now, we have a plan."

Bear went to the bow and pulled the anchor. The boat fell back in the current, drifting sideways until he took the helm. Casey stood in beside him. They floated down and out into the mainstream, waiting to fire the engine until they had well cleared the area. "Let's get the hell out of here," Bear cried out, firing the engine and throwing it in gear.

Chapter 26

Casey returned home well into the night. The struggle on the river still vibrated deeply within her bones. A night train clattered along the track that ran between her house and the river. Its impetus sucked away some of her present tension and pulled her onwards into an unknown future, illuminating thoughts about new places soon to be discovered. The reality of leaving struck home and quivered inside her. Like an arrow into a tree, it held firm. There could be no more reasoning about staying or going. She would have to go to where the life of a desperado awaited. Hiding, wanted, watching her back, etching out the new life experience yet to come.

Although still far to the finish line, she now possessed the key to retribution. With that reality under her belt, she turned her attention to the vengeful deed itself. She saw that what she would do was more profound and darker than anything she had ever done or imagined doing. She would have to connect to new realms unknown inside of herself. The Wolf shadowed her consciousness, bringing an answer. Transform, take on the robe of a vicious Wolf. Was the Wolf always there? Where was it when she cringed and withdrew when confronted as an unhappy child? She tried to answer the question by traveling back in time. The time clock ticked to a halt. She remembered seeing something. Too scary, she thought it a nightmare. Too intimidated by the world, she could not befriend it. But that was then. She growled, her power rising.

Silence came with the passing train. Casey's life's picture now shone more clearly. She saw the simple house as it had been for her these years passed, a place where she had gained friendship and experienced good times. A place where she had enjoyed the bliss of acceptance. The memories streamed by. They floated her ever higher until the needy present pulled the plug, sucking her away from fond memories and into a draining swirl of loss, leaving her stranded on an island of regret.

The accident had changed everything. Shaking off the mental spin, Casey pulled away from the car and held her chest proudly. She had returned home victorious. Her gear, wetsuit in the back seat, backpack in the trunk, remained in place. She'd deal with it tomorrow. Sticky and feeling dirty, she went straightaway to the shower before falling into bed. Laying there, she revisited holding the night's prize. Warming in satisfaction, she surrendered to the yield of the mattress—exhaustion releasing her from the chatter of her mind.

The sun shone, and the birds sang outside her window. Tiger curled beside her. She felt the softness of his fur. Cozy as it felt just lying there, no lingering in bed would happen today. On with the show. Fill in the remaining pieces. Absentmindedly, she scratched at an itching hand and rose from the bed.

As if returning from vacation, she strolled into the kitchen in her robe. "Well, if it isn't the mysterious Miss Casey," Frank said from the sink where he washed some dishes.

Jett's head lifted from his screen. "What you been up to?"

"Wouldn't you like to know," she said coquettishly and came behind him to rub his shoulders and give a kiss to the top of his head.

"Hey, I like this Casey in the good mood, woman. Welcome back," Frank said. He wiped his hands on a dishtowel and dug into his pocket. "I've got something that should keep you smiling," he said, pulling out a folded sheet of paper. He handed it to her, and she opened it. "Something from Tony," Frank said while she scanned the name, number, and Las Vegas address.

Her face went hard. Frank said, "What? Something wrong?"

"No. Just a reality check. This is great. Thanks, Frank. It's an important part of my puzzle". She hugged him. "And you, Jett," she said, bending over him, snugging his cheek. "Without you, this couldn't have happened. I'll never forget what you have done for me."

He scrambled for words. "Hey, it's not like I had to endure torture or something. I've decided to get into this twist of fate. Embrace my good fortune. You know it's not too late for you to get in too. At least I don't think you've done anything yet that makes you have to go?"

She pulled away, her chin bouncing like a bobblehead. "Nice try, Jett. Don't even go there."

He lowered his eyes. "You can't blame me, can you? I'll miss you like crazy. Maybe when all is said and done, you'll have to sneak back sometime and pinch our inflated big business egos. Go for a ride in my hot car."

She snickered. "Don't count on it."

"Summertime and the living is easy," Frank sang out. "Join me windsurfing on the river? Casey? Jett?"

"I'll come," Jett said, standing and stretching. "Some fresh breeze will do me good." His eyes met hers, searching, questioning. What had happened between us just the other day?

She questioned too, but for now, what had happened needed to remain on the back burner of her mind. "I have some stuff to do, so see you guys later." Moving to fix her toast, she brushed against Jett in passing. The contact pinged her. When he curved towards her, she knew he felt it too. Something was there—no denying that.

Outside in the yard, she walked towards her car. She thought of calling Lolly but pulled up short. Holding her head in her hands, prudence came over her. What am I thinking? I can't talk openly about these things on the phone. There can be no trace or connection to any of us. She needed the throw-away phones. She should go to the phone shop and get three more phones. Get time cards from a mini-market. Her gang will have their own network, then they would toss them. And, she remembered, check out the van rental situation.

Being careful, she called Lolly anyway. She couldn't bear waiting. Everything hinged on her arranging a date with the guys. The sacrificial ones. The tokens of the toxic system. They became faceless to her. No longer would they be people. They'd just be the evil ones, the mercenaries of the system responsible for Charley's death. She saw herself as an avenging warrior, summoned to strike a blow against the perpetrators of the poisoning of the world. Revenge a noble act. The Wolf grinned.

She made the call. The phone rang. No answer. She left a message. Lolly will call back. Casey would have to wait. She went to the car and removed her wetsuit from the backseat. She hung it to dry. Her hand scraped against her suit in the process. Her flesh stung. She stared quizzically at the hand while succumbing to another scratch. A frightening memory jerked into her brain. How could she have forgotten stumbling and plunging her hand into the toxic muck? "Oh shit!" she cried out to no one. Panic struck. Charley's scabby body leaped into her mind. She walked it off around the yard, worrying thoughts wanting to make her scared. Not touching the area, she paced until she calmed down. Steady girl, she told herself. The hand didn't hurt that bad. More irritating than any screaming pain. She remembered that aloe vera could be used for burns. She went to the bathroom cabinet and found a tube of the gel leftover from someone's sunburn and spread it on her wounded hand. The skin showed pink and irritated. Her phone rang.

"Hey, Casey, got your message. What's going on?"

"Lolly, so glad you called." She took a breath and got right into it. "You know that concert we were talking about? It's time to make the arrangement to go."

"Ah … yeah. Oh, that concert. No kidding. I didn't realize it was coming up so soon. So you want me to make the booking?"

"Sooner, the better. Get those tickets. You know how these things can go."

"All right, then. I'll let you know if I get through, then we'll plan on getting together. Okay?"

"Sounds perfect. Can't wait to see you. Hear from you soon. Kisses. Bye."

****

Lolly walked to the floor to ceiling window in the apartment of a friend where she stayed when in Portland Town and blankly stared out at the tall buildings of downtown. Her finger slanted between her lips. So, the plan is becoming real. I love Casey, but what a complicated girl. Always has been since we met. I'm going way out on a limb for her with little chance of crawling back. If I say no to the plan, the relationship will be over. Casey will be left desperate. She is so crazy about getting revenge. A disruption might cause her to have a mental breakdown or do something more nuts than what she has planned, whatever that is? Not the most stable person, is she? But, I love that wildness. Lolly pictured Casey's elfish face and flipped her reasoning. Someone must be held accountable for Charley and all the brewing toxicity out there.

I'm just scared of going to jail if Casey is caught. Fucking trying to chicken out, that's what I'm doing. Conspiracy charges, that's what I'll get. She shuddered at the idea of jail time. Considering her options, she could claim that she didn't know any more than her small part. Casey didn't and wouldn't tell her what she had planned. She knew Casey wanted revenge but did not know to what lengths she'd go. Set up the DOE guys and then hit the road fast. That would be her only part. Catch up with Casey later and build a new life. A better one, where they actually lived together. No more running up and down the highway. A simple, everyday life. Something she believed they both wanted. Something worth going after.

201

Slow stepping around the room, she pondered her situation while her vision viewed away from the city's high rises and out through the east-facing window where the Cascade Mountains stood tall on the horizon. Beckoning in the distance, they symbolized a western version of freedom found in the grandness of nature. The greenness of them, not so far out there, mixed with the lively city in front of her. They appealed sentimentally. Portland, a livable, small scale city where all types of lifestyles were acceptable. A unique, comfortable kind of place. But nothing like Las Vegas; that city of glamorous lights and exciting opportunity. That's what really got under her skin. Excitement filled her. She could be on the threshold of realizing a dream come true. She only had to get on with the show.

Finding her purse, she rummaged through, searching for the napkin. Damn. It better be there. She found it, folded up, stashed in one of those frustrating little side slits. Holding it, she took a breath and made the call to Bill's direct line. Three rings later, he answered. "Bill Glibson here."

"Hi Bill, this is your dancer friend from Riverside. How are you?"

"Oh, hey! What a sweet surprise. Great to hear your voice. What's up?"

"You remember that arrangement we talked about? I've been thinking about you and Richard and me, and it feels exciting. What do you say about getting together this coming weekend and having some fun?"

"Well, hey, make my day. Of course, I want to, but I've got to see how to work it out. You have me flat-footed, and jaw dropped. You know how I feel about you. Does it matter what day?"

She gave it a quick think. "I suppose Sunday would be best. End of my shift. See what you can do. I'm really looking forward to getting together. A little nervous even." She laid it on. "I don't usually do this kind of thing, you know. Kind of a special occasion for me."

A lump bulged in his pants at the sound of her voice, husky and low, full of anticipation. He had to make it happen. "I'll do everything I can to work it out. Sunday might be tough. Let me talk to Richard and check our schedules. Can I call you back at this number?"

"Don't take too long, baby."

"I won't. I've been dreaming about this for a long time. Holding you. Touching you all over."

"You're getting me hot. Hurry up. "

She let out a laugh. "These guys. So easy." The hook baited, she knew he'd come through. Her mind returned to working on the plan. After the setup, the running will begin. She will ride the Hound into the night for her getaway. Can't drive her truck. Can't leave traces. So, what about the truck? She sat and thought until an idea came. Swap out the truck for a junker. She could do it at her friend Stoli's car lot out on 82nd. Get a nice handful of cash too. The plan cleared. She could ditch the junker on the street that night before catching her bus. She recalled Casey saying something about going to San Francisco and then carrying on to Vegas, leaving no direct trail. She could be in San Francisco or gone on to anywhere in case someone investigated. Undoubtedly someone will.

****

Casey returned to her car from the bathroom and

took out her backpack from the trunk. She then went to the shed and rested the pack down on the workbench. It felt like a loaded bomb. Curiosity overcame her, and she drew the zipper open. The jars were there, along with the gloves and mask snugged together in the pack. She grabbed an old rag and pulled out the jars. She placed them on the workbench ever so carefully, handling them as if they were filled with nitroglycerin. Dark, when she gathered it, she wondered what the stuff looked like. She moved her head around the jars. Nothing irregular about the water. Maybe a little cloudy but otherwise, watery. She turned them to have a better view. The wound on her hand pinched her. Unsettled again by the flash of pain, she questioned what the dunking in the stream had done? What level of exposure did she have? Would her hair fall out? Would she miss her period? She thought harder. Her bowels acted a little runny, but that might be nerves. She blew out a big puff of air. What the fuck could she do about it if she did have a problem? Go to the doctor? Go to the clinic where someone would ask, "Dear girl, where did you get radiation exposure?" And then the inquisition would begin.

Couldn't it only be that she was just paranoid? Maybe it was only an itching pain she had to live with for a little while. If she put some makeup on it, no one will notice. She turned her attention back to the jars sitting on the bench and beamed with satisfaction. The unholy waters within represented a means to an end. An eye for an eye.

Regaining the old rag, she picked up the gloves and mask used the night before. Carrying them dangling from her hand like a dead mouse, she walked them out into the yard and dropped them onto the dirt. She went for a shovel. Burying them must be the right thing to do. Destroy the evidence. Allow no chance of contact with any living thing. Burning them just wouldn't do.

In the shed, she picked up the backpack, thinking to return the jars. Daylight peeked through the bottom. Damaged from contact like her hand. Some of the stuff must have run off of the jars. Did she get some on the outside? Did they need tightening? She checked and found them tight. She examined the eaten bag closer. Holy shit! The stuff is potent. She beamed wickedly. A taste of their own medicine indeed.

Impatient for Lolly's return call, she circled the yard in a holding pattern, putting off doing anything else until she got the word.

****

Bill called Richard to give the good news. Instead of excitement, Bill found his call met with a panicky reserve. Richard, so predictable. Big talk and scared silly of action when it came to women. "I don't believe you, Richard. What's there to be insecure about? She says she wants to do it."

"What if we get caught? It's illegal."

"Get that crazy thought out of your head. You think she'd set up a sting or something? This is cowtown Umatilla we're talking about. Hey, I'll go for it by myself if you can't get up the nerve. When are you ever going to get a shot like this? What, you forget how or something?"

"Heck, no, I haven't forgotten how. What are you talking about? I'm just not used to this kind of thing."

"From what I know, you aren't used to any kind of thing other than Rosy Palms."

"All right, all right, I'll do it. Book it before she changes her mind. You're right, Bill. How could I pass up a chance to have a piece of ass like this? Sunday works for me. I've got nothing going."

"It's usually a family night for me. I'll need a good excuse."

"Tell Janet you have to review our case for an important Monday meeting. She'd never suspect me as an accomplice in crime—know what I mean. It won't take that long to run down there, have some fun and get back."

"I want it to last as long as it can, buddy. I've got some blue pills to keep me going. Hump that bitch till she moans. Want some?"

"You know it. We'll give her a night to remember," Richard said, pumping himself up. "Make the date and let me know. Have you fixed the price?"

"Whatever it takes, big guy. Bring plenty of cash."

Bill wouldn't bother to check with his wife. He'd make her go along with the plan. He let her think that he cared about what she wanted, but he ruled the roost when it came down to it.

Lifting his head and swallowing, he gathered his cool and made the call. The phone rang long, but she answered. "Hey, gorgeous, it's me. You're on for Sunday night. We're both really looking forward to our little get-together."

"Oh, fantastic. I was wondering. It took a while to get back."

"Had a little sorting to do. Glad you agreed to make it happen. Don't worry. You know us. We're nice guys. Where and what time? Oh, and how much?"

"Of course, you're nice guys. You think I'd be

doing this if you weren't? I figure an even grand upfront package deal for the date. I'll arrange the room. All right, with that?"

"Okay, but anything goes. At least most anything. We're not into pain, only pleasure."

She smirked at Bill's words. "You're on," she agreed. "I start my set earlier on Sundays. Come around 7:00 and catch the last dance as a warm-up to what's waiting for you. Park around back, and we'll sneak out that way. We good?"

"Absolutely. See you on Sunday at seven. I'll be thinking about you, baby."

"I like a hungry man."

Chapter 27

Casey bit her nails down to nothing by the time the phone rang. "We've got tickets for the concert," Lolly announced. " I decided a Sunday night show would be best. Easier for parking and everything else. Be ready for seven," she sang.

"I thought you'd never call. Sunday sounds great! Good job. I like it. It's such an important show. So when are you going to be over?"

"Couple of days. I've got some last-minute things to do. Know what I mean? Need anything?"

"Not that I can think of. I'll let you know if something comes up. Hey, you can help me do my hair."

"Oh, cool," she said like nothing was happening.

Casey tucked away her phone and raised her face into the sunlight streaming through the blue spaces of the sprawling back yard oak tree. A ray of longed for satisfaction fell over her. The pieces were gelling. She had the nuke juice, and Lolly had the guys. All she had to do was get it into them. She wished she could chug it down their throats today, but there were more arrangements to be made. Perhaps, it might not be so easy. They could struggle against her. She didn't care what she would have to do as long as they got what was coming to them.

A 'to-do' punch list was needed. Time, ripping by like a run down the White Salmon River. Her mind spin accelerated. Her concentration skittered point to point like a ball bouncing on a roulette wheel. Something had to be written down. Otherwise, she'd drive herself crazy, rerunning the same circle.

Damn, Lolly was good. Smart of her to choose Sunday night. What a difference it could make versus a busy Friday or Saturday. The club will be slower, with less chance of being seen in the parking lot, also quieter down in Celilo. She admitted it was something she hadn't thought about. "Beware of the details," Bear had said. Unpredictable things could always happen, and people witnessing the guys being grabbed would be a catastrophe. The clock ticked. Pulling her phone back out of her pocket, she called Sam.

" Hey, what's up, girlfriend?"

"Could you meet me at the Trillium? I've got some new things to tell you about."

"Maybe later. I'm kinda busy right now working on this framing job. I'll be done at four."

"That will work. I can meet you before I start my shift. Meet me near four? All right?"

"Why don't I come by your bar and hang out?"

"Too busy. I gotta tell you some personal stuff."

" Oh Yeah? Sounds interesting. See you around four."

Uncomplicated Sam. No guilty consciousness on him. Everything fun and games. Danger exciting. A pang of guilt passed through her.

Jett had not come back from the river yet. No checking his part off. She fetched her new job phone from the car and pocketed a small pad and pen she used for grocery lists. Opening the new phone, she called Little Bear. His big voice responded. " Hey, Bear.

Carrying your new phone, huh? Ready for some action?"

"I'm ready when you are. What's up?"

"The plan is on for Sunday. Somewhere around seven."

"That's good news, Casey."

"What, no Woodpecker?"

"More like smart Raven now."

"I'll take that. Matches my new hair color."

"You did it?"

"No, but soon."

"Call me when the van is rented, and we'll work out the times, like when I drop you off on the river above the trailer."

"Oh, that's right. I almost forgot already." She put that on her list.

"Stay focused. I'll work out the times, and I'll check out the trailer. Need anything else there?"

She imagined the sting of a blade slicing flesh. "How about a big, scary hunting knife."

"Oh yeah? Okay—you got it. Ready to do what must be done?"

"Getting ready. Stoking the fire inside me. Chasing away fear. Hardening my heart. We have medicine. Now to get it down the fuckers' throats. I'm meeting Sam today. I'll call when the van is confirmed."

"Sam will be ready. Call me if you need to talk or anything. Know that I'm with you all the way."

"Thanks, Bear."

Closing the phone, she pictured the trailer and the big knife.

Across the river, in Oregon, where there was no sales tax, she picked up some phone cards at a Mini-

Mart and found the other job phones at the strip mall. She went to the nearby car rental office. "I'm looking for a van to rent for this coming Sunday. One with a sliding door."

"You want a two-seater or a three bench?"

"A two-seater upfront. Like a work van."

He scrolled the computer. "Looks clear for Sunday. Do you have a credit card?"

She had a quick think. "I do, but somebody else is going to rent it. Can you hold it?"

"I can put you down for it but no guarantee. Need to get the card number to complete the Reservation. Sunday is kind of a slow day, though."

****

Sam walked in, hot and sweaty, straight off of the job, to a full swing Trillium Happy Hour. He spied Casey at the bar and snuck up behind her. Slinging his arms around her, he squeezed and rocked her on the stool. She smelled his pungent sweat and didn't mind, for it fueled the emerging animal in her. He called for a beer.

His pint came. He downed most of it in a couple of gulps. " What you been up to? No good, I bet."

"Got that right. Finish up that first one, and let's step outside. I don't have much time before my shift starts."

"All business, huh. That's no way to be."

She tickled his ribs and scooted for the door. He jumped after her like a Doberman after a cat. She turned the corner and hung to their familiar wall and caught her breath. He pressed his weight into her. "Playful, huh?"

"Just to show you I am not all business," she said,

placing her hands upon his chest, fingers kneading. She allowed his knee to come between her legs as they both liked. " But I do have a lot on my mind. Our deal is going to go down on Sunday. Remember everything?"

"Yeah, the grab deal. I gotta come up with some plates, too, right?"

"Right." She pulled his new phone out of her pocket along with the charger and pressed it into his palm. "Special job phone. Don't use it for anything else and toss it when the job is done. I'll call with times and meet-ups. Sunday is soon."

He flipped the phone open and shut a couple of times. He liked the sound of the flap. "Job phone. Now ain't you the businesswoman. I could get into these partners in crime things. Turns me on," he said, flashing his teeth like a Jim Carrey character.

"Think again," she said, pulling away. "Gotta go to work. Go have another beer. You look like you need one. I'll call you."

"Okay, Boss," he said, with a thrust of his chin. She knew she was using him, but she needed him, and that was worth her little deception.

****

Casey entered her dimly lit house after work. The boys were slumped but still at it. Under The Bridge by the Chili Peppers crooned out of the speakers from the corners of the lounge. A pipe rested on the end table. The smell of its contents hung in the air. "There's beer in the cooler," Frank slurred, pointing to a Coleman on the floor holding some leftovers from the river. She grabbed one and plunked down on the futon. Frank offered the pipe, but Casey passed. Drink what she needed. Her brain was already over-stimulated. Jett sprawled on the lazy boy, somewhere over the mountain. " Nice on the river today, Frank?"

"Sweet, Casey. Don't you miss it? It's like you've chopped a chunk of your life off."

"True, Frank. I gotta admit that I'd be lying if I said I didn't miss it. So, when are you lazy bums going to get to work? "

"Waiting on the government. Got licenses and registrations to clear. Tony's people are working on the property end." He tilted his head and goofy faced. "Remember, we're only employees." Jett, apparently still in the room, shot double thumbs up and flew back onto his cloud.

"Okay, guys. Good luck with that. I'm going to bed. See you in the morning." Jett's head rolled towards her. His eyes opened. His gaze, soft and tender, as if she had been frolicking with him in his dreamland. She met his eyes with loving compassion. Dear Jett, he probably didn't know what to make of her tangled emotions. Love and hate all jumbled up, flaring from one to another at any given moment. Men and women intermixing freely into her intimate life. Yet, he accepted and seemed to understand the depths of her needs. She found this surprising; a man more like Lolly than Sam. His sensitivity awakening in her something always shunned and never understood, endearing him to her.

"Sleep well, Casey," he said.

She blew a kiss.

Chapter 28

The familiar sounds of Jett's morning ritual in the bathroom filtered through the crack under Casey's door. The differences between the two men's approaches were as apparent as the differences in how they interacted with life in general. Frank, loud and devoid of any consideration of anyone else. Getting into the shower preceded by ripping open the shower curtain. Washing in the sink involved water turned on full with loud splashing and abrupt drops of implements joined by medicine cabinet openings and banged closings. The toilet seat slammed up or down.—At least he lifted the seat—In contrast, Jett's manner methodical, smooth and considerate.

When the bathroom door opened, she sprang from her bed and intercepted Jett in the hall. He stood messy-haired in his undershorts. Her eyes moved over him in his next to nakedness. She admired his muscular leanness from yoga practice and how his undershorts hung on his thickened in the morning parts. Likewise, his eyes roamed over her, standing in her diaphanous nightshirt, nipples stiff against the cling, her darkness below, shadowing beneath the veil. She crossed her arms over her chest, unexpectedly becoming self-aware. She lowered her voice. "We need to talk after Frank leaves." Jett scrunched his shoulders sleepily and returned to his room while Casey slid into the bathroom for a quick pee before returning to bed.

She lay waiting for the sounds of Frank, running through what she needed to say to Jett. Tiger, always lazy in the morning, curled in a ball by her side. A morning train eased through town—its toot soft above the clattering wheels that slowly rolled along the track in a mesmerizing rhythm.

The slam of the toilet seat jerked her out of her doze. Frank was up. Hopefully, he'll buzz off soon.

She snoozed off again only to be reawakened by the roar of the V-8 engine in Frank's truck firing up. She washed, got dressed, and entered the kitchen to be greeted by Jett's chirping call of "Good morning."

"And good morning to you, Mr. Jett," she said, coming behind his chair and giving his shoulders an affectionate rub. "Got a little extra beauty sleep waiting for Frank to get going. Where's he off to today?"

"Gonna meet up with Cory at the Hood River sand bar." He lifted his head hopefully. "What did you want to talk about?"

Reaching for the coffee with her back turned, she let the news fall. "Our mission is on for this Sunday. Time to rent the van."

It wasn't what he wanted to hear. "Oh, so the mystery deed will be done, and you'll be disappearing soon."

"Something like that." She returned to behind him, resting her good hand on his shoulder. "Yes, over and done. Hard leaving friends like you, but there is no stopping now. I can't turn back what I feel inside. I need closure for Charley and justice for all the harmed people and creatures that have suffered. Just leaving it to karma to catch up with them hasn't accomplished anything. The World has called me to service, and I'm answering. Someone has to take a stance. Let these kinds of people know there are consequences for actions. You don't like me doing it or leaving, but I know that you know what I mean." It dawned on her that she sounded like a broken record, but it was her way of cementing her resolve.

He reached for her hand on his shoulder. Turning, he pulled it to his mouth and kissed it. Arching upwards, he searched her face. "Don't let anything happen to you."

She gently retracted her hand and returned it to his shoulder, her face turning to catch the shadow dancing on the counter from the movement of the trees coming through the open kitchen window. He rested his head against her belly. She bent and kissed his forehead. "I'll miss you the most. You're a special friend, and our relationship has deepened. I've been in denial about a lot of things, including you. I haven't forgotten what happened at the tree. I do have feelings for you, Jett. But now just isn't a good time to get involved. Can you understand that?" She let her question and declaration linger and stepped away, changing the conversation. "Could you be ready to check out about the van?"

A loud knocking came from the back door. Casey and Jett turned towards the sound. "Who could that be?" she said, going to the kitchen window. A sheriff car parked in the drive. "Holy shit! It's the cops!" Jett signaled for her to go to the door and made a visual sweep of the kitchen. She went towards the front door, watching Jett check the basement door to ensure it was closed. "Can I help you?"

She stared into the face of a uniformed officer with his brimmed hat on straight. "Does Frank Costa live here?"

"He's not here right now, but yes. Is there something wrong?"

"We got a report that his vehicle damaged a woman's car out by the river. He left without stopping."

"Oh. That doesn't sound like Frank."

"If you see him before we do, have him call me and come by the station voluntarily. Otherwise, we'll have to come and get him." The sheriff's mouth went thin, and he handed his card.

"We'll let him know for sure, officer."

They watched the car drive away. Exhaling, they gripped each other. Separating, Casey said, "The sharks are out there, aren't they. You think it's true about Frank's hit and run?"

"Nah. Doesn't sound right. But in that big rig of his, Frank might not have even noticed a little scrape. Sure don't want the cops around here, sniffing for whatever."

"Can we get back to what we worked on? The van?"

"Shouldn't we call Frank?"

She called. No answer. She left a heads-up message.

She put down the phone. "The van?"

"How about right now? We can go online and make a booking. Only takes a couple of minutes. For Sunday, right?"

"Yeah, all day. Return before morning. Probably do a drop-off."

Jett entered the details on the Enterprise site and waited. Doing a double-take, he turned to Casey. " You won't like this. The site is showing the van already booked for your day."

"That can't be. I talked to the manager. What's the phone number? I'll call them.—Hey, I spoke to you the other day about renting a van this weekend, and you assured me that it would be available. Your online site says it's booked. What's up?"

"It's first come, first serve, and I told you without a deposit, we can't hold vehicles. I'm sorry if this interferes with your plan. Can I help you some other way?"

Casey slapped her forehead, did a spin, and screamed into the phone. "What the fuck! I needed that van! Is there someone else you know that has a van?"

"I'm sorry. I can't think of anyone nearby. You could try in the Dalles or Portland. Can't you wait another day?"

"No! Get out of here. I'm not going to Portland. We talked, and you put me down, and I told you it was a done deal. Thanks for nothing, you jerk." Still pissed, she yelled at Jett. "Now what? Where am I going to find a van? It's not like I'm moving furniture."

"I don't know. It's not like I can ask a friend. Hey, can I borrow your van to do an abduction? I'll get it back the same day with a full tank."

"Yeah, yeah, I get it. Still, think about it. I've got to call Sam. He'll know what to do." She pulled out her job flip phone and called his. Sam answered. "We've got a problem. The van rental fell through. I can't change the date. I'm desperate. Can you come up with something from say four in the afternoon to eleven at night?"

"That's a tall order, sweetie. Daytime jacking ain't easy in a small town. Lots of eyes. Know what I mean.

I'm gonna have to get back to you. I'll check around. Best I can do, for now, honey."

"I'm counting on you, Sam."

"Sam, I am," he said with conviction. Jett didn't like what he was hearing. Sam again. Coming between them. Always rubbing him wrong.

Casey couldn't believe her luck. What happened to the roll? "Shit! It looks like 'Murphy's law' has set in—I hate waiting!" She screamed at the walls in frustration.

"I know you are all riled up and wanting to put everything in order, but waiting is what's on the menu. How about we make some sandwiches, grab some snacks and go down to Klickitat Canyon and be cool by the river. We can hang out down there and see if a new idea comes up. Bring your phone. You know, with everything going down, this may be our last shot at being together. Besides, there's nothing else you can do, is there?"

"Suppose not. They are the only rental outfit with a van around here. What a fuck up. Should have made the booking sooner. I'll have to count on Sam. All right, you win. Let's go to the river before I climb the walls hanging around here waiting." She put her head on his shoulder and calmed down. He put his arm around her and held her close while she tried to make sense of things. "Lolly is coming, so yes, this is our day. How strange to think of time vanishing away, where every day, every minute is rushing by, never to return again. I used to think I had all the time in the world. Anyway, it's early, so there's a good part of the day left before I go to work. Tonight and Friday are my last nights at the bar. Gonna need this paycheck. Don't exactly know where I'm going or what I'm going to do, but it's going to come up fast. Pretty crazy, isn't it."

"So, when have you been normal?"

She laughed. "In my own eyes, I guess I thought I kinda was."

****

Down within the basalt-walled river grotto, they waded around a massive stone buttress protruding out into the water, then found a sandy cove that offered solitude. They spread a blanket. "I'm hungry," Casey said. "All that van drama made me miss breakfast. Of all the stupidest things to go wrong."

"Something will turn up."

"It better."

They dug out sandwiches, chips, and grapes. "I suppose I can wait here as well as anywhere."

He placed his hands against the back of her neck and rubbed and kneaded. "Of course you can. Let it go. Things will work out. Remember, it's only Tuesday."

" Only Tuesday," she said, collapsing limply to his touch as he worked over her neck and back. She exhaled a deep breath. "I'm so wired up, Jett. You make me feel peaceful."

"Good. Now get some food in you, crazy woman."

She laughed a short laugh. "You think so?"

"Actually, I think you're the most intriguing, beautiful woman I know, but … crazy to boot."

"Oh yeah. What about you, Dr. Demento? The eccentric, lab rat."

She wrinkled up her nose at him and unwrapped her sandwich. "What a pair."

They rested on the blanket. Casey drifting off for a wink or two. The sun cooked while the melodic sound of the river eddying before them in a lazy swirl sang to their unconscious mind. Deep, wet, and inviting, the water enticed despite knowing well it's burning cold sting.

Their skin grew hotter, and the nearby water tantalized their heated flesh. Jett bent his head towards her, a sly smile upon his face. "What?" she asked with a bump to his shoulder, sensing he was up to something.

"I dare you to dip with me in that cold pool," he said mischievously, motioning to the water with his head.

"Not me, boy. You crazy? That water's freezing."

"Hot, that's what I am. Come on, chicken."

"You know you'll freeze your balls off in that water?"

"I don't care. I dare you to do it."

"Oh yeah. Nobody calls me chicken!" She jumped up, stripped off her clothes, and taunted him on the way to the water. "The last one in is a rotten egg!"

She plunged and burst to the surface farther down, the slow current pushing her up against a boulder where she clung tight, screeching from the cold. But, before her plunge into the icy river, she had stood, freeze-framed naked before his eyes—the Goddess he longed for. The sight stirred him. No cold could chill. He jumped into the river and shot up like a newly baptized man hollering for Jesus. The water burned like holy fire, jolting the blood through his veins. He drifted against her, and his body spooned into her warm, smooth skin for a heartbeat or two until they whooped and swam fast for the shore.

She rose from the water ahead of him, her skin taut, water beading upon it. She shivered and held herself while she waited for him to join her. The icy water, rather than numbing him, had stiffened his courage. He rose from the water, standing erect for love. Her surprised eyes took him in, dripping wet, swollen with aching desire. Dear Jett. His true heart waiting so long. She knew it time for them.

For an instant, he felt ashamed. Shyly he raised his eyes to meet hers. She reached out her hands to him. He took them, then melded into her arms, his stiff cock pressing against her chilled belly. "Come, lay down and make me warm," she said.

She rested back upon the blanket with her knees up and open. He gently placed himself on top of her, belly to belly, flesh all goose-bumped, droplets of water puddling. He rested on his elbows and drank of her face. How long he had dreamed of this moment. Their mouths joined, and the warming began. Each cried out when his desire found her welcoming home. He dug deep and ground, slow-building his motion, bringing her along, making the loving theirs, holding back the surging passion that wanted to roar.

How delicious, she thought, surrendering to their moving in unison. There was no ramming—only loving affection—a sensual and fulfilling motion lifting her higher and higher. And then it began—a deep burning inside of her. One that glowed and grew from within her heart, tingling her skin, hovering into a shiver, then descending to the junction of their union where it burst into a shudder that convulsed through her entire body. Brought on by her spasms and cries, he joined her. Peaking and falling over the hill, they tumbled down, clutching each other, wishing the moment to never end.

Side by side, skin to skin, they laid. "So beautiful,

Jett," she murmured against his cheek. "A first time for me … you know … with a man."

"I'm glad I could be that man. I've wanted you for so long. If only we had known sooner."

"Things work out the way they do for a reason. Don't ask me why, but I wouldn't have been ready for you before Charley and all. I've changed. Getting both harder and softer in different ways." She stroked his arm with the back of her fingers. " Let's not have the lovemaking change the way we are. Your friendship, the way you care about me, means everything."

Taking her honesty to heart, he combed his fingers through her hair then dropped his hand to cradle her neck like a baby. He loved her eyes. The delicious smell of fresh sex warming in the sun rose into his nostrils, and he began to rise again. "Friends forever we'll be. Kiss me and hold me." And with sweet sadness, "Soon, you'll be gone."

Chapter 29

Lolly swung into the Bingen house's gravel drive in a faded green, four-door '78 Chevy Malibu. She pumped the accelerator a couple of times to announce herself and then shut the motor down. Casey heard the engine rev and the heavy thump of the car door shutting on the second try. She opened the back door to see the dust still settling. "Hey, what happened to the truck?" She yelled in surprise.

"Cashed it in and got this classic ride. What do you think?"

"Funky."

"Hey, dirt cheap and disposable ... plus I got some good bucks for the truck." Checking the area, she leaned towards Casey. "More money for Vegas. How about you? You ready?"

Casey frowned. "Not quite. No van!"

"What? I thought you had that all worked out?"

Casey filled her in. "I know, I know, it's a fuck-up, but we have some time before I'll have to call it off with the guys. Sam's working on it."

"What about Little Bear?"

"I haven't called him yet. I'm too embarrassed."

Lolly hardened her face and blurted out, "Why the hell not? You better get everyone working on it. No van—no plan, girl!" Casey dropped her head in shame. Lolly spread her arms. "I'm sorry, Love. I'm a little wound up from the ride and everything. Come here, babe. Give us a hug."

Holding Lolly felt good, but something had shifted within. A memory of she and Jett at the river guiltily passed through. For the first time, she felt like she had cheated on Lolly. Letting go of their hug, Lolly went to her car and yanked open the creaky back door of her Chevy. She took out her bag as Casey ran her hand along the sleek front fender. She slapped her hand on the steel hood. "This clunker still running good?"

"Good enough. Pretty peppy, too. It got me here without a problem. The doors rattle going over bumps, and there is a mysterious engine noise, but the car gets up and goes. Got a 283 V8 in it. A friend at the lot said it should run fine for at least 5000 more miles, and all I need is one trip up the river and back."

"Smart idea trading in the pickup. I hadn't thought of anything like that. Can't take a car with us, can we? Maybe I should cash out the Honda? I need the money."

"Of course you should. Let's do it! Beats just hanging around all anxious and everything, worrying about the van. You know, get proactive. The Dalles would have the car lots. Find the title, and we'll make a run up the river. Hondas are always in demand. You'll have no trouble selling it, and you'll need all the cash you can get for where we're going."

Lolly seemed so upbeat. If she knew what Casey planned to do, she would be acting differently. Like heading for the door, Casey thought. "Can't take it with us," reverberated in Casey's head. Where they planned to go was distant, unknown, and strange—frightening in an insecure way. After all, she was just a small-town girl. Portland, the only city she had experienced in her young life. But Lolly would be there waiting for her to arrive. Lolly took care of business. She'll make sure they would survive.

Shrugging off her backwater of fears and pleased with the plan to sell her car, Casey raised her hand for a high five. "Right on, sister. We'll trade in the Honda, get some lunch at the Chinese, and pick up some hair dye, but first I better call Bear like you said. I can hold out until this afternoon to check back with Sam. If I haven't heard from him, I'll start making emergency back up plans. I could always run into Portland or the Dalles and get one, I guess. I don't want to, but it's only a van messing with the plan, after all."

Casey went to the house to get her job phone and search for the car title. Lolly followed with her overnight bag. The registration stayed in the car, but Casey struggled to remember where she put the title. There were only so many places to look. Most everything of importance landed in her top dresser drawer. She shuffled around in the drawer, and sure enough, the envelope holding the title lay there. It was satisfying to get a quick answer to a question. She picked up the flip phone from on top of the dresser, but no messages showed. She called Bear. It rang long. "What's up? I'm out in the boat. Might lose reception," he said.

She gathered herself and spoke calmly. "We've got a problem. I couldn't rent the van. After talking the guys ear off about needing the van, he still went ahead and rented it out to somebody else. Can you come up with something?"

"Not good, Casey. I told you shit happens. I can't think of anything off the top of my head. Give me some more time to think about it. I don't want to get friends involved. Know what I mean?"

"Yeah. Everybody is feeling the same. I screwed up; I should have moved sooner on it. Sam is working on coming up with something. I sure don't want to cancel. Lolly is here and ready to go."

"Me neither. I'll see what I can do. Something will come, but if not, we could get a vehicle out of town if need be. Don't worry. The spirits are with us."

"I hope so."

"I'm ready," Casey called to Lolly, who leaned upon her Malibu tapping her foot—the waiting for Sunday taking a toll on her nerves, too. Acting cool on the outside, inside, they both were churning. After a hurried cleanup of the Honda, they left for the Dalles, taking the State #14 and skipping the Button Bridge tolls. "I called Bear. He's working on finding a van too. Something is going to come."

"Where's Frank and Jett?"

"I don't know. They left earlier."

"How is their deal coming along?"

"Slow. Waiting on all the legal crap. But it seems like it's going to happen."

"Any regrets?"

Casey took her eyes off the road. "Please. Not you too."

Cruising the car lots at first didn't yield anything. It seemed the junkyards had already sucked up all the old cars. They decided to talk to a salesperson and describe what they wanted. At the next lot, a middle-aged salesman, who could have been mistaken for a preacher with his product slicked hairdo and southern Methodist split, dark-framed glasses, greeted them. "What can I do you for?" he drawled.

"Looking for a cheap old beater. Got a nice Honda to trade in," Lolly said.

"Not much call for old cars anymore. Kids nowadays won't be caught dead in anything unstylish. Would you take a little truck? I got one recently on a trade up." He pointed over to a faded blue Datsun parked on the side lot.

The women's heads turned to follow the salesman's pointer finger. The little truck had seen better days, but it was all there. Casey scratched her chin in thought. "That truck just might work. I could put my kayak in the back. What do you want for it, and does it run?"

"I'm asking $400.00, and it was running when it came in. I'll get the keys."

The women walked over to the little pickup, strolled around it, kicked the tires, and noticed the damaged upholstery. It had four on the floor.

He came with the key and opened it up, which released a musty, damp odor, killing the first impression. However, the blue Datsun started on the first try, a puff of matching the paint job blue smoke sputtering out of the tailpipe.

"Can I take it for a spin?"

"Hop in. We'll go up the street and around the block."

She put it through the gears and tested the brakes. Not much power, but it ran steady. Back in the lot, they checked the lights and turn signals.

Lolly pointed to the rips in the seat and a crack in the far side of the windshield. "This rig looks like you'll be lucky to get $100 from the junkman. We'll trade you the Honda for the old truck and $2000 cash."

Wagging and angling his head towards the ground, he said, "You're asking a lot. I could maybe go $1500."

"You're joking. Look at its condition. It's even got a rack for windsurfers and kayakers. You'd flip it in a week. We've already got an offer down the street for $2000, but we want the clunker."

He walked around the Honda rubbing his chin. again, his business mind calculating. "You got a clear title?"

"In my back pocket," Casey said.

"Tell you what. You got a deal. Let's go to the office. What you want that old Datsun for when you have this nice car?"

"I want some money."

They signed everything, and he counted out the money on the table. The cash swelled Casey's eyes. He slapped on some temporary dealer plates. Done deal and ready to roll, Casey said, "Still before two. Let's hit the Chinese."

They walked out with enough leftovers for dinner and stopped at Fred Meyers for hair dye. "I'm thinking brunette," Casey said as they hit the hair products aisle. "You know, normal-looking like any other brown-haired girl. I really would prefer black, but I think that color makes a statement. I need to blend in, be incognito. Know what I mean?" She muffled her voice." Do you think we'll be safe there? You know, in Vegas?"

Lolly took her hand and got close to Casey's ear. "It's a good place to start. Get those new ID's and see how it goes. I've always dreamed of working in Vegas. I could probably get a job pretty quickly. But we'll have to watch our backs. The guys will most likely think I set them up. Anyway, they will get blindsided in the lot, and if they don't see you or recognize your voice, they won't know who's responsible for the kidnapping. If we are careful and lay low, hopefully, it will all pass over. Lolly placed her arm around Casey's shoulders and gave a tug. "Can't say I don't love you now, can you?"

Casey picked up a box of Clairol with a glamorous, long wavy-haired brunette on front. Holding it next to her face, she flashed a cheesy smile. "How about this one?"

"Oh, girl. That's definitely you." Lolly slapped her thighs. "This is fun. I should dye mine when I get to Vegas. How about platinum? Go for the blonde bombshell."

"You could pull it off. You'd look great. Want to do it with me?"

"Can't do it now, silly. People would notice. It has to be my secret disguise for later."

By the bathroom sink, the playful job of dying Casey's hair began. It made for easy diversion. The transformation came almost immediately. Casey comically posed for Lolly and kept checking herself in the mirror as she became someone new. Her smeary painted eyebrows, which bore a resemblance to some old cigar-smoking comedian, cracked her up. Laughing let off some pressure, but her internal clock ticked relentlessly, like in Captain Hook's crocodile.

While Casey cleaned up the bathroom, Frank and Jett pulled into the drive. Fear and concern spiked their minds when they saw two suspicious cars parked in front of the carport. They turned to one another for a clue. Not any cars of friends that they knew. Quietly, they closed the truck doors and crept cautiously towards the house. Jett picked up a baseball bat leaning in a corner and slapped it in his palm. The thought ran through his head that someone might have broken in intending to steal his product. The back door remained open a crack. They silently crept in. Frank snuck into the kitchen, and Jett checked the basement. Lolly heard the floor creak.

"Hello. Somebody here?" Lolly called from the back room.

Casey picked up on Lolly's uneasiness and whispered, "You hear something?"

Frank jerked upright as Lolly turned the corner on him. "Lolly! It's you. Shit, we thought there were strangers in the house. Where did you get those old cars? " Casey stuck her head out from behind Lolly. "Wow! I guess there is a stranger here," Frank said. Jett heard the voices and came to support Frank, who gestured towards Casey. "Take a look at her."

The brown hair softened Casey and took Jett by surprise. The color did suit her. "You look great, Casey," he said, circling her appreciatively. "Sorta normal. Very pretty. Good choice of color."

She blushed. "Glad you like it, Jett."

Lolly thought Jett held his glance a bit long and curiously watched Casey's schoolgirl reaction.

"Sorry, we spooked you. Hello," Lolly said, throwing her arms around Frank and then Jett, jostling any remaining tension loose. Jett, still mesmerized by the new Casey.

Frank said with a laugh, "So what's with the old cars?"

Frank's comment reminded Casey of the police visit. "Speaking of cars, did you contact the sheriff's office?"

"Got it covered—done deal. Insurance companies are sorting it out—just a minor scrape on an old van. I never even noticed. The woman will get the paint job she was after, and I'll get my insurance jacked up. No charges. Innocent by ignorance. So, what about the old cars?"

"We got cashed out. We're leaving town."

"I see you got your disguise covered. So, the time has come?"

"This weekend. Time to roll the dice."

"Hope your luck holds out," he offered positively, thinking better of making a bad scene. His unaccepting feelings were already well known. " I'll miss you. Oh, I have to remember to get that cash to you. You know, for your stuff before you hit the road."

"Thanks, Frank. I'll need it."

Chapter 30

Sam roared away from the job site on his Harley, his intention set upon combing the town for a van suitable for heisting. Up in the Heights, he poked around in shopping malls, auto repair yards, and small independent shops. His observations confirmed what he already knew; stealing a vehicle in broad daylight was no piece of cake. Being thorough, he checked the hospital, the downtown blocks, and the commercial strip connecting to Interstate 84, where Wal-Mart, Les Schwab Tires, Safeway, and a host of fast food outlets and restaurants presided. Like a hunter seeking out the weak, vulnerable, wounded, or unprotected, he searched all the lots and alleys as well. Nothing showed itself. The Full Sail Brewery got a hard second look but no go. Everything locked uptight and, if taken, noticeably missed in a very short while. Only one place left to look—The waterfront.

He gunned it over the freeway and coasted into the industrial/tourist zone. He saw the commercial rigs parked behind the chain link. A tourist van seemed out of the question, it's owner would immediately report it stolen. Frustrated, he cruised the bike into the windsurfing parking lot. He kicked down the stand and strode towards the river. Letting his mind wander, he pictured all that lay on the other side. Park and Ride had cameras. Forget about the mill or BNSF railroad yard.

After avoiding considering it, he mentally came

back around to his job site. No other options had presented themselves. He thought of the work van that they kept on-site for storing tools and supplies. Scratching his head, he knew the storage vehicle was not his best option, being too close to home and connected to him, usually, a deal-breaker when planning his crimes. If things went wrong, he knew how fingers would point at him because of his history as a felon. Anyway, he knew that the van was available, and with no other options coming up, and wanting to please Casey, he figured that it would have to do. He hoped it ran strong and probed his memory as to the last time he saw it running. He recalled them using it from time to time to gather supplies, and he also recalled that the van was full of dirty construction crap. So what. The scum bag hostages didn't need a Cadillac. A comfy ride wasn't in the package deal for them.

He considered his plan. Because he worked at the site, he had a reason to be around if someone questioned. Jimmying the lock and hot-wiring the rig will only take a few minutes, back by midnight, no problem. A quiet Sunday, most likely no one noticing. And if they did, he'd not raise suspicion. He'd keep on his company T-shirt. Make like he was moving some furniture for a friend.

Firing up the scooter, he rode back up the hill to the job site and made a quick assessment. The van sat tucked around back, somewhat hidden. Good for take-off. He figured he'd have a closer inspection the next day when at work. He grinned an expectant smile. The man with the plan, coming through for Casey. She would be grateful and he liked the thought of that. If worse came to worse and his plan fell apart, what the fuck, steal something off the street. He only needed the rig for a few hours.

Casey's job phone rang. She took it into the bathroom. "Hey, it's me, sugar. I've got something worked out for you. The van is covered. Have you got a timeline yet?"

"Fantastic! Sam's my man! I'm so relieved. Nothing for certain on the timeline. Just the day. I'll call you soon, as I know. Good old Sam. I knew you would come through."

"You know it, baby. I think it calls for some special appreciation. Know what I mean? Let's get together and start having some fun again? What say?"

"Yeah, Sam, I'd like that. Let's get through Sunday, and we'll have smooth sailing after that. Thanks for coming through for me. I won't forget it. Sorry, I gotta go to work."

She returned to Lolly in the bedroom, who nervously busied herself with her nails. "Sam has a van."

"He has a van, or you mean he's going to steal a van?"

"Borrow, is the way he put it. Anyway, it means we're on for Sunday. He said he'll change the plates. We only need it for a few hours. Not my first choice but with the rental company screwing us over, what choice do I have? I've got to trust Sam."

"I've never met him. Is he some kind of outlaw? Where did you meet this guy, anyway?"

"At the bar. He's a regular, like Little Bear. We're friends."

"Odd sort of friend, isn't he?"

"I need help from where I can get it. Sam knows

what he's doing. Done time as well, so doesn't want to get caught."

"With a record, why does he even want to get involved?"

Casey hesitated. "He's sweet on me."

Lolly raised her head from her nails. "Oh, is that so?"

Casey left it there. "I need to call Bear." She went outside and rang him. "Thought I should let you know that Sam has a van for Sunday."

"A hot one?"

"Most likely. What else can we do? He said he'd swap out the plates. You come up with an alternative?"

"Nothing any better. At least Sam's van doesn't connect anybody else. I'll call you tomorrow, and we'll agree on the schedule. Dropping you above the camp will be step number one. Anybody else know what you intend to do?"

"Nobody but you and me. They know we're grabbing the guys and probably think I'm going to scare them or something." Her voice dropped down a notch. " They're going to be scared, all right."

"Good. The She-Wolf is still with you."

"She is eager and waits. We'll talk tomorrow."

Frank knocked on Casey's door. "Wanna do some dinner together?"

"Thanks, Frank, but we have tons of leftover Chinese to polish off," Casey replied through her closed door. She caught herself listening to her words. She seemed to be brushing off his good intentions. Leaving Lolly, she leaped off of the bed and pulled open the door. She managed to catch him before he got away. She put on a happy face. "How about we do a BBQ tomorrow night. Make up some salads and stuff. Have a proper going away party."

He broke into a grin. "Awesome. I'll pick up some things to grill and some beer. You make the salads. Chicken breasts and steak sound good?"

"Sounds delicious."

"We'll do it up in style. Last Tango at the river house," he said, dance shuffling down the hall.

Even though Frank appeared to be taking the changes in stride, Casey sensed his uncomfortableness. She tossed an explanation she thought he could understand. "Hey, Frank. No worries. No fear. I'm going with the flow, right? This is where it's taking me. Great idea for tomorrow. Promise? No sad stuff ?"

"You got it. I'm cool," Frank said from down the hallway.

The first pinks of evening streaked the changing sky. Frank and Jett prepped for 'the last supper' in the kitchen. Frank cleaned and seasoned the meats while Jett shucked some fresh corn. Lolly and Casey arrived from the store with salad-making supplies. Jett cleared space on the kitchen table for them. "I'll make the potato salad," Casey said, and she dumped some potatoes into the sink for washing. Jett bent down in front of a cabinet and fished out a large pot to boil them. He came alongside her, put his shoulder to her shoulder, and placed the pot into her hands. She smiled. A memory glanced her mind. A sensation remained. Lolly couldn't help but notice the closeness between them.

"Hey Jett, while you're at it, can you find me a salad bowl?" She said, breaking their moment.

He knew where to find one and pleasantly handed

it to her. Her questioning eyes searched his face. He held steady, knowing in his heart that he loved Casey, too. "So, how about a beer? Let's get the party rolling," Lolly said. Frank opened and passed some beers around. They clinked bottles. "Here's to it to those that do it. I'll fire up the grill!" Frank said. He covered the meats and headed for the back door, leaving an awkward silence behind him.

The waxing moon shone in the night sky. Refreshing evening breezes breathed from the nearby river. Around the weathered, wooden picnic table, one that had hosted them on many a prior occasion, they gathered as old friends. Smells of smoldering BBQ coals kept the taste of dinner on their lips. The meats, seared over wood charcoals, and the potato and green salads had been delicious. Jett grilled the corn to a nutty brown, which gave a caramel chew to one of the summers' favorite garden treats. The talk and laughter rambled easy and simple, albeit slurry and sometimes silly. They remembered past times and fell into a lighthearted banter about the cannabis business and what fun it would be to live in Vegas. No hard questions spoiled the mood. They rolled with the flow.

"We probably won't stay there that long. We'll have to see how it goes. Maybe take off for New Orleans or Miami Beach. Miami, now that would be cool," Lolly said, leaving their future whereabouts left unknown and up for grabs. They fell back into memory lane; how they had met and all the good times.

After a good many beers already, Casey lifted her bottle for a toast. "Thanks for everything. I'll miss you guys." They raised their bottles and joined her in saying, "Good friends!" And left it at that.

Unspoken were their inner feelings. Each held their concerns for the future, but no one wanted to unsettle their last get-together. They all knew Casey's course. Their commitments had already been given. The strike against nuclear waste, something, in principle, they could agree upon—except for Frank, who felt it a useless waste of time.

What Casey would do with the guys was left to her friends' imaginations. They didn't press her. Jett and Lolly worried about the price Casey and they would pay for her actions. Would she get redemption? Would they forgive her and she, herself? Casey held her secret close. Her She-Wolf heart caged within a separate self. Only Little Bear grasped the darkness lying and waiting to escape from inside of her.

Frank cut a resounding, beer fart.

"Ewwww," the others cried out and moved away.

"That's what I've got to say. Great dinner, huh?" He took a long guzzle of beer. "Hey, next time you come around, you can visit me and Jett living in the big house—driving new pickups—weed tycoons. That's what we'll be—legal drug dealers. Speaking of, fire something up, Jett. Toast the future with getting toasted." The pipe went around, and they lifted to the stars—everyone spinning in their own orbit.

Casey pulled back the sheet, and they climbed in, tipsy from the drink and smoke. What had hung in Lolly's mind throughout the evening began to unravel. "You and Jett seem awfully close. What's going on between you two?"

The truth stuck on Casey's tongue. A small piece fell out. "You're not here most of the time, Lolly. Sometimes I need a friend."

Lolly turned away, her imagination ballooning.

"Come back here," Casey said, spooning her body against Lolly's. Her love had never left. She kissed Lolly, where the hair curled in front of her ear and whispered, "We'll be together all the time soon. That's what matters. Tonight is our night. Be with me. I need your love."

Lolly rolled and embraced her. Tonight's all that mattered.

Chapter 31

With little more to say, Lolly set out for Umatilla. From her rolled down window, she waved and called, "Good luck Casey! I'll see you soon, babe." She blew a kiss, tooted her horn, and shoved off to where her part in the abduction awaited.

Nerves jangling, she put a chewing gum square into her mouth and jawed away while her mind ran on. Casey had changed. Her whole obsession for revenge had made her into a different person. And, there was the Jett thing. What was all that? Had the spark between them grown dim? The love-making in the night had been intense, but a life together in Vegas remained a fuzzy, far-away concept.

Casey walked the lazy street, aware of being ever closer to the eventful day. What pieces remained undone? Where did she leave her punch list? Tonight would be her last night at work. Packing her things came to mind. She figured traveling light with only a backpack of clothes and toiletries would be the best way to go. She walked back to the house. Her hand burned. The aloe vera and makeup had helped put the irritation out of mind over the last couple of days, but the redness had gnawed deeper.

She searched and found an ace bandage in the bathroom and examined her hand closer. A scab had formed. Remembering Charley in that room, she turned her eyes to the heavens and fought to stay focused. She applied more gel, laid down some gauze, wrapped it, and pushed back her fears. She thought of last night with Lolly and shifted her mind away from the wound. She would deny its existence if she could. Let it wear it's self out and heal like any other scrape she had encountered in the past. She prodded herself. Stop thinking and get on with what needed doing.

She went to her room and packed the few articles of clothing she planned to take. The rest, she stuffed into boxes. Frank could take them to Goodwill or whatever. Not a clothes horse or collector of decorations, it didn't take long to be down to her bureau top and special drawer. On the bureau, meaningfully arranged, were some objects she had gathered over time. She touched them one by one and drew from them the energy that had inspired the attraction. The pieces were mostly odd bits collected from nature: a sturgeon vertebra from the dinosaur fish that fed on the bottom of the Columbia River—a bird skull, beak intact—some smooth, green stones that she rolled in her fingers—a shell gathered on the beach from a trip to the coast.

All of the pieces held the power of nature that had touched her soul. She took their essence in for the last time and then released them. She would place them somewhere in the yard. Her jewelry box remained. She opened it and pawed through her scant collection, passing over a couple of her favorite pieces to fondle a freshwater pearl necklace that Charley had given her. She placed it in the pack. Oddly, nothing much wanted to stick to her, as if she was meant to go with a clean slate.

She reached for the photo album that held the story of her life. Album in hand, she lowered herself into a comfortable position on the bed and reverently turned the pages. Mulling over the images, she recalled the sadness and the joys, the victories and defeats. She found a picture of her mother smiling gayly in one of her better moments and a tattered shot of the father she never really knew but was coached to despise, leaning on a pickup truck in front of their trailer. Proof that he existed, there, at some point in time. Sheila and she, one of her few friends, arms hanging over each other's shoulders, chunky new teeth too big for their mouths displaying proudly in their smiles. Out of all the snapshots of her and Charley, she selected one of him as a teenager. She pulled another one out of its sleeve. One of her beaming happily in the sunshine, holding her kayak, the White Salmon river sparkling behind her. She paused, holding that remembrance, the joy that the river and her boat had brought to her that day. Lastly, she collected the picture of the two of them, brother and sister, by the tree that she had kept on his altar. The accident seemed so long ago, but in reality, not that long at all.

Her phone rang, reeling her in from her memories. Little Bear spoke. "How are you doing? You all right?"

"Working on keeping it together, Bear. A lot of emotional stuff pulling at me, you know? Lolly left today, and we had a 'farewell' party last night. You caught me getting my things in order. I have my last shift at work tonight, which should give me a break from thinking. No changes on my end." She caught herself. " Wait a minute. I did my hair! It's brown. How about you?"

"Good choice on the hair. I've been figuring out the timeline. Get paper and pen and write down some times. You, me, Jett, and Sam got to be on the same page."

She found what she needed. "Okay, I'm ready."

He gave her the times, then added, " I didn't forget. There is a sharp, scary knife in the top drawer of the trailer kitchen."

"Good. I will need it."

"There is something else … Granny wants to meet you."

"You told her about me?"

"She knows my mind. We live together. She knows about the Wolf and that we plan to do something for the river. That's all. She is a wise old woman, and you'll know that when you meet her. The Wolf has meaning to her. She wants to feel it inside you. Check out who is running with me."

"We were supposed to keep this to ourselves."

"She doesn't know what will happen. Like your friends."

Casey wondered about Granny, wanting to know more. Maybe Granny could help. "Why not. I have a couple of hours I could fit in. Where?"

"You know where the river camp is past the Bridge of the Gods?"

"Seen it from the road."

"That's where I live. Fifth trailer in on the riverside. One thirty?"

"Okay, I'll be there."

She pulled off the highway and slowly rolled down the gravel incline in the blue pickup. Pieces of rock popped under her tires, announcing her arrival into the quiet flat of land lying along the side of the river. A misfit collection of trailers and converted to living in vehicles lined the narrow drive. Purposeful disarray held sway. Counting down the trailers, she located Bears' place. Aware of being a white girl entering a tribal camp, her unease blew away when she saw familiar Bear out by his truck. "Okay to park here?" She called out.

"You're fine," he said and waved her in. "New truck?"

"Traded up for it."

He smiled, and they came together in a warm hug, aware of how their friendship had deepened over the last few weeks. "Nice hair. Welcome to my humble home."

"Thanks. Not much different than from where I grew up."

She pointed towards the swift flowing river, not far from Cascade Locks and the Narrows. Her point followed the short path through the broadleaf maple trees out to the river's edge. "I see you have a fishing platform. Those things always amaze me. How do they stay there rooted somehow into the bank? They seem to want to fall over the way they hang out over the water like that."

No expression showed on his face. "Indian magic. Come on. Let's go in. Granny Ceci is expecting you."

Inside the long room that was both lounge and kitchen, Granny sat at a table in front of a picture window that looked out to the river. The close air smelled of burnt sage and fried eggs. A silent television screen flashed from the opposite end of the room. " Granny, this is Casey, " Little Bear introduced. He took Casey's hand and placed it in the older woman's. Ceci placed her other hand over Casey's and cupped it. She gave a slight squeeze. A warm current passed up Casey's arm. Ceci held firm and pulled Casey towards a chair beside her.

"I am glad to meet you, Grandmother."

"And I, you. You have joined hearts with my Bear." Her eyelids fluttered, and the line of her upper lip curved slightly into a hint of a smile. She then directed her voice towards Little Bear. "There's some tea steeping in the pot on the kitchen counter. Pour us a couple of mugs, would you?"

Granny's eyes floated in milky pools of faded color. How much could she see, Casey wondered? The older woman answered her thoughts. "I can feel you, Casey. You are a strong, young woman. Your spirit is aware. There is much to see without eyes. I think you understand. Do you see inside?"

Casey felt a camaraderie with the older woman. She trusted her and answered, "I see the eyes of a Wolf inside me, sometimes."

The old woman nodded and rocked while Bear presented the tea and left them to themselves. She squeezed Casey's hand. "Are you afraid of the Wolf?"

"No. It strengthens my resolve. Gives me support for what I must do."

"That is good. Thank you for sharing your heart. Have some tea with me and imagine your spirit in this circle spread on the table." Casey's eyes roamed the circle, taking in the pattern of bones, shells, feathers, and stones positioned in a way that pleased her but brought forth no hidden meaning. She drank the warm tea. Rooty and earthy, herbal and floral, more bitter than sweet, it tasted like nature. Ceci drank, and resting her cup, lit some braided sweetgrass. She passed the sweet smell of morning meadows over the circle of odd things lying on a woven cloth on the table and blew some smoke in Casey's direction.

Casey drank more tea. Heat blossomed within her. Ceci lit a bundle of sage and fanned it with an eagle feather, the smoke engulfing them. She intoned the four directions and above and below in her language. Granny motioned for Casey to lean towards her. She circled Casey's head with the smudge before resting it in an abalone shell. She blew three short breaths to the heavens over her fingertips and began to hum a song. The tonal sound of her song and the richness of the sage transported Casey into a dreamy trance. Her body seemed to sway but was stationary to the touch. Something moved inside of her. The Wolf's eyes opened.

Ceci took back Casey's hands and, cradling them, pulled them to her chest. "Are you trusting your Grandmother?"

At that moment, Casey would have given anything, feeling like a tamed small bird in the woman's hand. "Yes, Grandmother."

"You have suffered, and you are troubled. Bring forward the Wolf that you feed. Allow me to meet with its eyes."

Casey surrendered. Grandmother merged with Casey and felt Wolf's presence. Sensing the woman's approach, the Wolf stepped from behind concealing shrubbery, head down, eyes deep and wary. Sniffing out the old Grandmother, She connected with the tribal link. One they had shared for millennia. She sensed no challenge and shifted to sitting proud, chest out, and waiting. Grandmother gave respect and gratitude to the

Wolf Spirit and linked their worlds. Wolf Spirit had helped her tribe before. She was much revered by Native peoples as a powerful and fearsome ally, and one did not want to be her enemy. Wolf assured that She had come to help, not harm Casey. Ceci questioned how that happened? Casey, a white woman, not schooled in the spirit world. Leaving the question unanswered, Grandmother gave thanks to Wolf and respectfully lowered her gaze, and returned within. She grasped Casey's hand with a jerk as her eyelids snapped open.

Casey found herself standing within the wheel one moment and sitting in her chair the next. The wheel lay on the weaving as before. A strange sensation followed her. What was in that tea? She finished the cup, searching for an answer.

Grandmother plucked a bone from the circle and offered it to Casey. "Keep this for protection. The Great Wolf Spirit has joined with you. She is unpredictable and can be a ruthless killer. If her family is threatened, she knows no limits to her vicious retribution. How did she come to you?"

"I don't know. She just came. I think it was after joining forces with Little Bear for the river."

"Ahh, Little Bear, and the river. His beloved river. It is true that the river is wounded. I know Little Bear's heart and that he cares deeply. Although preserving Nature is worth the fight, the battle, like all battles, can claim a price. Your Wolf may help you, but she cannot save you. Be careful how you move, my dear." She turned away and called out in a commanding voice, "Little Bear, Little Bear." His big head came apprehensively through the doorway. "Did you call the

Wolf Spirit to this young woman?"

He stood head down like a scolded little boy.

"She holds the old guardian of the tribe. Why?"

"We are helping River."

"Wolf and Bear is strong medicine. Know well what you do."

****

Casey left Little Bear's home in a fog. She had hoped to gain clarity from her meeting with Grandmother Ceci, but all remained uncertain. What was the connection to the Wolf? She was not part of their tribe. Or was she, in a greater sense, since becoming a water protector? How did the Wolf come to be a part of her, and how could Bear call a Wolf? What did it matter? She gave thanks for it, glad that the Wolf empowered her. It brought the violent edge that pushed her past her moral constraints. She knew she would need that in the end. A viciousness came into her teeth and gums when she drew upon the force. Her revenge for Charley would come. Not long now, she steered towards what came next.

After a couple of attempts, she got hold of Sam. "Hey, Sam. How's it going?"

"Finishing up at the job site, trying to make a dollar an honest way. What's up?"

"Can you meet me at the usual place after you get off and before I start my shift? I have something important to give you."

"I like the sound of that."

"Not what you are thinking. This is about business, partner."

"Business, business. Come on, girl. I'll be glad when this trick is over, and we can get back to doing our thing."

"Almost over. We have to get through this weekend. Just a little longer. So, I'll see you soon ?"

"Yeah, sure, Casey."

She hung up and held her head between her hands. She needed him.

Casey slid a copy of the written down times across the table to Sam. He quickly reviewed the times, stuffed it into a pocket, and began his incessant pawing. Needy and turned on by her different hair color, he thought having her would be like making it with a new woman. She stood to go, carefully brushing away his hand. "Sorry, Sam, but I got to go to work. Make sure you get those times down, okay?"

"Yeah, sure. A little uptight, aren't we?" he said, turning his head away from her in frustration.

She gave his arm a rub. "I know, I know, Sam. The weekend will soon be over."

She walked the few blocks to work. Keeping Sam on board hung in her mind. It had become more difficult. Enticing promises felt abusive. But, she did what she had to do. Getting what she needed in the present all that mattered. In the past, his hunger had reassured her desirability. She had worked past that and no longer allowed her insecurity to hold her captive. Her destiny was her own, and Sam, a fading phase.

****

The bar got busy. Friday night had a rock and roll band playing. The music drew a crowd, and she busily slung drinks and beer until closing. The mindless flurry of transactions across the bar whisked her through the night. She kept her arm covered by a long-sleeve T-shirt. No one noticed anything wrong. Closing time came, and she cashed out her check and split, singing out a silent 'adios' to the workplace that had put bread in her jar. She gave no notice. Disappear, cash in hand, her final play. One more collection added to the bankroll needed to start over in that unknown place of Las Vegas. She went to her car, got in, and moved on.

Crossing over the Button bridge in the wee hours of Saturday morning, the bridge was empty. She paused the Datsun midway on the bridge and sniffed the breeze off of the river flowing in through her open window. Not the first time she had done this, pausing in the middle of the bridge, over the center of the river, watching the water move through the grate holes in the bridge deck. She felt her moment in place and time, and a bittersweet recognition fell like cottonwood fluff. It might be her last time across the bridge. A dirge hung suspended in air, playing a song of the good things that came to her while living by the river—a place where she had bloomed and found acceptance.

Before her lay the unknown, where she knew not the landing of her heart or what price she would have to pay for Charley's revenge and her retribution for all of the victims; past, present, and future of atomic waste. She hardened her face and locked in her determination. They would pay regardless of the price. Damn them for all the wickedness done and for all that they stood for. She placed the truck in gear and crossed the bridge.

Chapter 32

She ascended towards the light of a new day. Stroking in liquid air, short of breath, she aimed for the guiding light pulling from above. The light drew her from the consumptive sea of her dreams as if being summoned by a dazzling fairy Godmother. Slipping out of the confining membrane, she birthed into the new dawn, rising abruptly in bed, the dew dripping away. Tiger lay by her side, connecting her to the physical. She stroked him and a purr vibrated from within his outstretched body.

Still blanketed by her dream state, she slid off the bed. On the toilet, she yawned and wondered why her period still had not come. She itched her hand and arm. The Wolf paced behind her eyes. Just one more day of gathering and waiting. She held her troubled head.

She heard the men talking in the kitchen. Frank, sounding restless to get to the playground of the day. She brightened. Like a big kid, he seemed never to get tired of playing. Perhaps, merely his way of holding the world at bay, forestalling the inevitable passage into adult responsibilities.

She entered the kitchen. "Casey, what happened to your arm?" Frank said, tossing the first curve of the day. The small ace bandage on her wrist had never been seen before.

"Got burned on the coffee machine last night at work. It's nothing."

"Does it hurt?"

"Only a little. Don't worry about it, Mom."

"Somebody has to worry about you—Never know what's up with you—What are you doing today?" Excessive coffee bunching his words.

"No plans, Frank. No job either. Last night was my last. I'm all cashed in."

"Oh, that's right. I've got money for your gear," Frank said to the air while zooming out of the room.

Alone with Jett for the first time in days, Casey irresistibly slunk behind him while he sat in his chair and coiled her arms around his shoulders. She pressed her head against his cheek and sought to regain the peaceful closeness they had shared by the river. He grounded her. The physical contact worked, and their connective energy flowed. Abandoning his self—inflicted repression, observed out of respect for Casey's relationship with Lolly, he stood and put his arms around her. She surrendered to his touch.

Frank charged back into the room, his ramped up momentum coming to a screeching halt. "Yo, like what's going on here, guys?" he said, shocked at seeing them ardently entwined.

"Jett and I are secret lovers," she said provocatively. Frank's mouth dropped. She took advantage. "Didn't know, did you? I'm leaving tomorrow, so no more secrets. It doesn't matter anymore."

He gripped his head, his mouth wide open. "This is blowing my mind. I thought I saw something going on between you two, but I guessed it had to be about the plan." A glaze of disbelief pasted his face as he drew closer to them. "I never would have guessed." He shook his head, still working on getting over the shock. "Wow! You never know." He held out an envelope. "So Casey, here's your cash. Put in a few extra bills as a going-away present."

She had forgotten about selling her gear to him and was pleasantly surprised when she peered inside and saw the wad of money. "Aww, Frank. Too much. What a true friend." She hugged him. Jett watched them. An unspoken hands-off agreement about Casey had always been in place, out of respect for her relationship with Lolly.

They pulled back to arm's length. "You know what? I've always been a secret admirer too," he said with a wink.

She punched his arm. "Get outta here, you joker."

"No kidding. I'll miss you, Casey," he said with his head angled in concern. He had no idea what she would do the next day, and he didn't want to know. All he knew was, that she needed to leave town because of it.

"That's sweet, Frank." She hugged him again and stepped back beside Jett.

"Okay, you two. I'll leave you to it. Have a nice day. Catch you later," he said, breezing for the door.

They heard his truck pull away, and before finishing her coffee and toast, she had Jett by the hand, leading back to her bedroom. With so much brewing inside of her: excitement, fear, anger, and the edge of the Wolf, sex served as a way to unload her taxed mind.

"Do you have any more preparations to make for tomorrow?" Jett asked, propped on his elbow in bed.

"Only in my head and heart. It's just waiting now, and I hate waiting!"

"How does a long walk in the woods sound?" Jett

said while stroking the hollow of her back. "Get clear-headed, away from the spin. Pretend like it was just us, and we were free to be any way we wanted. This could be the last time to enjoy being in the forest for a while. You know, you going to the desert and all."

"That's a fantasy. Free to be any way we want to be. It's how I used to feel. Going to the woods does sound centering and peaceful and, most of all—distracting! Damn, I wish tomorrow would hurry up and get here. Otherwise, I'll be grinding my teeth all day. I'm freaking wound up tight, Jett. Getting moving will help. Got somewhere in mind?"

"How about hiking up in the headwaters of the White Salmon where it's coming off of Mt. Adams? We'd have to drive above Trout Lake to reach the trailhead but not too far. Think the old Datsun could make it?"

She had a quick thought and said with confidence, "I think she'll make it—no huge hills. The grade is pretty gentle. Aside from blowing some smoke when she starts up, she's been running smoothly. Just has to make it to the Dalles and into Portland, and then she's done."

"What do you mean?"

"I'm ditching her, Jett."

"Hey, could I take care of her? I'd like to have something of yours."

"Best you stay clear of anything connected with me. Tell me more about the trail before we start going in the wrong direction. Remember, keep it light. Like being a pair of fluttering, carefree butterflies," Casey said, then fluttered her eyelashes against his and pressed him with her lips.

He arched his hands dramatically skyward. "Oh yeah, I can see us now. A pair of happy butterflies flittering in the sunlight, dancing up the trail by the singing stream."

"Yes, that's it, that's exactly it."

He yanked back the sheets. "Come on then. Let's get dressed, pack some water and snacks, and go!" He got out of bed and offered an outstretched hand. She slid across the bed and grasped the offered hand, rising to stand before him. So irresistible, her soft-skinned beauty standing there before him, he wrapped her to him and then said those three magic words. " I love you." A tear puddled in the corner of her eye.

****

The old Datsun chugged along up from the river and into the mountains. Downshifts kept her revving up the grades and on to the dirt road turnoff that led to the trailhead. No other vehicles at the trailhead; the trail belonged to them. Jett slipped the day pack onto his back, and off they went. Streams of sunlight filtered through the towering cathedral of green firs and pines, dancing a patchwork in front of them upon the trail. Entering farther into the ancient, coniferous forest, they heard a hidden gurgling stream running beneath the brush that banked a pitched canyon. Light dust rose from the dry-dirt, summer-time trail. Gentle breezes floated it behind them as if the breath of the forest walked with them. It was so alive, invigorating, and refreshing that they skipped along as light as the butterflies they had envisioned. Following the headwaters, the glacier shrouded peak of Mt. Adams awaited somewhere around the next bend.

The hallway to the mountain dipped, ascended, and

switched back and forth. A cry from a broad-winged wood hawk drew their eyes upwards. A rustle perked their ears. Holding still, they waited for a glimpse of what mysterious creature moved in the brush or skittered on a limb or scampered up a trunk. And then, around a sword fern clumped bend, the forest opened to the snow-white mass of the mountain jutting into the deep blue sky in all its majestic glory.

The sight stopped them dead in their tracks. Humbled, they found a seat upon a massive, smooth boulder. Half buried, it perched out from the edge of the forest in the shade, overlooking fuzzy lichen encased rocks strewn across a meadow painted with grasses and wildflowers. The mountain king broke the sky before them. Jett passed the water and began to speak. She raised her finger to her mouth and silenced him. Held in the arms of nature, beneath the mountain's presence, the peace that had eluded her came trickling down from heaven. It soothed like warm rain. Her open heart filled, basking in the redemptive feeling of being part of the love found in all things. So sweet, but how to make that love stay?

Her peace dissolved when her vengeful path in the world stood painstakingly bare before her, awaiting judgment. She saw herself standing between the mountains of right and wrong. The accepted ways of the world said that what she will do was wrong. But the forces of truth, justice, and righteousness reinforced what she knew she must do. If she is damned, at least she recognized her dance with the devil. She held to her mortal moral choice.

She turned towards Jett, who was having his own meditative moment. He noticed the shift that had come over her. He reached out to her with a smile, pleased to see the lost joy within her returned. "It's beautiful here, isn't it?"

His touch brought her back. "I love it. So inspiring. Can we go find the beginnings of our special river?"

They hopped off the boulder and had another staring at the glacial mountain rising above them. So close and immense, hard to believe it wasn't a mirage. Jett bowed to Patoh, the native name for their sacred mountain, and they began to make their way down along a twisting, vine maple lined deer trail that brought them within view of the musical, cascading stream.

"How tiny our river is," she said.

"It springs out of the ground not far from here. Fed by that beautiful mountain."

She had a desire to be cleaned inside. Washed and forgiven for the darkness she plotted—baptized anew before the life-changing acts of tomorrow. She went to the streams edge and splashed water on her face repeatedly, wiped her face with her arm and said, "Let's find a rock to sit on in the middle and have the water flow around us. Be one with it."

They found a spot where the light broke through and warmed the stone against the cold of the creek. Feeling a part of the stream, they drank of the delicious air that surrounded them. Fresh and pure oxygen, an elixir of life that washed her as she rested, snuggled between his legs, savoring the music of the eternal spring.

Her Wolf growled into her bliss. Her fiery eyes were telling Casey not to lose her purpose. A pair of blue dragonflies lifted off of the water and rose into the leafy canopy. Time to move on. Time to return to the hard reality of her choice. Time to fulfill her pledge of revenge for her brother. She made her transition, wondering if coming to the woods was the wrong thing to have done. A tease of a reality that she must forsake. A memory of what might have been.

Back out of the river canyon, they stood in awe of the up-close mountain for the last time. The late afternoon western sun turning it from snowy white to golden red. They turned away and headed back down the trail. Senses heightened, they noticed small things that they had skimmed past on the way in, a brilliant gold reflected off a limb, a tiny wildflower, a hidden, clear trickling waterfall within a ferny glen.

The sun lingered warm and soft as it began to sink behind the forested hills. Seeing the Datsun was strangely comforting. She had yet to bond with it but was pleased nonetheless to have it start right up. With spacey heads, they left the National Forest and wound their way down to the village of Trout Lake, the pressure in their ears building into a thankful, clearing pop. She focused on the road ahead until the restaurant sign called to her stomach. "I'm starving," she said and pulled over into the gravel lot beside the roadside cafe.

"Good call, Casey. The Buzzard Burgers are awesome."

"Let's get one of those," she said. They sat outside at a picnic table next to a small stream where Pacific Crest Trail trekkers, with their gaunt, dry sweat appearances, hunched at tables with their massive packs resting beside them. A craven, protein starved packer stared in anticipation as another chomped on a mouthful of the famous burger, holding his eyes to the heavens while he chewed.

They went for the works: Buzzard Burger, fries, and huckleberry shake. When the platter came, they quickly assessed that their eyes were bigger than their stomachs—oozing over before them was a double meat patty, topped with ham, turkey, bacon, cheese, and a fried egg, plus the standard lettuce, tomato, and pickle. Could have been a condemned man's last request. They managed half and bagged the rest. The huckleberry shake, made from berries harvested in the nearby hills, the best they ever had.

Bellies bursting, they motored steadily downhill into a setting sun. Jett rode silently by her side. Anxiety regained its grip. He sensed the dark shadow overcoming her but had to let it be. Her choice made the change inevitable—what lay ahead no longer an abstraction—tomorrow only a night away.

They arrived to a dark and empty house. Saturday night, Frank out on the town. The comforting bed gave sanctuary. They nested there with little more to say, for living in the moment was all that mattered. They held on to each other through the night. Time ticked and the song of the mountain stream ran in their hearts, delivering them to the dawn of the day.

Chapter 33

Eyes ablaze, the She-Wolf pounced onto Casey's dreamscape, causing her to spring up out of sleep into a sitting position. A fierceness rippled through her. She slipped out of bed, leaving Jett to slumber, dressed, went out the back door, and walked the few blocks down to the park by the river. The river drew her into its flow. She imagined herself upon it, in her kayak, paddling towards the Celilo trailer. Her fists clenched. Her blood pulsed. She threw her head back and howled at the sky. Hate spilled over her. No more holding back, she opened all of the flood-gates. Today, vengeance will come. But, not soon enough. She walked briskly on the riverside path, charging her body and mind.

When she returned to the house, the smell of pancakes permeated the kitchen. "Hungry?" Jett asked.

The smell of food appealed to her animal. " I guess I should eat something. Any sign of Frank?"

"Nope. He must have hooked up with Cory last night. Wanna eat outside?"

"Sure." She reassured herself that there was plenty of time. Only mid-morning. Too early to leave.

Jett brought the pancakes to the table and noticed the faraway expression on Casey's face. He tried to turn the conversation his way. "When you get settled in Vegas, can you send me a card or something so that I know you're all right?"

She stared at him and shook her head briskly. " No

way, Jett. No links. It's bad enough that you and Frank know where we might go. If the Feds ever put heat on Frank, he'll squeal like a pig. Maybe you would too."

Jett attempted to hold eye contact but sensed her slipping away. "Your secret is safe with me."

She squeezed her lips. Being with Jett this morning was not working at all. His words made her think about being busted. She didn't want paranoid thoughts running in her head, but they slipped in anyway. Did she deserve to be caught? She twisted her neck in irritation and spoke past Jett between bites. " I have a lot going on in my head. Best that you don't talk to me."

"Is there anything I can do?"

"Just back off is what you can do! Don't you get it? Today is showtime. I'm sorry if you don't like it, but it's better if you leave me alone. Play in your lab or something. I need to get my head together."

"Casey, you don't have to be mean to me. I know I have to let you go."

For a moment, she felt a tug. Pulling away from Jett was difficult for her, too. He deserved an explanation. "You have to leave me alone, Jett. I am transforming. I don't want you to see me. You will not like who I become. I don't want you to remember me the wicked, destructive bitch. Don't you get it?" She stood abruptly, making her break. "This is where our beautiful little interlude ends." She walked away. Thoughts spun in her head, and paranoia snuck back in. Lolly was the weak link. How to separate her connection to the victims? An idea came. Lolly should take her time getting changed, making sure she is seen by everyone on her own, getting ready to journey onwards as usual. Maybe even having a drink with the barman before she leaves. Everything like a typical end of her tour. So what if she goes to Portland and decides to split town. Dancers do it all the time.

She called Lolly. "Hey, got some last-minute thoughts." She explained her idea to a drowsy Lolly.

"I like it. I'll do that. How about you? Everything all right?"

"Antsy. You?"

"Nervous as hell and a little hungover, but I'll be okay as soon as the show starts. I'll hear the music, and the moneymaker will go to work on cue. The rest will fall into place—I hope. I'll be glad when this is over, Casey. This dangerous stuff isn't my thing. So, guess it's on with the show for you. Get your satisfaction, darling, and call it a day. Good luck. Love you."

"They will get what they deserve. See you in Vegas."

Jett stood defeated, watching her walk away, hoping in his heart that she and they would survive the fallout from the abduction and whatever plan of retribution on the DOE men she will do. He did not want to accept that this could be the end for them. Her mental condition concerned him. He feared that whatever acts she will do might scar her forever. What price will they all pay for facing up to evil with another evil? Will the acts against the establishment lead people to wake up and fight back? Resist lethargy? Take action against the continuing dark shadow of nuclear waste? Will it halt the threat of the world's extinction or clean up the degradation of the beautiful Mother Earth and the river's poisoning? Out of the questioning, his mind became clear. He saw the planet as a whole integrated system that we had to protect as a species. No other blue and green paradises were floating around in the heavens. At least not in this solar system. Nature, from the beginning, meant to nurture lucky us. So yes, protect and save her at all costs.

He wanted to go after her, cheer her on. Leave her knowing that he was behind her all the way—wish her Godspeed to victory. Instead, he honored her request to be alone and slunk away to his lab, leaving her to prepare as she had asked. Downstairs, he half-heartedly tinkered around while playing at imagining his life as a businessman. Armed with a fully equipped lab, he could pump out a product for the people's enlightenment rather than the numbing to all-cause and responsibility. It felt shallow compared to what she will do, but then, he wasn't her.

She went to the sanctuary of her room, shut the door, and regained her transformation. She thought of Charley. Venomous anger quickly returned to her veins. The first taste of revenge flashed through her heart. It tasted righteously good.

She gathered her day bag, stuck in her money pouch, and had a last look around. Had she forgotten anything? She closed her eyes and concentrated. Nothing came but the smirky faces of them—the betrayers, the perpetrators of nuclear waste, the poisoners of her brother. She journeyed, reaching for Charley's spirit in her mind. He came in front of a storm of billowing clouds to stand beside the She-Wolf, sharp-toothed and determined to bring down her prey. Joining with them, she became their redeeming warrior and strode straight ahead for the door. The past already behind her.

She walked directly down the corridor, out of the house, and into the drive where the pickup waited. Like she did many times before, she loaded her kayak and paddle and secured them. Her wetsuit she threw onto the front seat with her travel bag. All that remained was to add the reinforced pack with the jars of poisonous water that she had stored in the shed. She gathered them and placed them on the passenger floor—time to get herself out to Spearfish Park. Be by the river, by the dam, engaged in the plan. Firing the Datsun, she let it warm for a couple of minutes.

Jett heard the start of the truck and sprung for the stairs. He needed to catch her and tell her all the things he had thought of before she left. Hold her one more time if he could.

She placed the truck in gear and drove away— never looking back—never seeing Jett standing in the drive waving fare thee well.

Chapter 34

At the stone cliff, above the big river, on the windswept point of land called Spearfish, Casey stood transfixed upon the river below. The spray from the rumbling waters off of the dam's spillway swirled around her. Static and wind electrified her face and hair. Native American fishing platforms made from poles and scraps of wood poked over the rocky cliffs lining the gorge. The Dalles Dam, a massive concrete wall, sluiced the river into a channel, blasting the water through its turbines, generating electricity. To harness water power and convert its force to energy was an outstanding achievement of humanity, but not obtained without loss. Casey thought of sacred Celilo Falls buried by the damming and the diminished salmon runs. Everything had a price. Cause and effect. Action and reaction. She became aware of stepping into the laws of karma. Let the chips fall as they may. She will live with the consequences of her actions. She believed she was in the right, and they were wrong. Her eyes and her heart went out to the beauty and power of the river. Vowing to protect it, her resolve unwavering.

A shadow moved behind her. Little Bear approached. The roar of the river obliterated the sound of his movement. He greeted with an uplifted hand, then motioned her to come away from the roar of the falls. They hugged and then walked towards the trucks. "You ready?" he asked.

"Yes," she said firmly. "I haven't watched the time. Been with the river."

"What does she say?"

"Protect her. Help her."

"True. We're okay for the time but should get moving to the drop spot."

They transferred her boat and gear to his truck. Placing her day pack out of sight behind the seat and feeling comfortable with where she parked, she locked the Datsun and with a pat on its hood said, "See you later, Blue Boy." In Little Bear's truck, Bear asked, "So you'll beach the kayak above the dam and walk here to your pickup?"

"That's the plan. Then high tail it to Portland and catch a bus."

Bear gave her an encouraging nod, locked his jaw, and placed the truck in gear. He turned onto the freeway and drove towards an exit above the trailer site. They spoke not a word. The doing was all that remained. They passed the fish camp, exited off the freeway, and traveled along a deserted side road until they found a pullover with access to the river. Bear carried the kayak while she hauled her wetsuit, paddle, and pack to a sandy launch spot.

She placed the pack holding the jars into the boat and slid her wetsuit over her shorts and t-shirt. She cringed at the contact with her hand from the wetsuit. Bear noticed. "The seep get you?"

"Yeah. Strong stuff. I'll deal with it later." She stood face to face with Little Bear. "For all those who have suffered, this day will be in remembrance of them."

He held her by her shoulders. "I am proud to know

you. Be the hand of justice and be safe in your journey."

With a nod of her head and her paddle in hand, he pushed her off the beach. The river embraced her kayak and carried it downstream. She sat tall in her boat. On course to the trailer, at home on the water, she set her mind to her deadly purpose.

****

Sam hated having to do a daytime carjacking. Hard time already served; he harbored no self-destructive wishes about returning. He had to laugh to himself over 'the things a man would do for a woman.' He left his motorcycle at home. It drew too much attention. Instead, he parked his old pickup a block away from the construction site in an unsuspicious place. Acting completely natural about what he intended to do, he put on a straight face and walked to the worksite. He already had staked out the van while at work, pretending to hunt for a tool out of the back. He checked and loosened the wiring under the dash while no one watched.

Sam opened the van door that had been left unlocked, stuck his head under the steering column, and found the right wires. The engine fired. He smiled to himself at his expertise, got behind the wheel, and backed out of the gravel drive onto the street, nonchalantly driving away. The van's gas gauge hovered around a quarter tank. He had enough to make it to the station over on the Washington side across the toll bridge. He didn't like having to use the bridge because the bridge had cameras, but he had to collect Jett. The sooner he got out of Hood River, the less chance of the van and him getting recognized by someone who worked at the site.

Even though the van had rusty dents and construction wounds on all sides, it seemed to be running well. No misses in the engine, air holding in the tires, and no wobbles from the front end. He crossed his fingers, willing the van to make the trip. He didn't want to have to revert to 'Plan B.' On the other side of the bridge, he pulled into a gas station to fill up. He used the self-serve and kept the engine running while pumping.

****

Jett checked the clock for the third time in the last five minutes. It was still twenty minutes until pickup. His armpits dripped. He knew that his actions made him part of a kidnapping ring, which unnerved him to no end. The thought of working with Sam frightened him more. No telling what that goon might do. The idea of Sam involved at all left a sour taste. He never did like the guy. The way he postured with his badass attitude irritated the hell out of Jett, and the belittling dismissiveness Sam showed whenever around the house rubbed him raw. Besides, he'd been fucking Casey in the room above, more times than Jett wished to admit, causing him to cover his ears with his pillow and wait for the pounding to end. Jett reminded himself that this gig was for her, and that thought brought him along. He figured that she had to use the people in her small circle to pull off her scheme. Badass Sam was good for the part. He granted her that. And, after all, he was sure that Casey loved him more than Sam. A smile broke onto his face. Holding that little victory cheered him on.

He didn't have a problem with Little Bear. He couldn't claim to know him, but Casey spoke highly of his integrity. He trusted her judgment. The Bear will balance out Sam and won't take any shit from him. Anyway, it didn't matter. He reckoned the whole thing would be over in a blink of the eye. Do his part, then do his best to forget about it. But not her. His breath fell. Casey would be long gone by the end of the day.

The van pulled into the drive. Jett pulled himself together and went out to meet it, ready to ride. Sam swaggered out of the van, leaving the motor running. He grinned his cocky grin at Jett. "You ready for this, man? Being an outlaw and all?"

"I'm doing it for Casey."

"Yeah, me too. Give me a hand straightening out the stuff in the back. I had to borrow the van from the job site. I thought you were supposed to rent one?"

"Yeah, but they fucked us at the rental company."

Sam opened the side doors and left the rear doors shut. Inside, scattered about, lay mostly hand tools, and some regularly pawed through supplies. A layer of construction dirt lined the floor. Sam jumped in and arranged the back, stacking bulky items against the rear door. Long-handled rakes and shovels they placed against the side. It didn't take long to clear out a sizable space in the middle. Jett found a trowel and scraped chunks of dirt and stones out the door, then took hold of an old towel and slapped some more dirt out the side door. The dust settled. Sam grabbed a bag of zip ties and a roll of duct tape and pushed them behind the seat. He had a last look around. "Good enough for a joy ride with our boys, don't ya think?" He checked his watch. " We'd better hit the road. Keep this show on time. I know you're supposed to be the driver, but if you don't mind, I'll take us to the Dalles. I'm too wired up to ride shotgun. I'll give you the wheel when I have the Bear to keep me company in the back."

They rode the Washington side of the river, planning to cross over on the free bridge, that had no cameras, into The Dalles. Riding by Spearfish, Casey's car hid out of sight from the highway. Through town, they pulled into the Cousins restaurant parking lot and searched for Little Bears truck. Outside, leaning against the bed, it wasn't hard to miss him. He came to the driver's side when the van pulled up and filled the rolled down window with his buffalo sized head. Sam, he knew. Jett, he acknowledged with a dip of his head.

Sam motioned towards the side door. "Let's get it on. Climb in the back like a good Indian," Sam said with a cackle.

Little Bear pointed a thick finger. "Don't get me started—Samuel," and slung open the creaky side door. "Where you get this piece of shit?"

"Job site. Get in. Time's a-wastin'."

Bear checked out the back of the van. "This old van will work. We can lay them out and use them for a rug if we have to," he said with a rare smile and climbed inside.

"There are some duct tape and zip ties behind the seat," Sam said, getting out to switch with Jett, who took over the driving.

Bear pulled some bandanas out of the small bag he had. "I've got these and some duct tape too. So we all set? We're good on time. Got gas, I presume, so any last questions?"

"I could use a pit stop before we go into action," Jett said, his stomach queasy.

"All right, we'll hit the truck stop at Biggs

Junction. Make it a quick one. Get a snack or a drink if we want. Once we're on to making the grab, there will be no stops until the drop."

"So, let's go get the fuckers," Sam snarled. Jett swallowed the lump in his throat, put the van in gear, and headed for the freeway.

****

Lolly had had too much time to think while traveling on the road to Umatilla. Worries about what Casey might do plagued her mind. She wondered how badly Casey would hurt the DOE guys? Casey never said what she was going to do, but from the sound of what she did say, a happy ending was not in store for them. Lolly knew that Casey was angry, obsessed, and vengeful, but surely she wouldn't commit the ultimate act? Kill them? Really? Lolly struggled to get her head around that possibility. The thought left her stranded at the crossroad. If, by some horrible chance, Casey did kill them, how would that change their relationship? Could she be lovers with a killer? Pressure built to the point where Lolly shouted out loud — "Have some sense, girl!"

Lolly arrived at the club, wishing it just another Friday night at just another strip club. With her nerves frayed from running all of the thoughts around in her head as the miles passed by, she went directly to the bar, pulled up a stool, and ordered a Manhattan.

"Little early for you, Lolly. What's up?"

"Just life, Tommy. Sometimes it gets complicated."

"Don't I know? Want to talk about anything? I'm a good listener," he said, mixing her drink behind the quiet, empty bar.

"Too personal, Tommy." She wished she could

spill her guts and take off the edge. Instead, she touched his hand affectionately when he placed down the drink. She kept her turmoil to herself. Tommy had always been a good friend. Part of the team. Part of her inner circle of people working the edges of the sexual game they played. A caring friend, there to soothe the tangle of emotions bound to come unraveled in the interplay of dancers egos mixed with the stirred desires of the marks. A protective, sympathetic male who could resist the temptation of coming on to the dancers. He didn't need to, for he was held on a pedestal by the girls, who regularly shared their troubles, slipped him a share of their nightly cash, and sometimes something else when the need struck. "Thanks, Tommy. Just have a lot on my mind. I'll take my medicine, and it will all be fine." She gave the cocktail a stir with the swizzle and sipped deeply, savoring the smooth fire on her throat, knowing the warm glow would soon come. She played with the cherry, rimming it around the glass. The filmy cling of the liquor hung behind. She thought of Vegas and smiled. That's where she wanted to be.

Sunday morning, Lolly's head spun in an achy swirl. The drinks had flowed throughout the weekend. In a boozy blur, she'd made it through two nights of shows—only one more to go. A night to mark as the highlight of her acting career. The bedside motel clock flipped numbers. She gripped her throbbing head. Getting up and wobbling to the bathroom, she tossed down a couple of aspirin. Back in bed, she covered her head with the blankets and tried to resume her slumber in the air-conditioned, cheap motel room on the strip that ran past the bar. Plenty of time until she'd shower and get something in her stomach before showing up for work. Tonight her show started early but today had a long finish. She envisioned herself at the bus station in Portland later that night, stepping onto the platform and leaving it all behind. Time to sober up and get a hold of herself. Too much at stake. But it was early. For now, she'd sleep and nurse her head if she could. Her phone rang. Casey.

****

Richard picked away at his fingernails. Skip lay beside him on the sofa. The television blared while the real show went on in his mind. The TV served as background chatter, connecting him to the world in which he belonged. A privileged, white male thread that sanctified his day-to-day existence and held his life together through a steady stream of detached security achieved through a Fox consciousness.

His fear of hooking up with the dancer thrashed his insides. The gorgeous young woman was way out of his league. Never had he even had sex with a typical hooker before. In fact, he hadn't had sex with a real woman in a very long time. Instead, he wanked to porn, satisfying himself enough to suppress coming up with enough gumption to pursue a woman in which he might actually be interested. But then, real women didn't interest him.

He doubted if what he and Bill had arranged was in his best interest. The last thing he wanted, the something he most dreaded was to be a poor performer. His pride couldn't take it. He struggled enough with ordinary confidence, and this confidence concerned an intimate nature that challenged the core of his manhood.

Imagining her wet, warm opening, he practically

shot in his pants just at the thought. He feared that's exactly what might happen, him blasting off on contact. An embarrassing and belittling blow. What will she think of his shrinking little dick going off like a schoolboy? He could hear Bill's laughter. Richard, no man at all. And worse yet, what if his trepidation kept him from getting hard at all, at the crucial moment? He groaned at the movie playing in his mind and stood and irritably paced while the clock ticked. Bill will soon be there. Fired up and ready to go. Full of confidence— like always.

****

Bill kissed his wife goodbye. He told her that he shouldn't be too late but not to wait up for him. He apologized for having to go out on a Sunday evening, missing dinner and all, but tomorrow's meeting demanded his and Richard's preparations. She asked if he wanted poached or fried eggs in the morning.

Entering into the attached garage from the hallway, Bill clicked to unlock his BMW's doors and hit the garage door opener. A blast of hot summer air flooded in as the doors lifted. The tight sound of the opening door of his car filled him with confidence. He loved the hot little number of a car, and tonight it would carry him to what he anticipated to be a very— memorable— event. But, first, there was Richard to pick up. He, most likely in a tizzy. Bill wondered why he even bothered. He'd rather have her all to himself. But that wasn't the way it came down. Maybe another time if things went well. What the heck. The two of them going at her would spice things up. Big dog and little dog—he'd show Richard how to get it done.

Getting the AC blasting, he drove towards

Richard's. He glanced at the gauges and realized that he'd have to get gas. Shit, that meant having to go back towards town. He hadn't planned time for getting gas. He decided to pick up Richard first.

Skip came attacking the door when he arrived but settled down to jumping up and hand licking when he knew who it was. "You ready? Time to go. Let's get moving. We have to get gas. We'll have to step it up, or we'll be late."

Richard looked at his shoes. "I don't know, Bill. Maybe this isn't for me."

"What! Are you scared again? Come on, you dufus. Let's go. You'll get over the jitters on the ride." He saw the fear on Richard's face. "Look, I've got a vial crammed full of blue pills. Don't worry. You'll be a man of steel. Rock hard."

Richard lifted his head thankfully to Bill as that vision took hold. Thank goodness for blue pills. "All right. I'm in. I'll meet you in the car. Sorry about being such a scared kid, buddy. I get thrown off by women."

They backtracked to the closest gas station. The Sunday evening line up at the end of the weekend, moved slowly. Bill checked the time. Late.

****

Music pulsed in the dimly lit den of desire—stale perfume hung in the air. Lolly waited in the curtained dressing room doorway. Men scattered around the half-full stage, typical for a lightly attended Sunday night. Sandy entertained the lads. Lolly up next. She moved the curtain and scanned the ring observing the men. Her guys were not there. She checked the time. Damn. They should be here.

Sandy finished her routine, and the DJ touted her

talents. He began his pitch for the next act. "And now prepare yourselves for the lady you'd love to lick ... Lollyyyyyy."

Her song came on, and she sashayed onto the stage like so many times before. She spun on the pole thinking, fuck those guys. If they don't show, I'll go to Vegas anyway. Fed up with the whole scene, she knew it was time to hit the road.

Chapter 35

Tires spit rocks as Bill's sedan swung hard into the near-empty gravel lot. The BMW came to a skidding stop in the back parking lot, and Bill and Richard jumped out. "We'd better get in there fast, or we'll miss her act. Don't want to piss her off now, do we?" Bill said, hustling for the rear door entrance. Inside, they adjusted their eyes to the dim lighting of the club. Lolly already worked the stage. They took a seat ringside, and Lolly's heart lifted when she saw them. Now she could come through for Casey. They settled in, focusing on the beautiful woman moving on the stage that would soon fulfill their sexual fantasies.

The second song came on, and she crawled into her floor routine, stretching, posing, and spreading for the men's pleasure. She pawed towards her guys, arching her back and wiggling her ass to expose herself to the gawkers watching from behind. Hanging her hair over Bill's head, she enveloped him and pressed her mouth to his ear. "Had me wondering. Glad you could make it," she whispered with hot breath. "Leave and go out the back door as soon as I get finished dancing. No one can see me leaving with you." He nodded and rubbed his head against her. She dragged her hair over him and went to Richard, who perked to her scent, the first pill starting to kick in. She rolled and spread legged sideways to an eager customer and spun back onto her knees. Her bottom slowly circled in front of her two guys. She had them where she wanted them; eyes glued onto the hypnotic ass of their dreams, minds running on as to what they intended to do in only a little while.

Set over, she slipped on her flimsy robe and collected her money and costume bits. Making her exit, she caught Bill's eye and nodded encouragement discretely over her shoulder. The men stood and walked towards the back door as planned. "Vegas, here I come," she muttered as she exited the stage and the next dancer came on. Too bad the money didn't get collected upfront. It would have been a nice closing bonus. They're all yours, Casey.

****

A steady wind came up from out of the west, blowing against the downriver current. It forced Casey to earn the few hard miles left to the Celilo camp. If it didn't let up, she'd have a more demanding journey later than she had planned. 'Expect the unexpected,' isn't that what Bear had said? What the Hell. No time for worries—she felt prepared for anything. Her adrenaline pumped. She paddled hard against the wind, believing that nothing could stop her payback. "Just bring them to me," she barked out loud, sticking her paddle into the water again and again as if into them.

The wind lifted white caps out in the channel. Hugging close to the edge of the river, she kept her kayak out of the main force. Spooked ducks shot into the air as her boat sliced through their shelters. Their necks stretching forward, they lurched out of lapping waved lees protected by thin-leaved willows grasping to the transient shoreline. As seasons changed, so did the River. It's changing, harmonizing with the migratory birds, insects, fish, and people.

Shapes of the fish camp appeared. Her anticipation grew, joined with relief for almost completing the first leg of the plan. Her Wolf's mouth stretched wide in her face. Did She have a name? No answer came. Wolf would do. Casey squeezed her bag of jars with her legs and stroked hard towards the camp. The hunger to have the evil ones at her mercy growled in her belly. Mercy, she didn't intend to give. Mercy they and the waste station did not deserve.

The hull of the kayak scrapped against the small stoned beach-head. The crunching sound scratched her acute tension. She dragged the boat over onto the sandy beach in the protected cove that she and Bear had scouted. Tying her bowline to a sturdy, young willow tree, she took no chances. The water might rise or fall depending upon the regulating of the dams.

She stretched her limbs and pulled back her suit to check the time, inadvertently brushing her injury from the seep. She winced but welcomed the pain the contact brought. It took her out of her mind and into her body. It hardened her edge.

Still time before the planned arrival, she spread the willow branches on the bank and reconnoitered the area. Spiders crawled along her nerve endings. She saw a pickup truck parked on the dirt road in front of the trailer. It being there an unanticipated part of the plan. Why was it there? It pissed her off. Didn't Little Bear make sure that no one came around? She sat in the sand and backtracked her mind to the times that they had been there. What did he tell her? Something about how fishermen friends used it sometimes but hardly ever. She figured that it had to be next to impossible to tell everyone not to be there on any given date? Today is sometimes.

If the van with her guys showed up, then what? Think fast. Maybe drag the victims out into the bushes, hold them down and make them drink? Not bad, but the incoming van might alert whoever was in the trailer. They couldn't risk that. She pulled out her phone. She didn't want to, but she felt she had to call Little Bear. "Somebody is in the trailer," she said in a deep voice. "What are we going to do? Yeah, there's a truck parked outside." She described the truck.

"Wouldn't you know," he said with a snort, knowing whose truck it was. "Stay calm. I'll call them and try and get rid of them. Send them on a goose chase." She told him of her idea to drag the men into the bushes. "Pretty good. Glad you got your brain working. Whatever you do, don't panic. We're about fifteen minutes from the grab time and close to an hour out from you. Call me if they leave. If not, I'll call you when we're getting close, and we'll make an alternative plan if we have to. Take it easy, and let me sign off and call the guys."

Casey remained in her willow blind and waited for something to happen—or not. She held faith that if the people didn't leave, Bear would come up with something. She sat with her bag of jars by her side, the river flowing on behind her. It never stopped, did it? It carried on. Just kept on rolling, like her life would, no matter how the plan unfolded.

Hot with the wetsuit on, she peeled it off, accidentally rubbing her wound again. A burning pain shot up her arm. The sore had etched deeper, and she feared that it might spread into her arm. It remained a constant reminder of her connection with the stuff,

Charley's, and soon to be theirs. She'll have to deal with it later when she is far away and long gone. For now, the pain served her purpose.

She heard the creaky squeak of the trailer door opening. Repositioning herself deeper into the willow blind, she watched and waited. The door slammed with a shudder against the flimsy metal house on wheels. Two Native American men in plaid cowboy shirts came down the rickety steps and walked around outside, one man going to the front of the truck and the other coming in her direction. She ducked down and hunkered. Holding silently still, she heard the splatter on the nearby ground and smelled the rising odor of his urine. The pissing man shouted back to his partner about that crazy Little Bear. He moved away. Doors shut. The engine fired, and the pickup drove off. She watched them drive out of the park and towards the freeway ramp. When she saw the truck on the ramp, she grabbed the bag and stealthily crept to the trailer, no one else in sight.

Putting on her gloves, she tugged at the door. It took a couple of serious pulls, but the rusty hinged, ill-fitting metal door swung open. A blast of burnt frying pan, greasy food smell assaulted her nostrils—hamburger grease. The men had left a mess, but what did she care. They were gone. The smell only improved the atmosphere for her guests arriving soon for drinks. Placing her bag upon the floor, she brushed aside a collection of junk sitting on the sofa to prepare a place to sit for her guests. Where had Bear left that knife? In a drawer? She checked the drawers and pulled out the knife. Wide, long, sharp-edged and pointed, better than she had imagined. A real Bowie knife that could intimidate a soldier. She held it in her hand, feeling it's steely power. She grinned wickedly, thinking of what it could do, then turned and rested the knife on the counter for later.

Better call Bear. She checked the time. They should be on the way. He answered his phone. "They're gone. Whatever you said worked. I'm inside."

"Good. We're on our way. "

"I'll be waiting."

Her prey approached. Let nothing else stand in the way. Wrath blazed within her belly. Clearing the counter, she brought the jars out of the bag and placed them down within the sink. The faded light coming in through the window dimly lit the scene. She searched for the kerosene lamp and found it full of liquid, in its place, in the cabinet below—Bear, true to his word. She only had to remember how to light it. She ran her hand down the side, and the mantle jiggled. She wiggled it some more, and it started to come off. Her fingers touched the burnt wick with the cover removed, and fiddling with the metal knob on the side, the wick lifted. She struck a wooden match from a box lying on the counter and lit the wick. Placing the mantle back, she tucked in the wick, and a soft light spread through the trailer. Shadows wavered around thick cobwebs embedded in the dark corners, their inhabitants peering out from deep inside their furry tunnels.

Fine-tuning her ears, Casey listened for the approaching van. The sounds of waves lapping against the river bank and the rumble of trucks passing on the freeway were all that she heard. She sat upon the dirty sheeted sofa and waited. Tattered pieces of cloth and stuffing poked out at the edges. She breathed and turned inward, her Wolf keening in anticipation.

****

Richard and Bill spilled out of the back door of the dance club, laughing casually, drunk on expectation, excited thoughts of impending good fortune lighting their faces. Jett spun his head to the back of the van and croaked, "They're out!" Sam and Bear jerked themselves into a squat and prepared to lunge. Jett shifted the van into gear. Smooth and silent as an advancing shark, the van slow-rolled towards laughing Bill and Richard. The sliding side door remained slightly ajar, primed for the attack. Sam and Bear pulled down their masks.

The approaching van halted Bill and Richard in their tracks. Nonchalantly, they waited for it to pass. All of a sudden, they heard the sliding side door roll open and were shocked to the bone when two masked brutes leaped out of the van, grabbed hold of them, smothered their mouths, lifted their bodies off of the ground, and slammed them onto the floor of the van before they knew what had hit them.

"Go, go," Bear called out in a gruff voice. He slid the door shut while pressing his heavy knee into Bill's back. The van slow-rolled ahead. A struggling commotion coming from the rear of the van assaulted Jett's ears. Even though the cries scared the shit out of him, he kept his cool. He motored to the main road, eyed the street, and eased onto the highway, all the while resisting the urge to gun it and get the Hell out of there fast. On the road, his eyes darted back and forth between the speedometer and the pavement in front of him. Every headlight and movement sparked his nerves. His use of turn signals at every junction impeccable.

The smacking sound of a fist slamming into a body came from behind and he winced. A moan echoed off the metal walls of the back of the van. Another thump sounded, followed by squealing. "Shut the fuck up," roared out. Another whack brought whimpers.

Cries became muffled as Sam and Bear slapped duct tape across the victims' mouths. Zip ties seized the guy's hands behind their backs and shackled their ankles, a wrap of duct tape added for extra measure. Folded, cloth bandanas covered their eyes. Hogtied and subdued, Bill and Richard lay passive as bundled rugs on the van floor.

Sam lifted the creepy nylon stocking he wore off his head and sucked in a breath of fresh air. Bear bunched his ski mask up and took stock. Satisfied with the situation, he punched fists in celebration with Sam, who decided to explore the guy's pockets. Extracting their wallets, he leaned back against the side of the van, rested his feet on a body, and checked the contents. He yanked out a thick wads of large bills and grinned at Bear. Lolly's payment. Sam counted the score and passed some to Bear. Jett turned the van onto the freeway entrance, Celilo bound.

Bill couldn't budge. Dazed and confused, he lay on the van floor in disorientated pain. Everything happened so hard and fast. He had enough time to put up about as much resistance as a stuffed doll. What did these guys want with them? Money, most likely. The guy already had his wallet. Some kind of ransom thing? Or could it be something else? His side ached from the punch, but it could have been worse. No telling what these guys might do. Judging from how easily they tossed him around, he wouldn't argue with whatever the strongmen wanted. Get the money and feel glad to walk with his life. Isn't that what his training told him to do?

Tears drenched the bandana wrapped across Richard's face. His soggy—wet pants clung uncomfortably to his legs. Laying in a puddle he shivered with fear, petrified by the abrupt brutality done to him. He wondered if he had cracked ribs as he achingly drew breath. His fearful mind pinged fantasies about what other horrible things these bad men might do to him. Helpless to his capturers, he found the claustrophobia maddening. He always had a problem with darkness since a child, and even tight blankets sometimes brought hyperventilation. Worst of all, was his taped mouth. The fear caused him to pray to Jesus while he recalled his past sins and begged for forgiveness as if he knew a cliff awaited.

Bear held his nose and pointed to Richard. His phone rang, and he answered in a calm voice. "Good. We're on our way."

****

Taking her time changing into her street clothes, bag in hand, Lolly made her usual pass by the bar on her way out. She stopped to say goodnight to Tommy. "What, no drink tonight?"

She laughed. "What, after the last couple of nights, you think I need one? The binge is over, man. I've got a long drive ahead. How about pouring me a large coffee to go?"

"Sure. Headed to Portland?"

"Yeah," she said, resting her bag on the bar seat. He handed her the coffee. "Safe trip, doll."

"Thanks, Tommy. See you next time around."

Trepidation rising, Lolly pushed open the back door of the club. Outside she froze, taking in the whole back lot before going another step farther. She saw no sign of her guys, only a sleek BMW parked at the rear of the lot. The car might very well be theirs, but no way of knowing for sure. No one sat in the car, and she didn't see anybody anywhere. Chances are they got nabbed as planned, or, just a crazy maybe—they searched for her at the motel. Fuck them, anyway. Her bit of drama in Casey's scheme was over. Time to hit the road and not stop until safely landed in Nevada.

Lolly reached Portland around eleven, just in time to catch the last bus to San Francisco. She parked a few blocks away from the bus station near a homeless shelter and left the keys in the ignition. Maybe some homeless woman will get lucky. She thought of handing the keys over to a random person in need, but that would only bring recognition. Tossing her job phone into a trash bin, she moved on. "Done," she said and slapped the disgust off her hands. She walked on, pulling her travel bag with her head held high, only a few short blocks to reach the station.

Blurry lights streaked past the bus as it traveled down the interstate. Lolly gazed out of the window into the night, knowing that leaving was the right thing to do. She should have gone sooner. She wondered how long she might have kept herself wrapped up in her secure, comfortable routine, going nowhere fast. Thinking of Casey, her hopes went out to her. Loving feelings remained deep in her heart despite all the strangeness connected with the abduction plot and the recent twists to their relationship. They'd get back on track when they were away from it all in Vegas. With luck, the vengeful consumption would be finished by now. Whatever horrible deed Casey had planned, over and done. Casey, on the road, following not far behind. Lolly blew her breath through puckered lips and sank into the high-backed bus seat, relieved to believe that Charley had finally been put to rest. Tonight, the end of one story and the beginning of another.

Chapter 36

Casey circled in the confines of the trailer. Flames of anger and hatred coiled through her body. Her emotions freed, she ritually drenched herself from a well of hateful elixir, gassing the fire of her intentions. Her eyes burned black as she clenched the long knife in her hand; the lantern light reflecting on its blade. She twisted it and empowered it, imagining the point pricking into their skin, stinging and drawing a line of blood while fear pounded in their blindfolded, expectant minds. Her She-Wolf gums pulled back. Setting down the knife, she held each of the jars in her hands. She admired the promise that they held. Her wound scowled reddy brown. "Bring them."

****

The Celilo exit sign reflected in his headlights, causing Jett to slow the van and swing off of the interstate into the riverside compound. The destination so close, his heart throbbed in expectation. He consoled himself by running the simple plan again through his mind. Drop the guys and be done. Be free of the criminal conspiracy. The whole deal had turned worse than he had imagined. He feared what Casey would do? At Bear's direction, he navigated towards the lonely trailer that sat backed up against a dark field of brush. He halted out front.

Hogtied, blindfolded, and lying face down, Bill and Richard stretched their hearing for any clue as to a sense of place and purpose of their capture. But none came. All they knew was that the van had stopped and that things were changing. They silently prayed as their hearts lumped up in their throats.

With the van parked, Jett leaned towards the back to see what was going on. He heard Bear speak to the captured men in a gruff voice. "I know you can hear me. Keep your mouths shut and do what you're told— or else." He jabbed a thick finger into each man's ribs to bring his words home. Jett cut the headlights but left the motor running in the van. Bug-eyed scared, he hurried around the front of the van to slide open the side door. Sam and Bear gripped the captives and slung them over their shoulders like meat carcasses. Jett climbed back into the front behind the wheel. He turned his head toward the trailer. He saw Casey standing at the doorway, harsh and stern as cold steel. Her face twisted into an executioner's mask. Her eyes, blank dark holes. Someone he didn't know. Repulsed, he didn't want to see this person. At the same time, he felt sad and sorry for her: the whole beat-up trailer, bound victims, and burly rough guys scene, a macabre dreamscape to him. He detached himself from the spectacle and set his sights on being done with the terrible revenge business for Charley.

Casey stood at the entrance of the trailer in the fading light. The door hung open. A glow from the kerosene lamp starkly framed her as she waited in the doorway, a dark figure with her tangled hair hanging askew. Her face, hard set, and distant. She stepped back inside as the bundles approached, and she pointed with an outstretched arm to the ragged couch. Little Bear and Sam flung the constrained bodies upon it. Bear jostled the men into sitting positions. He grabbed their cheeks in his oversized hands as if squeezing the heads of salmon and again commanded, "Do what you're told."

On the way out, Little Bear halted to grip Casey's shoulders as a comrade in arms. She grabbed him back in stoic solidarity and moved her head in recognition. Sam, bewildered by her detached trance that didn't recognize or notice him, returned to the van in disbelief. "What the hell is she up to?" he muttered under his breath, and came around the front of the van to open the driver's side door. "I'll take the wheel from here, jump in the back." Jett didn't argue. Whatever it took to get done with the bad dream. Bear climbed into the other front seat to ride shotgun. Sam drove the van onto the freeway ramp and made for The Dalles. First, drop Bear, then Jett in Hood River. Forget about going over the bridge again. He turned to Bear, grinning like a twisted frog. "That went pretty smoothly. Maybe we ought to go into the business. Man, Casey was a real gone girl. Felt like I was walking into the flames of Hell back there."

"Pay attention to your driving, Sam. We've got a hot van, and we're not out of this yet. It's only beginning for Casey," Bear said, holding on to a psychic connection, going to her, standing beside her, giving her strength to fulfill what she must do.

****

The bound, blindfolded, and gagged men squirmed on the couch, sickened by the stale odor of garbage and fry pan grease mixed with decaying fish scales. What horrible place was this? They struggled against their constraints, feeling a reprieve from the overwhelming dominance of the van ride. To Casey, they showed themselves as pathetic, wiggling worms. Disgust and rage overcame her. She growled through gritted teeth, "Sit still!" Grabbing the Bowie knife off of the counter, she took Bill by the hair and stretched his head back until his windpipe bulged. She dragged the flat of the long blade slowly across his throat. He silently screamed. Holding restraint, she pricked his face with the point of the blade furthering the reality of the knife. He jerked in pain. A bead of blood streamed down his face, and his eyes teared beneath the blindfold. What sort of Satan was this, ran in his mind? She slid the knife again, enjoying the feel, this time across his cheek, emphasizing the full length and breadth of it. "Do what I say," she rasped. His head bobbed in short, rapid nods.

Muffled groans and lurching body movements on the couch alerted Richard to something happening to Bill. The cries rioted his fears. Being blind and constrained, he squirmed in a living nightmare while he anticipated whatever might come to him. His fingers dug into his bound hands as terror lashed his brain. His head rolled back when the air moved towards him, his captor's sweat assaulting his nostrils. The touch of her blade slid along his face. He cringed and cried inside with every slow inch of it. Nerves stung him like shards of glass ripping in his veins. His teeth clenched. His eyes squeezed. "God, no! Not a knife!" He whimpered uncontrollably. She pricked his darkest fear—knives. He quivered, softening within her touch like a rabbit before its neck wrenched. He would do anything, give anything. If only he could say so. Not the knife. Oh please, not the knife.

****

Silence left a hollow sound in the van. On the short ride to the Dalles, each man stayed in his mind. Little Bear's truck waited. With no more than a wave, they left him at his truck in the lot. Jett moved up to the passenger seat. Sam spoke out of the side of his mouth, eyes on the road. "Change of plan, Jett. I don't want to go back across the bridge. Going to drop you in Hood River and get this rig back sooner than later."

"That's okay with me. I can get a ride," Jett said, more than happy to get away from Sam and out of the vehicle. The whole incident gripped his mind and body with a sickening feeling. What had he allowed himself to be a part of? He needed a breath of fresh air, denied when in the close company of Sam.

Jett called Frank and begged a ride from Hood River. He walked to the nearest bar and slammed a couple of shots, then settled into a beer while he waited for Frank and for his nerves to relax. He decided to tell Frank everything. Get the creeps off him. Frank was his closest friend, and like it or not, also involved with Casey's plot. He held his head in his hands. What he had seen in Casey freaked him out.

Sam steered the van out of downtown and up the hill towards the construction site. Charged from the thrilling intensity of the abduction, he unwittingly sped to his destination, grinning with satisfaction as he made the last few turns towards the drop-off. A whoop-whooping siren assaulted from behind. Bubble lights swirled in the rearview mirror. His old prison cell flashed in front of him. "What the fuck!" he cried aloud. Realizing he had nowhere to go, he pulled over and fumbled in the glove box for the documents. Where the Hell was the registration? Think fast, shot through his head as the officers approached him from both sides. His hands rose to his face as the flashlights shining through the window blinded him.

Bear rested in his truck after Sam pulled away, fine with just sitting there for a while. He didn't need a drink. Instead of celebrating the night being over, he remained fully engaged with Casey in the trailer. He closed his eyes and traveled. He chanted a song of protection and power and merged with the Wolf Spirit and Casey. Together, they would go for the kill.

Chapter 37

Bill's and Richard's heads hung limp and defeated on their chins. All the fight gone out of them, their bodies slumped into the greasy, smelly couch. They prayed that if they obeyed, no further pain would come. The knife had scared the bejesus out of them. Like good little schoolboys, they would do what she said. Something that came quite naturally to them. They had submitted all their lives, yielding to the demands of pastors, schoolmasters, parents, employers, and society as a whole.

The knife dangled in their minds. They dreaded its return to their flesh—not seeing made it worse. Their clothes stuck damply to them. Their mouths were dry and parched for want of water. Bill rolled his tongue. If only the duct tape would come off his mouth, to slake his thirst and give him a chance at negotiating. What is this all about anyway? It had to be merely a matter of money. But then, he reconsidered. It might not be so simple. This guy, who held them captive, seemed to be some kind of a sicko, taking pleasure in their suffering and speaking in a devilish voice. He remembered Helter-Skelter from the past.

****

Casey's hands pressed into the counter in front of her jars. She observed them. The two jars holding the liquid gathered from the poison seep seemed like ordinary water. But it wasn't that at all. Instead,

Charley juice awaited them. Her lips spread wide. Her eyes glared with her rising power. All her forces, her vengeance, Bear, She-Wolf, channeled together. Her hands held steady.

She spun to her captives and paraded slowly back and forth in front of them, willfully increasing their anxiety. She stopped in front of them and spoke in a kindly voice, not hers. "Look at you two. You're sweating, aren't you? It's hot in here, isn't it? You must be getting very thirsty. I bet you would like a nice drink of water?" She took a loud gulping drink of her clean water and exhaled an exaggerated "Ahh" at the refreshment it gave. "You're going to be sitting here a long time waiting for the others to come back. Tell you what I'm going to do for you," she said, coming close and poking the knife tip into each of their cheeks just enough to hurt. "I'm going to take off the tape and give you a big drink. Show you I can be nice when you, DO LIKE YOU ARE TOLD! Drink up because it will be your last chance for water for a very long time. Try to talk or yell, and the tape goes right back on. Understand? You make a peep, and you'll get no water, and you'll feel my knife sawing on your skin." She stepped away, then whirled back. "Got that?" she shouted, kicking them both in the shins. They jerked their heads in response.

Choosing Bill first to set a precedent for Richard, she ripped off the sticky duct tape from his face. He gasped for air and swung his head side to side, mouthing speech. Quickly she grabbed his face and squeezed his lips into a fish face while jabbing the knife into his neck. "What did I say?" His mouth went slack. She rested her blade and brought Charley's water to him. Tilting back his head, she placed the lip of the glass jar against his dry mouth. It opened, and she slowly poured half of the liquid into his thirsty mouth. He gulped it down before sputtering and wincing up his face. She let him catch his breath and brought the jar back. "Good boy. A little more, and you'll be all hydrated for the trip." She poured again, and he struggled against it. She wondered how badly it tasted. The water finished, she slapped the tape back across his mouth. He lashed side to side in protest. "I said to keep quiet!" she spat in a guttural voice into his face, and taking the knife, she slashed him across his exposed chest. He arched in spasms from the stinging pain as the blood wept from the thinly drawn line.

Richard listened, horrified by Bill's muffled scream. Blindly, he felt Bill's jerking against the shared couch. Richard wet himself again. He could tell that Bill was hurt. Just like Bill to not listen to the instructions. Probably hurt with the knife, Richard feared. It became still in the room. Richard waited. The reeking smell from his soggy pants soured the space even further. Blinded anticipation had him on the edge of panic. He willed himself to do whatever.

Casey returned to the counter, where the other jar waited. Sneering, she thought of how Charley must be pleased. How brilliant this plan. A taste of their own medicine—drinking from the well their hand poisoned. She felt Little Bears eyes upon her and knew he was pleased too.

Richard sensed her body coming towards him. Its approaching heat altering the energy field in front of him. Its mass looming large, hot, and threatening. Tears fell beneath his blind. He sniffled as the capturer spoke in that eerie voice.

"You must be thirsty like your friend. Last chance to have a big drink." She waited, allowing the suggestion of thirst to penetrate. Her words came hypnotically from deep in her throat. "You are thirsty now. I'm going to remove the tape across your mouth. Make a peep, and I'll cut you," she hissed towards his ear and slid the cold steel of the long blade down his cheek. He shuddered. "Then I'll gag you, and you will not get any water for a very long time. Understand me?"

Terrified by the thought of the knife and the thought of no water, he nodded. Where had he heard that voice before?

She ripped the tape off, and he squealed. "What did I say?" she scolded. He tensed to stillness. Her voice settled back down. "Time for a refreshing drink." She brought the Charley water to his lips and poured. Some went down his throat before he involuntarily choked. His throat contracted from fear. Water seeped out the corners of his mouth. She pulled the jar away, waited for him to clear then tipped the jar back to his lips. "See, I can be kind if you behave." Her tone relaxed him, and he was able to swallow some more before the choking resumed. The chalky and swampy tasting water appeared difficult to ingest.

"No!" she yelled, setting down the jar and slapping the tape back over his mouth. He wiggled in protest, his movements pissing her off. She grabbed the knife and squeezed the handle, wanting just to stab the pig and get done with it. Stepping away to rid herself of that temptation, she searched the trailer for an answer. In the trash, she found an empty paper towel roll. She lifted it from the plastic garbage bag and, making a slit in one end, twisted the paper tube to form a funnel. Skulking back to Richard, she stuck the point of the knife into his belly. "I ought to slit your belly like a pig. I'll give you one more chance. Let's try that drink again." She ripped off the tape. Grabbing his cheeks, she yanked his face center. "Open your mouth." He opened, and she shoved in the cardboard tube. His head wagged side to side. The paper towel roll stuck up like a tooting horn. Another dig with the point of the knife settled him down. She reached for the jar of seep juice and poured it, not so fast that he choked again, but slowly and deliberately administering the liquid straight down his throat. She watched his Adam's apple bob up and down until the jar emptied. Tears seeped out from beneath his blindfold. She removed the tube and abruptly taped back his mouth.

The empty jars rested on the counter. Casey leaned into the sink, and gripping the edge, allowed the mists to come over her. Charley faded into them. Her eyes joined with the She-Wolf. Together they bounded along a trail of Little Bear's lineage. She found her hands on the empty jars. She placed them back into the pack and, after adding the knife, had a good look around for loose ends. She found none.

Her victims became agitated. They cast their heads side to side as if to expel a lump of burning coal from their gut. Taste of their own medicine indeed. The Hanford seep waste ate at their insides, joining them with all that had suffered. Dispassionately, she observed them struggling and bound on the ratty couch. She felt no sympathy. Let the water finish them. Let them feel as Charley had.

She gripped their shaking heads as if to kiss them goodbye. They prayed for a reprieve. Instead, she stretched a fresh layer of duct tape over their mouths, running it back to below their ears. She stepped away. All hope lost to them.

Casey blew out the kerosene lamp, and the room went dark. She had no last words for them. They disgusted her. She opened the trailer door, and the starlit night shafted in through the opening. Crossing over the threshold, the She-Wolf receded. The woman awakened to the fresh air of the night. The bodies twitched on the ratty couch. She shut the door.

Trembling, she had to steady herself with the handrail running alongside the short staircase down to the ground. A stiff, northwest wind blew across her face. It slapped her into action. She slung her pack over her shoulder and wound her way towards the river, parting through dry brush and willow branches until she reached the shoreline. The trailer scene peeled away like a second skin. Her raw, exposed self grappled with what she had done. A chilling moment of shame came over her, but pride in achieving revenge reset her jaw. She turned her focus to the getaway.

The kayak remained tied as she had left it. She removed her gloves and scrubbed her hands with some sand and water, then she splashed water on her face, blinked her eyes, and exhaled deeply. She donned her wetsuit. Before launching her boat, she threw back her head, cast her eyes to the stars, and opening her arms, let go of any remaining rage. Heaven could judge her as it may. Her job phone bulged in her shorts pocket. She opened the wetsuit, extracted it, considered it, and then threw it into the river. She placed her pack into the boat and shoved off, the wind sweeping back her hair.

Chapter 38

Steady winds out of the Northwest buffeted her kayak. It bobbed like a cork upon the choppy surface of the water. Rudderless, her boat was more like a water bug than a finned fish. With several miles to traverse before reaching Spearfish Park, she got to work; stroking side to side with her double-bladed paddle, she kept the kayak's bow pointed into the wind. She gained favor from the current pushing from behind. The trailer faded away. The new life that awaited was the carrot that drew her on.

A swell began to build and roll. The added waves worked against her. She knew that she had to cross to the other side of the river to make a landing at Spearfish where her Datsun awaited. She decided to cross the river before conditions worsened. Years of river experience helped determine the angle of her tack. She put her bow head on to the wind, then slacked off the nose, finding the niche between the wave and direction of the wind. Digging her paddle deep with each stroke, she slowly forged her way. The safety of the shoreline shifted to the rolling sea of the deepwater channel.

The wind blew the night sky clear of clouds. The river's far side showed a shadowy silhouette in the distance—a bevy of stars and a half of a moon lit the sky. The shining stars touched her wounded heart. They inspired hope for a life beyond. Boat length by boat length she gained to the west. The deeper into the channel, the farther away she went from what she had done, each stroke drawing her closer to what will be.

Her life since Charley's accident screened upon her mind as she bashed through the swells. The splashing water struck against her body with each passing memory. Like a well-oiled machine, she relentlessly pushed onward, the river threatening to end it all out in the midstream.

The wind, the memories, and the river had her at the point of exhaustion. Alone, she called out for help from the people that had stood by her through all her struggles. She called for them to come to her now. Lolly, who risked so much, waiting for her at the end of the line. Little Bear, who revealed the pain that lived in his heart. She saw him standing immovably behind her every step of the way. A great Bear. Nothing little about him at all.

Sam, who proved how much he cared, gallantly serving her needs beyond sex. And then, Jett. His face brought a smile even though she was nearly breathless from fighting to keep the boat moving forward, across and down the river. She gave thanks that the eyes of Jett and the Wolf never met when she stood possessed at the doorway of the trailer. Jett, the good man who opened her to what she thought she could never have. Will she have that again? Will her feelings for Lolly change or only deepen after all they had gone through? A surge of desire came to her paddling. She will have to get to Vegas to find out.

The far side beckoned as a dark coastline, and Casey's arms ached to get there. The fierceness of the trailer had extracted a toll on her. She willed herself onward, again reaching into her depths. Recalling how she crossed the river in the dark to fill the jars, she took courage. Her faith stiffened from knowing that she had done it before. She will do it again. She thought of Frank and snickered when remembering him saying he was a secret admirer. She must have some good qualities that managed to attract so many people to her. Maybe not the loser her mother always made her out to be. Maybe her cocky, aggressive attitude made her attractive? She didn't think herself pretty. A wave slapped up into her face, threw her off balance, and she coughed and spat water before righting herself. She made a resolution. If she made it across the river, she would dedicate herself to being a softer, kinder person. Be what Jett showed her a person could be. Make a fresh start.

The shoreline grew close, and she hoped that the wind might slacken there. She plunged her paddle with renewed vigor. A vision of her struggling victims snaked back into her head. What chance did they have for someone to find them before the poison took their lives? Slim chance in Hell. The only possibility, if she had called it in, but she tossed her phone into the river, didn't she?

The Dalles' lights came plainly into view, a backdrop to the massive dark shadow of The Dalles Dam. Closer to the shoreline, the winds did ease off, boosting her morale. She will make it, after all. Pride thumped in her heart. Once again, she took on the river and won.

Her kayak came into the lee of the dam, and the wind dropped to a balmy breeze. Her boat slipped through the water on smooth, relaxed strokes, allowing her some drift time between paddling. Her muscles relaxed and settled into powering on without the strain. Leaning back in her seat, she savored the accomplishment of the crossing and realized that, indeed, she would miss being on the rivers when out in the desert land. She drifted under the stars in the strengthening current with the warm summer wind caressing her face. The dam and the craggy outcrops of Spearfish Park rose before her. A flush of excitement veined through her as she felt the first tugging suction of the dam water. Listening ahead, she heard the roaring fall of water. The side spillway of the dam was open. The music of the falls spoke to her like it would to a returning Salmon. What a way to finish her journey, cap her night of accomplishment. Ride it over like any of the countless waterfalls she'd conquered in the past. Shoot off into her new life with a leap of faith.

The current gripped her boat. She leaned forward, surrendering to the pull. She thrust her paddle down like a rudder and positioned the kayak to the center of the approaching entrance. The thundering roar of spilling water over the edge deafened her ears, and then she blasted into the dark tunnel of the spillway. Curling, twisting side waves funneled wildly into the middle of the chute. They randomly slapped and broke against her boat, rocking her balance from side to side. She tipped. The river reached, grasped her body, and slammed her down. She heard the thud of her head against the concrete. She tasted the water. Darkness came. The river possessed her and tumbled her down into the bubbling cauldron, burying her like Celilo Falls.

A word about the author…

R R Rowley has lived coast to coast in the USA, in London, UK, and has spent many years on his farm in Grenada, West Indies. He has owned and operated several companies and was involved in start-ups. Currently, he resides in the Cascade Mountains of Washington State.

Thank you for purchasing
this publication of The Wild Rose Press, Inc.

For questions or more information
contact us at
info@thewildrosepress.com.

The Wild Rose Press, Inc.
www.thewildrosepress.com